What could he say?
That he desired her?

That he…what else did he feel, besides desire? He shied away from the thought.

"Please," she said. "Do not be angry with me."

"Angry with you? It is you who should be angry with *me*. I never intended to…I swore no harm would come to you."

She looked away, biting her lip. When she took a deep, shaking breath, her breasts swelled in her neckline. He stared unwillingly for a long moment before forcing himself to look elsewhere. He could not stay in this chapel where the very stones seemed to speak of carnal hunger while frustrated desire throbbed sullenly in his veins and other, unnamed emotions made him a stranger to himself. If he did not escape, he would take her in his arms again, and if he did that, God help them both…!

Dear Reader,

Have you ever been tempted to turn Mr. Wrong into Mr. Right? In each of our books this month, you'll delight in the ways these least-likely-to-marry men change their tune for the right woman!

We are thrilled to introduce debut author Katy Cooper, who has written a captivating and emotional story set in Tudor England, *Prince of Hearts*. The hero is the younger brother of the king of England, and is caught between preserving his father's dying wish to protect the throne at all costs, his brother's commands…and the woman he has come to love. You won't want to miss this powerful story!

Also new to Harlequin Historicals is the talented Julianne MacLean. She brings us *Prairie Bride*, a sexy, fast-paced Western about a recently jilted—and angry— Kansas farmer who advertises for a mail-order bride and finds himself falling in love with her, despite her secretive past. Ruth Langan has written a new medieval novel, *The Sea Witch*, book one of her SIRENS OF THE SEA miniseries. Here, a female privateer and a dashing sea captain team up—in more ways than one!—to thwart a villain's plot against the king.

And be sure to look for *The Paper Marriage*, a darling marriage-of-convenience tale about a young widow in financial trouble and a steel-coated mariner who needs help raising his adopted daughter, by mainstream historical author Bronwyn Williams.

Enjoy! And come back again next month for four more choices of the best in historical romance.

Sincerely,

Tracy Farrell,
Senior Editor

KATY COOPER

PRINCE OF Hearts

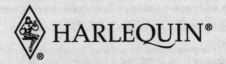

HARLEQUIN®

TORONTO • NEW YORK • LONDON
AMSTERDAM • PARIS • SYDNEY • HAMBURG
STOCKHOLM • ATHENS • TOKYO • MILAN • MADRID
PRAGUE • WARSAW • BUDAPEST • AUCKLAND

ISBN 0-373-29125-6

PRINCE OF HEARTS

Available from Harlequin Historicals and
KATY COOPER

Prince of Hearts #525

Please address questions and book requests to:
Harlequin Reader Service
U.S.: 3010 Walden Ave., P.O. Box 1325, Buffalo, NY 14269
Canadian: P.O. Box 609, Fort Erie, Ont. L2A 5X3

To Denise, Terry, Debbie, Carole and Nina for chocolate and "grammaring" and never letting me give less than my best; to my sisters Gill and Megan for believing in me before I knew how to believe in myself; and to my husband, Jim, for teaching me about true love.

Prologue

The Tower of London
October 1508

There was no blood on the Bloody Tower. Squat and unremarkable, it stood in a cluster of gray stone buildings near the Water Gate with nothing to show that it had been the site of a murder. Edmund Tudor, nine-year-old Duke of Somerset, stared at it for a long time. Maybe if he looked long enough, blood would leak from the mortar, oozing between the huge blocks of stone.

A pleasurable shiver of distant horror skimmed him from head to toe. His uncles had died in the Bloody Tower years ago. The younger one had been no older than Edmund was now, a fact that exerted a strange fascination over him. Edmund had heard that the boys' uncle had murdered them, but he thought it was a lie. The uncle had been King of England and Edmund could not imagine a king creeping through the darkness, intent on murder. Kings killed, he knew that, but they killed openly, using the law. So if his uncles had not been murdered, how had they died?

He shivered again. The early autumn dusk filled the spaces between the buildings of the Tower with shadows, darkest where the red-gold sunlight splashed across the battlements. The Tower rooks, settling for the night, called to one another; for a moment, their raucous voices were the only sound he heard. He ought to be lonely or afraid; surprisingly, he was neither.

He caught a glimpse of movement in the passageway bisecting the base of the Tower. The flicker became a lone girl, wrapped in a cloak just slightly too long for her. She held its folds bunched against the front of her bodice with one hand while the other rubbed furiously at her eyes. Faintly, he heard the hiccup of her sob.

"Who goes there?" he said in a soft voice.

She jerked to a stop and looked up. "Who are you?"

"I asked first."

She had dark eyes and dark hair that escaped her linen cap to cling to her damp cheeks. Judging by the material of her cloak, she was well-born, though he could not be certain how well-born in the tricky light.

"My name is Cecilia," she said. She started walking again. Impulsively, he moved to block her path. She jerked to a stop, the folds of her cloak flicking his ankles. "Let me by."

"No."

She scowled at him. "Let me by, I said."

Did she not know who he was? Did she not recognize the king's youngest son? Perhaps not. She had paid him none of the usual marks of respect; there had been no curtsy, no lowered eyes, no waiting on his pleasure. *She thinks I am a nobleman's son.* He grinned. How could she think otherwise? In a fit of annoyance, he had dismissed his attendants, one mark of high station. And his clothes, another indicator of rank, were not very rich since he had expected to spend the day in studying.

"Do not go," he said. "I will tell you my name if you stay."

She looked past his shoulder at the buildings and towers behind him, chewing her lip. He could see the reluctance in her face. Did she wish to leave him? Or was she loath to go within? She sighed and then met his gaze, the corners of her mouth beginning to lift. "Very well. I shall not go."

"Good." Now that he had persuaded her to stay, what would he do with her? She turned her head so the light caught on the marks of her tears. "Why were you crying?"

She scrubbed her cheeks with a fold of the cloak. "I want to go home."

"Home?" How strange, to have a home away from the Court. Sometimes he lived apart from the Court but when he did, it felt like exile.

"Wednesfield Castle, in Hertford," she replied.

Now he knew who she was. "You are Lord Wednesfield's daughter."

Her chin lifted. "Yes, I am the Earl of Wednesfield's daughter. But I still do not know who you are. And you said you would tell me."

"My name is Edmund."

"Edmund?"

"Edmund Tudor," he replied, and waited for her to realize who he was.

She bit her lip and then took a deep breath. "Do you like Court?"

He let his breath out in a sigh. She had not recognized him. "Yes. Do you not?"

"I do not like the staring. Or the mean things people say." She lifted her arms out from her body so the cloak hung like brown velvet wings and then dropped them. "But I expect it is different for boys."

Or princes. "I expect so." He searched for something new to say, but nothing came to mind. The grumbling of his stomach broke the quiet between them. All at once he was so hungry he could eat a beefsteak all by himself. That morning, he had put a few sweetmeats in the pouch hanging from his knife belt and he was fairly certain he had not eaten them all. Plunging his fingers into the purse, he rooted through the other useful things he had put in there: stones, a plover's egg, a penny someone had given him, pearls that had torn off a doublet sleeve that he kept meaning to give to his tailor to sew back onto the doublet. Finally, his fingers closed on the soft, sticky sweetmeat. He pulled it out and examined it in the waning light. There were bits of lint clinging to it, but it still looked edible. He bit it in half and then remembered Cecilia.

He held out the uneaten half as if he had always intended to give it to her. "I am sorry it is not more, but it is all I have."

A smile broke across her face. "Thank you." She popped the sweetmeat into her mouth with no more regard for the lint than if she had been a boy.

Why were none of the girls he met like this? She made him forget he was a prince and that did not seem like a bad thing. Wiping his fingers on the front of his doublet, he said, "I can stand on my hands like a mummer. Do you want to see?"

She flung one corner of the cloak over her shoulder. "Oh, yes, I do."

He took off his short gown since it would only get in the way. The first time he tried, he hesitated so his legs only lifted half off the ground. The second time he used enough force to fling himself into balance. "Watch me!"

He began to walk on his hands, his heart pounding. She could not be any more surprised than he; he had only learned to stand on his hands last week.

"Cecilia!"

Edmund overbalanced and landed on his back, the impact driving the breath from his body. He lay still on the ground for a long, stunned moment, then rolled onto his stomach and looked for the owner of the sharp voice that had sent him reeling.

A girl stood at the corner of the White Tower, her hands on her hips. At this distance, it was hard to be sure but Edmund guessed that she was a few years older than he and Cecilia.

"I must go," Cecilia said, pulling the folds of her cloak more tightly around her.

"Who is it?"

"My sister, Beatrice. We are leaving tomorrow so I do not think I shall see you again. Farewell."

"Do not go!" He stretched out his hand to grasp the cloak. It was hard to be commanding lying on his stomach in the grass.

She took a step backward and stumbled a little on the hem of the cloak. Righting herself, she shook her head. "I must." She turned around and hurried to join her sister.

Edmund crouched in the grass, wondering if he should stand and call her back. *If I command it, she will have to stay.* But the only way to command it was to reveal who he was. He pressed his forehead against his clasped hands. What should he do? Lifting his head, he saw Cecilia turn the corner of the White Tower and disappear behind its ghostly bulk. His question was answered. He was too late.

He looked for her later when he went to his supper in the King's Hall but she had not joined her parents. He looked away, disappointed. He wanted to see her again. She made his rank invisible, lifting the weight of being Duke of Somerset off his shoulders. *How strange.* He liked being someone other than the king's youngest son. That could not be right. He ought to *want* to be a duke.

Later that evening he joined his father in his private rooms for one of their frequent games of chess. Save for a gentleman usher, a pair of hounds and a man playing a harp, they were alone.

For a long time he and his father played in silence, absorbed in the intricacies of the game. His father made no concessions to Edmund's youth and won more often than not; Edmund prized his few victories. Tonight would not bring one of them: his pawns were in disarray, his queen much threatened. No matter what he did, he could not bring himself out of danger.

"I am told you dismissed all your attendants today, Edmund," his father said into the quiet.

"Yes, Sire, I did." He chewed his lip and gripped the seat of the chair, afraid he would betray what he saw to his father.

"Was that wise?"

Edmund glanced up. His father was apparently studying the board between them, but Edmund was not deceived. All his father's attention was focused on him.

"I needed to do something. Alone."

"A king's son should never be alone." His father moved the pawn. Edmund moved his bishop, his shoulders tightening. "But you know that. What was so important you must ignore that knowledge?"

Edmund adjusted his slippery grip on the chair. "I wanted to see—" His father would think him a fool. He glanced up again and found his father watching him. The affection in his father's normally cold gray eyes gave him courage to continue. "I wanted to see if the Bloody Tower was bloody."

He knew by the way the corner of his father's mouth quivered that his father was trying not to laugh. Then his father's expression altered, his eyes looking inward. His mouth drooped at the corners.

"Do you know why they call it 'bloody,' Edmund?"

"The murdered princes."

His father's eyebrows lifted and a little of the coldness crept back into his eyes. "Who told you about the princes?"

His brother would thrash him if he told; his father would have him beaten if he lied. Edmund swallowed. He might be able to avoid his brother. "Harry told me."

His father sighed. "I should have known. Do you know why the princes died?"

"An evil tyrant murdered them."

"That is partly true. They also died because a man broke his promise to his king. The Duke of Gloucester promised his brother the king that he would protect the king's sons and then, when the king was dead, he killed his nephews and stole the throne." His father gripped the edge of the table so hard that the chessmen rattled on the board. "He burns in hell for his sins, Edmund. Do you understand that?"

His father stared into his eyes, his thin mouth a seam in his face. Edmund wiped his palms on his hose. "Yes, Sire."

"Promise me that you will never betray your king."

Those eyes could winnow his soul. "I promise, Sire."

"Swear it by the love you bear me."

For a moment he had the notion that this man was not his father, but a stranger who happened to look exactly like the king. "I swear it, Sire."

The man relaxed and became his father once more. "England was torn to ribbons by civil war for thirty years because men could not keep their promises to the king. I will not let that happen again. Nor should you."

Edmund crossed himself. A great burden had been laid on his shoulders, greater even than any a king might bear. "No, Sire."

Chapter One

August 1516
Eight Years Later

Cecilia swung her bare feet and shifted in the crook of the tree limb. Her stomach grumbled as a trickle of sweat crawled between her shoulder blades. She had not taken the time to snatch something to eat before escaping her duties after Mass and now she could not climb down without running the risk of being seen. Hurry, John, she thought, and pushed clinging wisps of hair off her damp forehead. Shading her eyes against the glare, she peered southward. No dust on the road. No sign of her brother John.

Her eyes wandered to the sprawling bulk of Wednesfield. Her nurse, Mistress Emma, stood just outside the gatehouse, exasperation clearly expressed by fists planted on her hips. Cecilia stiffened, resisting the urge to leap from the tree and flee. Dressed in brown linen and screened by oak leaves, she should be invisible. The only way Mistress Emma would see her was if she gave herself away.

She held her breath until her nurse turned away, disappearing into the courtyard. She released the breath in a gusting sigh. Still free. Last night, Mistress Emma had requested her help with the mending and her mother had reminded her she wanted Cecilia to spend some time working in the herb garden. Cecilia had awakened before sunrise knowing she would do neither. Today was hers.

She looked toward the road from London again. No dust. No John.

Out of the corner of her eye, she saw a flicker of movement at the gatehouse and turned her head to look more closely. Her older sister Beatrice stood in the archway, dressed in one of her plainer gowns, a broad-brimmed straw hat shading her face and a cloth bag hanging from her hand. Cecilia's eyes sharpened. She watched as her sister sauntered down the lane, glancing back once or twice as if for pursuers, and swore softly to herself. Here was an opportunity to pay Beatrice back in her own talebearing coin and Cecilia couldn't take advantage of it without getting into trouble herself.

Beatrice drew closer. Sweat shone on her flawless skin, golden curls clung damply to her white brow, dust powdered her hem nearly to her knees but she was still beautiful. It was unfair. *She* never moved as if her hands and feet had wills of their own. Words never tumbled in disjointed knots from her mouth. Worst of all, she had never been small and awkward and dark-haired. Cecilia thought, Go away. Go away and never come back.

Stopping beneath the branches of the oak, Beatrice looked up. Cecilia expected her sister to scold her for being too old to climb trees like a child, that at sixteen it was past time Cecilia comported herself as a noblewoman.

"Madam my mother and Mistress Emma are hunting for you," Beatrice said.

Cecilia scowled to conceal her surprise. "Are you going to go back and tell them you found me?"

"No, I shall not betray you if you will not betray me," Beatrice replied calmly.

"A pact, then," Cecilia said. "You keep my secret, and I shall keep yours."

"Done." Beatrice wiped her upper lip on the cuff of her shirt. "Why are you in the tree?"

"Waiting for John."

"He has been gone for six months—you cannot be sure he will return today."

"I know."

Beatrice smiled and for a moment, despite the fact that John was as dark as Beatrice was fair, she looked like him. "How long have you been up there?"

"All day."

Beatrice wrinkled her nose. "You must be bored."

"No." Cecilia lifted the books she held in her lap. "I have my friends Virgil and Erasmus to keep me company."

"Does our father know you brought books outdoors? If it rains—"

"They are mine, given to me on my name day."

Beatrice sighed. "Then I'll warrant you're hungry. Here." She reached into her bag and tossed something to Cecilia. It was an apple, firm, warm and a little green. "Will just brought a basket in."

Cecilia took a bite. The apple was sour but her stomach growled in relief. "Picked too early," she said with puckered lips.

"But better than nothing," Beatrice said, and turned toward the river.

"Beatrice!"

She turned around. "Aye?"

"Tell Sebastian I said good day."

Beatrice smiled slyly. "I shall."

Her heart in a tangle of longing and resentment, Cecilia watched her sister walk down to the river until she was lost in the mist of green willow branches.

She was kind to me. I wish she liked me. She pushed away the treacherous thought and clung to the familiar image of vain, mean, tale-telling Beatrice.

Looking toward the road, she saw a cloud of whitish dust hanging over the hedgerows. Was that John, home at last? She swung her feet in excitement. John had not been home since Candlemas and she had a hundred things to tell him, everything she had been unable or unwilling to write in her letters for the last six months.

A rider trotted into sight but he was not John. Her stomach dropped and she blinked back quick stinging tears. He *will* be here today, she told herself fiercely, he will. Throwing the half-eaten apple aside, she dug her fingers into the strands of ivy swarming over the trunk of the oak as curiosity pushed through the pall of her disappointment. If this wasn't John riding toward her, who was it? A guest, obviously; she hoped it would be someone important or interesting, someone who would distract her mother and Mistress Emma.

The rider drew close enough for her to see he was a young man of perhaps her age, well-dressed, astride a very fine horse. Tawny-gold hair glinted beneath his blue cap; strong cheekbones and jaw balanced a proud, high-bridged nose. He put her in mind of a young, half-fledged hawk.

I know you. But when had she known him? And where? She closed her eyes.

Against her eyelids, memory unfurled like a flag. She had been eight or nine, truly a child, when she and Beatrice had gone to Court with her parents. Every moment of her stay had been a torment of boredom. Every moment but the one that came at the end of the last day.

She had met a boy who gave her half a sugarplum and walked on his hands like a mummer. He made her want to laugh at a time when she felt as if she would never laugh again. If everyone at Court had been like him, she would have gladly stayed.

Later she had wondered about him. The old king had a son just her age, named Edmund. Could the Edmund who had shared his sucket with her have been the king's son? It had been a foolish thought; kings' sons did not wander the precincts of the Tower without attendants. No, her Edmund had been a different boy.

But was this man the boy she remembered? She peered through the flickering leaves of the oak, narrowing her eyes against the glare. He was too far away.

She leaned forward, clutching the ivy for support. Please God, it would hold her. He rode beautifully, graceful in the saddle as he turned his head to examine the property. She leaned a little bit further out. The ivy gave an inch or more, and for a heart-stopping moment, she was certain she was going to fall. The books slid out of her lap and crashed to the ground.

She dragged herself backward and thrust herself into the safety of her former seat. "God's nightgown!" She closed her eyes, her heart thumping against her breastbone and her breath coming in gulps. "Sweet Jesú, thank you for saving me. Saint Cecilia, thank you for watching over me." She pressed her hand to her throat, trying to calm the fear there.

"How now, what is this?"

Opening her eyes, she found the stranger riding toward her, coming closer until the hooves of his mount were inches from her books. Her heart gave a great leap and then subsided into quivering.

"Mind your horse, sir! He is going to trample my books!" she said sharply.

He looked down. "So he is. I beg your forgiveness." Chirruping, he backed his horse away from the books and leaped from the saddle in one easy motion. He looped the reins of his horse around a nearby sapling and returned to the tree. Bending, he retrieved her books, opening one and then the other to read the front. He looked up at her, his brows raised. "You grow strange fruit in these parts, mistress. Latin?"

She leaned forward to see him better. His gray-blue eyes, framed by stiff brown lashes, glinted like river water. His mouth curled up at one corner in a smile that was friendly and sly and clever all at once. She had seen those eyes, that mischievous smile before; there was no longer any question in her mind that it was he. She smiled back, happy laughter tickling like bubbles in the back of her throat. "May I have my books, sir?"

"It is my pleasure to deliver them." He tucked the books into his doublet and tightened the laces. Seizing a fistful of ivy, he dragged himself up the trunk of the tree.

Was he mad? She scrambled backward into a higher perch to make room for him, managing skirt and petticoats with the deftness of long practice. And was she mad to allow it? She would do penance for this as she did for all her sins. For now, she could not worry.

He sat where she had been a moment ago, larger than he had looked from above, so close he filled the sky. She thought, He is just a boy, no older than you. He could be anyone: a neighbor's son, one of Sebastian's cousins, a scholar returning to Oxford or Cambridge. It did no good. He was too big, too close, too alien. She needed room.

Suddenly breathless, she leaned back against a branch and tilted her head up to gaze at the dense, dusty leaves overhead.

"I know you," he said.

"Do you?" She tilted her head, glancing down at him. She could not make herself confess her suspicion.

He cocked his head and grinned at her. "I do."

That smile.... She pulled her scattered thoughts together. "Who am I?"

"Cecilia Coleville. But you do not know me." His eyelids lowered and his mouth curled. How sure of himself he was.

I shall bring you down a peg or two, braggart. Or she would make a fool of herself. She closed her eyes and resumed her relaxed position against the branch. "Edmund Tudor, who could walk on his hands like a mummer."

He laughed. "I am caught out."

She peeped through her lashes at him and fought against the corners of her mouth as they tried to curl up in a smile. With the color in his face and the laughter in his eyes, he looked abashed and amused at once.

He took the books from his doublet and held them out to her. "I give you your books, mistress, though I beg leave to doubt you read them."

She opened her eyes wide at that, ignoring the outstretched books. "You have a proper wit, sir, to think I risk the loss of valuable books for no better reason than they are an ornament to my linen."

He laughed. "Then read to me, O Mistress Scholar." He tucked Erasmus back into his doublet and offered her the *Aeneid.*

"Do you not fear I shall find a portion I have committed to memory to impress skeptics such as yourself?" She pushed the book away. "Select a passage for me, Master Doubter."

He opened the book and flipped through the pages, plainly searching for something in particular. "Ah!" With the book open near the middle, he turned it so she could read it, his finger marking his place. "Read this."

It was somewhere in the middle of Book Four. Cecilia began, "'All-pow'rful Love! what changes canst thou cause/In human hearts, subjected to thy laws!/Once more her haughty soul the tyrant bends:/To pray'rs and mean submissions she descends...'" She looked up at Edmund, her eyebrows lifted. "Is that enough, or do you require more?"

He released the book into her hand, laughing ruefully. "You have proven your point, mistress."

She grinned at him before closing her eyes and sitting back. All around them, the leaves rustled as the breeze, heavy with the clean green scent of new-mown hay, moved through them. Cattle lowed in the water meadow near the little river Wednesford and the heat of the afternoon was heavy and soft.

"How peaceful this is," Edmund said.

"It is my favorite place in the world."

"The whole world?"

"I would rather be here than in the Grand Cham's kingdom." She blinked, trying to drive her sudden drowsiness away, and then glanced at Edmund.

Their eyes met and held. His were intent, as if he saw nothing but her. Her heart jumped, her mouth growing sticky. The moment spun endlessly and she felt like a woman under enchantment.

"What a peculiar pair of birds," a deep voice said from below, breaking the spell.

She looked down to find her brother John leaning on his

saddle as he eyed the pair of them nested in the tree. Her drowsiness vanished. "John!"

"Ceci." Her brother's black eyes glittered as he looked from her to Edmund, sitting together in defiance of every precept drilled into her.

"Oh, John, I am so glad you are home!" She shifted in her seat, longing to leap down and into his arms, longing to escape the peculiar intensity of Edmund's eyes and the uncertain way they made her feel. Edmund was in the way, blocking the only safe path out of the tree. Belatedly, she remembered her manners.

"John, allow me to present..." she began and then realized she knew nothing more about Edmund than his name. Assuredly, she was mad to be in this tree with him.

"Edmund Tudor of Pembrokeshire," Edmund said, rescuing her.

"Good day, Master Tudor of Pembrokeshire." John nodded at Edmund and then glanced at Cecilia, a tiny crease between his brows. Her heart plummeted. Not only would she be obliged to endure a scolding from her nurse and perhaps a whipping from her mother but she would have to survive one of John's rare rebukes.

"My brother, Lord John Coleville."

"Sir." Edmund nodded back.

"Let me get this brute to Tom Stableman and then the three of us can take a walk by the river."

"Beatrice met Sebastian down there," Cecilia warned.

"All the more reason to take a walk. Do not go without me. I will be back in a trice," John said lazily, and turned his horse toward the castle.

She did not need to be told that at least one reason for walking down by the river was to get her out of the tree. Heaviness settled against her breastbone, surprising her.

Why was she reluctant to join him when she had waited for him all day? What ailed her?

Understanding came like a slap. She wanted to dally with Edmund. Not only did good manners demand she depart, but also the hard facts of life. She was too old to be sitting in a tree with a young man, especially one who did not meet her in rank. She looked at him, his eyes full of distance as he looked south, past the castle, and her breath caught. What a fool she had been. This man was dangerous to her.

She handed Edmund her copy of Virgil. "Will you carry this and climb down?"

He tucked the book into his doublet and clambered out of the tree, dropping the last few feet and lifted up his arms. "Jump down. I'll catch you."

"Get out of my way." The last thing she dared do was leap into his arms.

He stepped back and she climbed down, swinging easily to the ground beside him.

"You are not like anyone I know," Edmund said.

She looked up at him. "Do you have no sisters?"

"I have two, but neither of them is anything like you."

Unsure of his meaning, she turned her head toward the castle, in time to see John pass under the gatehouse into the lane, moving with that deceptively relaxed stride of his. He never looked as if he hurried but whenever they walked anywhere together, she had to trot to keep up. As he walked, he carried the battered canvas satchel that contained his drawing tools: paper, charcoal and an oak board to draw on. The satchel meant John would spend time under the trees with them, rather than detaching Sebastian from Beatrice and bearing him away. But they must join him—he had bidden them wait for him but that did not mean he would wait for them.

She turned back to Edmund and smiled at him. "Come. We must hurry or we will lose him." She lifted her skirts and ran toward her brother, Edmund shortening his long stride to keep pace as he trotted at her side.

They found Beatrice and Sebastian where Cecilia expected, near a still reach of the river. Beatrice sat with her back against a willow trunk, her knees drawn up with her arms around them, a hard little smile curling her lips. Sebastian lounged on the soft turf beside her, scowling.

"Who is that?" Edmund whispered, his breath soft as feathers against Cecilia's ear.

"Which one?"

"The beauty."

A chill rippled across her skin, as if the sun had gone behind black clouds. She would warrant no one asked after her as "the beauty." "My sister, Beatrice."

"Is she going to Court? She will be pursued by everyone if she does."

"She has a post in the new Duchess of York's household. She is to go to France next month, when the ambassadors go to fetch the duchess."

"Fetch! You make her sound as if she is a bone and the ambassadors are dogs," Edmund said.

"I don't know how else to put it. It *is* what they are doing."

John said, "Beatrice, Sebastian, allow me to introduce Edmund Tudor from Pembrokeshire. Edmund, my sister, Lady Beatrice Coleville. And Sebastian Benbury."

Introductions made, John sat down beside Beatrice, nudging her away from Sebastian. She muttered something that made him grin, but he did not move. Cecilia assumed Edmund would choose to sit with Beatrice since her sister gathered men the way a honeypot gathers flies. Cecilia moved to sit in her usual place on the high bank above the river, bunching her skirts underneath her and slipping off her shoes to dangle her feet in the cool water. She had learned to abandon her escorts before they abandoned her for Beatrice. Cooling her feet in the river gave her something to do as well as the appearance of indifference.

But Edmund flung himself down on the turf beside Cecilia, propping his head on his hand. The sun came out; he had not gone to Beatrice. She glanced at him. He was watching her with the same focused intensity he had shown in the tree. She turned her head away, suddenly shy. She lifted her foot from the river and watched the drops of water sparkle as they fell from her toes. Anything rather than look at Edmund.

"Who is Sebastian?" he asked softly.

"The only son of Lord Lionel Benbury. Benbury Manor is over that hill." She nodded eastward.

Male voices murmured behind her. John spoke first, then Sebastian, then John. Laughter, and more talk. Beatrice was silent. Cecilia scooped water with her foot, letting it run over her ankle.

Edmund leaned close. "And you, mistress? Do you go to Court?" His breath tickled her throat, the tickle curling deep inside her.

"No." She took a deep breath and let it out slowly. "My father attempted to obtain a post for me in the new Duchess of Somerset's household, but they had been filled."

"Then you must know German."

Surprised, she turned to face him. He was looking at the ground, rolling a pebble under his forefinger.

"I do not, but I have heard the Lady Anne knows enough French and Latin to get by."

"I have heard the Germans do not educate their women,

so perhaps she does not." He began digging a hole in the soft ground with his finger.

"That cannot be so. My father says a woman must have an uncommon wit to succeed at Court."

He rolled the pebble into the hole and buried it. "She is a child of eight. She will have time to learn."

He sounded almost sad. She laid her hand over his without thinking. Warmth flowed through her hand and up her arm. He turned his hand to clasp hers and the flow of warmth became a flood.

"I am going home," Beatrice said suddenly.

Cecilia turned. Her sister stood under the tree brushing bits of grass from her skirt. Nothing could destroy the perfection of her features, but her wan face and shadowed eyes dimmed the glow of her beauty.

"I will go with you," Sebastian said, rising.

"Please do not," Beatrice said coolly. "I should prefer to be by myself."

"Do not be a carping misery, Bea," John said abstractedly. He had pulled out his sketching materials and was more than half absorbed in the work on his lap. "Stop awhile in the sunshine."

"I stopped before you came," she said tartly. "If you had been home sooner you would know it."

John looked up from his sketch. Cecilia watched her brother and sister intently, knowing from experience how his black gaze could bend the will. Beatrice glared at him but did not move. The silence between them stretched to the snapping point. Cecilia stole a quick glance at Edmund, curious to see what he thought. He watched Beatrice and John as if he, too, could see the battle of wills taking place.

"Oh, very well," Beatrice said. "If you will make such an issue of it." She sat back down, graceful even when annoyed. If Cecilia sat down when she was irritated, she thumped.

"Turn 'round, Ceci. I want to draw you," John said.

Pulling her hand free of Edmund's, she moved so John could see her face. She had been his chief model for as long as she could remember and was used to sitting still in the poses of his devising while he sketched. If nothing else, it had taught her the appearance of patience. Her reward was to see his sketches, even the ones he showed no one else. Through the gentle burble of the water against the bank and the soughing of the wind through the thick grass, she could hear the rasp of the charcoal on the paper. The soft scratch was the most soothing sound she knew. The paper rustled.

"Relax, Ceci. I've finished. Now you, Edmund."

"I beg your pardon?"

The barest note of arrogant surprise rang in Edmund's voice. Cecilia looked sharply at him, intrigued and disturbed. How dare he? He had not sounded like a gentleman's son a moment ago. The old suspicion that he was a king's son stirred, and with it the old objection. Logic insisted that a king's son did not go anywhere without a dozen or more attendants, nor did he put off the deference due his rank. This Edmund, whoever he was, did not demand a prince's due, so he could be no prince. She made a very neat argument, but the doubt remained, fed by the unthinking arrogance of Edmund's question.

"I am going to sketch you. Turn 'round so I can see your face." John spoke so mildly Cecilia wondered for a moment if she had mistaken Edmund's tone. But no, she saw the consternation in Edmund's face, wiped away in the instant before he turned.

Who are you?

John drew quickly, his hand dancing over the paper rest-

ing on the board on his knees. The sketch of her rested at
his feet; she could see enough to distinguish the shape of
her face. Before Edmund had the chance to break his pose,
John was done. He laid the second sketch beside the one
of Cecilia and began another. Edmund crawled over,
picked up both sketches and returned to Cecilia's side.

He studied the sketch of Cecilia first. Looking over his
shoulder at it, Cecilia's first reaction was despair. She was
still not beautiful. Her eyes were dark and narrow, their
expression suspicious, her nose without character or defi-
nition. Her mouth was too wide. God had given all the
family beauty to Beatrice, leaving her with nothing.

She picked up the sketch of Edmund. John had captured
his hawk look as well as an indefinable air of otherness.
She had not seen it clearly before; now she wondered in
earnest who and what he truly was.

"Is that how I look?" Edmund asked, resting his chin
on her shoulder. She was suddenly conscious of his body
pressing lightly against her from shoulder to hip. A pulse
beat in her throat and her mouth went dry. *I am going to
make a fool of myself.* Her flesh did not care that he had
almost certainly lied, nor could she make herself feel outrage or anger.

"Yes," she managed to say. "It is very like you."

"It is very like my brother." He held out the drawing
of her. "This is exactly like you. May I keep it?"

Her blush burned all the way down to her bones. "With
my great pleasure." She hesitated. "May I keep this?"
She lifted the drawing of Edmund.

"I cannot imagine why you would want it."

A sly little devil took hold of her tongue and spoke. "I
imagine for the same reason you wish to keep the one of
me."

She felt his start of surprise then the shaking of his

frame. She turned her head and saw he was laughing silently. "Keep it with my blessing," he whispered and stood. "It grows late. I am expected at Hatfield and must not tarry."

"You will not make it before nightfall," John said, frowning at the oak board.

"In August?" Sebastian asked. "It will be light enough to see for hours longer and there is a moon tonight."

"You need not fly to Hatfield tonight, whether there is light to see or not." John looked at Sebastian for a moment before turning back to Edmund. "I offer you the hospitality of Wednesfield."

"I thank you, but I may not accept." He bowed, first to the trio under the tree and then to Cecilia. He took a step toward the Wednesfield lane and then stopped, his mouth quirked up at the corner. "I do not know my way." He held his hand out to Cecilia. "Mistress, I should be glad of your instruction. I pray you, show me the way."

Her hesitation lasted only an instant. "Gladly." She rose and took his hand.

"Ceci—" John said.

"John." She had never defied him before; she did not know if she had the courage to do it now. *Please, do not say it. Do not forbid me.* She looked into his eyes, hoping her heart was in her own. *Do not shame me before him.*

His black stare softened. "Do not tarry."

It seemed only an instant before they were back at her tree, his horse drowsing on three hooves beneath it. Why was the journey back always shorter than the journey away? She did not want him to leave.

"Hatfield is that way." She pointed past Wednesfield, glowing golden in the late afternoon sun, its hundred windows glittering.

"I know the way," he replied, stepping closer to her. "I said I did not because I wished to say farewell to you alone."

The heat of his body, shimmering through the warmth of the afternoon, brushed her like a caress. She reached out and stroked his horse's nose, aware as never before of her hands and feet, arms and legs. She did not know where to put any of them and feared that looking up at him would only worsen her awkwardness. "You are welcome to return when your business at Hatfield is finished," she said, staring at the long sunlight glittering on the brass rings of the bridle. People came and went from Wednesfield in every season; one more visitor would be unremarkable.

"I do not think I shall return this way, mistress." He reached into his doublet and pulled out her small books and John's sketch. He handed the books to her and tucked the sketch back into his doublet, patting it so it crackled. "But I shall not forget you."

"Nor I you," she whispered.

He took her hand and raised it to his mouth, his lips soft and cool against her knuckles. She looked up, daring to meet his eyes. They stared into hers, blue as the sky above. She began to tremble, the inside of her mouth drying. He murmured, "God keep you, mistress."

Unable to bear the intensity of his stare, she broke her gaze from his, looking at the white velvet of his mount's nose instead. "And you."

For the first time in her life, she did not feel as if everything she said or did was wrong. He had liked her erudition; he had understood her oblique remarks, never once giving her the blank stare she had come to expect. How could he leave her, when she had never known anyone like him? Yet she was glad he was leaving—for all that he followed where her wit led, he unsettled her more than anyone she had ever known.

She heard the whisper of his feet through the grass and then the creak of leather as he mounted. She loosed his rein from the sapling and handed it to him, daring to look at him once more.

His beauty caught in her throat, all tawny-gold and soft, English gray-blue. Her fledgling hawk. He touched the brim of his cap and turned his horse. Within minutes, he had ridden out of sight.

When she returned to the river, Sebastian and Beatrice had disappeared. John remained where he had been, still intently sketching. He glanced at her swiftly as if he had just become aware of her, but she knew otherwise. John always knew when someone came near to him.

"Sit with me, Ceci."

"You are going to scold me," she said, pleating her skirt with her fingers.

"I shall not."

She had no doubt he lied but she also knew his persistence. Let him speak his piece and be done with it. Settling beside him, she waited for him to begin. When he did not, she kicked off her shoes, closing her eyes and listening to the river burble against its banks. Soft as the gentle breeze, so softly she barely heard him, John sighed. "So, poppet, you have your first swain. Not as noble as our parents would like, I'll warrant, but pleasing enough."

Her eyes opened as her calm dissolved. She could not speak of Edmund. "Do not."

"You ought not to have walked him to the road—you are not a child any longer—but no harm was done." His voice was flat, as if he spoke the words without truly knowing their meaning, and some darkness in his eyes as he stared at her spoke to her of dread and excitement mingled.

"Is that all you wish to say?"

"No."

He took her hand, clenching it in his own. Her heart pounded against her ribs. This was going to be worse than a scolding; she had no desire to hear anything more. Yet she was more afraid not to know. He whispered, "Promise me you will not tell anyone what I am about to tell you."

She swallowed, her throat hot and sore. It must be very bad, the very worst thing he had ever done if he was swearing her to secrecy. She nodded, unable to speak.

She fought the obstruction in her throat. "I promise." The pain in her hand was nothing.

"I am leaving."

"Leaving?" The tightness in her chest grew to suffocation as her sight clouded. *I am dreaming. This is a nightmare and I shall wake. Now.*

"I am going to Germany, to find a painter, Master Hans Holbein. I am hoping he will let me study with him."

"A painter? Germany? John, I don't understand." This was growing stranger and more awful by the moment.

"I cannot stay here, Ceci. I cannot. Father has arranged a place for me in the Duke of Norfolk's household. I cannot go. I cannot go on pretending to be a nobleman."

"Pretending? John, you are a nobleman. You were born one!" She had never felt so stupid, her mind resisting his words.

He released her hand and pulled her against him in a quick rough hug. "I am not a nobleman. I have no desire to live at Court, or make a great marriage, or do any of the things expected of me."

"That's sinful!"

"Oh, Ceci," he said, looking down at her in the curve

of his shoulder, his eyes full of doubt and pain, as if he feared she would repudiate him. Worse, he looked as if he expected it. She clutched the edge of his doublet with her free hand. "Do you really believe God would give me the ability to draw and then make it a sin for me to use it?"

"He might. It might be a test." Her voice broke on the last word. She bit the inside of her lip to forestall tears. Something, some clear cold part of her mind said she must not go back to the castle with red, swollen eyes. Her mother would badger her until she was driven to confessing John's secret. The only way to keep her word was to avoid the interrogation. The same passionless part of her suggested that if she betrayed John, their parents would force him to stay. She thrust the thought away. Anything, even breaking her heart, was better than that.

"And it might not. Perhaps all the worldly glory of being a Coleville is the test, hmm?"

"Don't go, John. Don't leave me." She threw her arms around him, burying her face in his shoulder. Maybe if she held tightly enough he would stay.

"Poppet, I promise you I *will* come home. I promise."

"You could die. It's dangerous in Germany."

"It's dangerous in England. I won't die." Gently, he pushed her away, pressing a kiss to her forehead and tucking a strand of hair back from her face. "Whatever it takes, I will come home."

Chapter Two

April 1521
Five Years Later

"This night rail is too ragged to take," Cecilia's nurse, Mistress Emma, said decisively, holding the nearly transparent linen up to the light. "I shall add it to the ragbag."

"It is the softest one I have," Cecilia protested. "It is my favorite." Her mother, who was nearly too busy to sew, had stitched the smocking and Beatrice had embroidered apples on its cuffs and collar, a kindness that had begun healing the breach between them. When she was sick or unhappy, this was the nightgown she wore for comfort.

"You cannot have threadbare garments when you wait on the queen." Beatrice turned from her post by the window. She was dressed magnificently enough for Court herself in blue velvet almost invisible under silver embroidery; diamonds and pearls glowed in the soft spring light. "Mistress Emma is right."

"Very well. I will not bring it to Court. But do not add it to the ragbag, I beg you." Mistress Emma shot her a disapproving glance but checked the reproof she might have spoken before Cecilia received her appointment to wait on the queen.

"Let her keep it," Beatrice said. "It is pleasant to come home to Wednesfield and find some things unchanged."

She met Cecilia's eyes and looked away. Nothing was the same, nothing would ever be the same. John had never come home. After studying in Germany, he had moved on to France and then Italy, studying with painters along the way. He had written letter after letter, explaining why he needed to go farther away instead of coming home, but nothing he wrote made any sense to Cecilia. She longed for her brother, for his kindness and affection. And almost as soon as she and Beatrice had become friends, her sister had married and left to live at Court with her husband. Cecilia missed her sister more than she would have dreamed possible five years ago.

"Ah, there you are, my dear." Beatrice's husband, Thomas Manners, stood in the doorway, a pleasant smile fixed on his worn face. He was years older than Beatrice, twice widowed with grown children. His furred gown and slashed velvet doublet, both in the height of fashion, did not disguise his skinny legs, wattled tortoise neck or protuberant stomach. Under his jeweled cap with its jaunty plume, his head was bald. The scent of cloves, underlaid with a faint tang of decay, followed him wherever he went. Cecilia's skin crawled.

"I am assisting my sister. I thought she might benefit from my counsel," Beatrice said tonelessly.

"I should like you to walk with me in the garden," he said mildly. Cecilia saw Beatrice's hand clutch the window frame.

"I am not finished here." While Beatrice did not cringe,

her voice lacked its old firmness and her statement nearly sounded like a question.

"I am sure they can finish without you," he replied. Beatrice's mouth thinned. Cecilia put her hands behind her back to conceal her curling fists. She did not know how he did it, but Manners had a way of speaking kind words cruelly without using sarcasm or raising his voice.

"As you will, my lord."

Beatrice left the window and paused to kiss Cecilia on the cheek. Her hand, briefly touching Cecilia's, was cold. Manners offered his arm to his wife, who laid her hand on it. They left the room, a picture of domestic bliss.

"I hate him," Cecilia muttered fiercely.

"He is your brother," Mistress Emma said.

"He is no brother of mine! He is merely her husband. While he lives."

"What do you say, mistress?" Mistress Emma asked. All at once, she was Cecilia's nursemaid again, trying to guide her charge on the path of proper behavior.

"Merely, he is old and she is young. She will be his widow."

Mistress Emma crossed herself. "It is unchancy to speak of such things, Cecilia. She may well die in childbed."

"They have been married for how many years? And she has not quickened once. I do not think she has ever been pregnant." Resolutely she refused to think of what Beatrice must face to become pregnant.

"Beatrice is not barren." Mistress Emma scowled at her.

"No, a field is only barren when it is well plowed and does not bring forth." Cecilia waved her hand dismissively. While it was common knowledge that childlessness was the woman's fault, she could not help thinking of fields planted with damaged, diseased seed.

"You should not say that," Mistress Emma said.

"It is the truth."

"It is country talk, and will do you no good at Court."

Cecilia paced around the room, suddenly restless. She opened the chest at the foot of the bed and closed it, then went to the window, opened the casement and leaned out. The courtyard was empty, clouds gathering overhead. She ducked back inside.

"Country talk may do me no good at Court, but at least I know enough not to walk in the garden in April. It is going to rain again." She moved from the window and sat on the chest at the foot of the bed, looking up at Mistress Emma's familiar face. "I am afraid, mistress."

"I know, chuck. It is a big world when you are in it alone."

"But I shall not be alone. Beatrice will be there, and my brother Jasper. And Sebastian, too."

Cecilia bounced up from the chest and seized Emma in a robust embrace, pressing her cheek to her nurse's. "Dear Mistress Emma, may I pack you in a trunk and carry you with me to Court?"

"What should I do at Court, then?"

"Keep Beatrice out of trouble. Lighten my heart. Make the queen laugh."

"Do not worry about your sister. She will come right, never you fear. And once you get settled at Court, the other maids will lighten your heart and you yourself will make the queen laugh."

"Shall I? I cannot imagine how."

Emma's arms held her tight. "Chuck, my old bones tell me none of us can imagine what is before you."

Cecilia pulled out of the embrace, a strange dark note in Mistress Emma's voice making her uneasy. "What do you mean, Mistress?

"A turn of speech," Mistress Emma said. "I was not paying heed to my words."

"No. I do not believe that. Tell me the truth, I beg you."

Mistress Emma sighed. "Promise me you will tell no one what I am about to tell you."

"I promise."

Mistress Emma's eyes met hers searchingly, one woman to another. It was the first time Mistress Emma had ever looked at her so. A rippling chill ran over her arms.

"Very well. My bones sometimes tell me things. I knew your brother Henry was not long for this world even as I helped him from your mother. And I knew your brother John would break your mother's heart."

"What do you see now?" Cecilia whispered.

"I *see* nothing. I listen to my bones. And they tell me that you will not go where I or anyone else expect."

"I am not going to Richmond?"

"Do not be literal, child." Mistress Emma pulled her close once again and rubbed her back, the way she used to when Cecilia was a very small girl, crying her eyes out. "All will be well. I do know that." Cecilia listened for masked fear and heard only love. She relaxed against Mistress Emma's familiar softness. She had not fought a Court post because duty demanded she do all she could to advance the family, but now that her departure was upon them, she did not want to leave home. The nest was too small, the sky too big; she was a bird that didn't know where it belonged.

"I wish I knew what was going to happen to me," she said, pulling out of the embrace a final time.

"You will go to Court, earn the queen's favor, dazzle a rich, noble Gentleman of the Bedchamber, marry and live to be a wise woman like your mother."

Cecilia giggled. "The only rich, noble Gentleman of the

Bedchamber I know is Sebastian Benbury and I could not dazzle him if I was covered head to toe in cloth of gold and diamonds.''

"And you need not go away to Court to meet him, either," Mistress Emma replied. "There are other men at Court with their eyes open for a rich, pretty wife. Mark my words. I was at King Edward's Court with your mother."

Abruptly, Cecilia remembered the stare of blue-gray eyes and a touch that had made her pulse flutter in her throat like the beat of a lark's wings. Where was he now? Waiting for her at Court? She sighed and set those thoughts aside. "King Edward's Court was a long time ago, mistress."

"But it was a Court. I was at King Henry's Court, too. You could scour the length of England and not find two men less alike than King Henry and King Edward, nor have two Courts more different in any number of ways. But one thing was the same at each. Men met maids and matches were made."

"Like my mother and father."

"Aye, like your mother and father." She shook her head and sighed. "I have forgotten the bags of herbs to tuck into the folds of your clothes. It won't do for you to arrive at Court with your clothes smelling like mildew." She left the room.

Cecilia walked to the window and watched the rain pour down in sheets. Had Beatrice gone outdoors, after all? Or had she, more weatherwise than Cecilia, seen that a stroll in the garden was folly and persuaded Manners to stay within? Cecilia had never understood what had compelled Beatrice to her marriage. Manners had been no choice of their parents; in fact, their mother had done everything she could to prevent the union, short of forbidding it. That ill-favored toad had been of Beatrice's choosing.

"Ah, you are here."

Cecilia turned. Her mother stood in the doorway, hands folded against her waist, one of the serving boys staggering past her and dropping a large box on the chest with a booming thump. Sliding a look at Cecilia, he tugged on his forelock and then, bent at the waist in a bow to her mother, scurried from the room.

Her mother swung the keys that hung from the end of her belt into her hand and crossed the room to the box. Moving swiftly without appearing to hurry, she unlocked the box and flung open the lid. Pale, clouded light spun gently on gold and silver, sparkled in diamonds and sapphires, heated to blood in rubies. The box was crammed with jewelry, more wealth than Cecilia had imagined the family possessed.

"Mama!" She was too surprised to remember to be formal.

"Five hundred years of royal service are in that box," her mother said. "You will need jewels at Court."

"Oh, Mama." She sighed, unable to imagine wearing any of it.

Her mother lifted the box and spilled its glittering contents onto the bed. She leaned over the piled jewelry and began sorting it by kind. Cecilia crept closer to the bed and gripped one of its posts, watching her mother's deft white hands moving over the jewels like the cook's when he sorted eggs.

When the contents of the box had been sorted, Cecilia's mother glanced up. "Hold out your hands. We must choose rings." Cecilia did as she was bidden. Her mother picked through the pile of rings until she had a fistful. "See how well these fit you."

Only one ring, an ugly knot of gold stuffed with a cloudy diamond, was too large. ''Bring me your jewel coffer,'' her mother said. Cecilia turned back to the chest at the foot of the bed and lifted the lid. The little brass-bound coffer in which she kept her few pieces of jewelry was buried in a corner, resting on another box. She pulled the coffer out, her fingers brushing the long thin box underneath it. Dare she open it? She straightened, closed the lid of the chest, and set the coffer on the bed.

Her mother lifted the coffer lid and put the rings inside. ''The fashion is to wear a ring on every finger.''

''It will interfere with my playing,'' Cecilia said.

Her mother's eyebrows lifted. ''That is what royal musicians are for, Cecilia.''

Cecilia lowered her eyes. Would she be forbidden to play the lute and the virginals at Court? Beatrice had told her that the queen's ladies entertained her with music and Cecilia's heart had soared in pleasure. Was Beatrice wrong? ''Yes, madam.''

Her mother chose pendants and neck chains, bejeweled belts and bracelets, piling them all in the coffer with instructions on how and when to wear each item. Finally, her mother drew out a circlet of pearls, a W made of rubies dangling from it. ''This has been made for you.''

Her breath left her in a gasp. ''Oh, Mama.''

''It is a carcanet, to wear around your throat. You have the skin for pearls and rubies, better skin for it than Beatrice or I.'' She undid the clasp. ''Turn. Let me put it on.''

Cecilia turned, bending her neck so her mother could refasten the clasp. The pearls were smooth against the skin of her throat, the W cool in the opening of her shirt.

''You will not wear a shirt with this. Your bodice will be open, like so.'' Her mother's hands reached over her shoulders and untied the fastening of her shirt. "Come. See yourself." Her mother walked to the chest against the wall and held up Cecilia's silver mirror. Cecilia followed her.

She saw a distorted image of a woman in a white linen coif, dark hair peeping out from underneath it. Circling her neck were pearls as smooth as the skin of her throat, rubies burning like blood against her breastbone. If she were dressed in her wine-red velvet bodice and skirt, with the French hood that matched....

Her eyes burned and she blinked. "It is beautiful," she whispered.

Her mother lowered the mirror, the blue of her eyes deepened by tears. "You are beautiful, my child." She stroked Cecilia's cheek with the backs of her fingers. "My little one." Clearing her throat, she wiped her cheeks with her free hand. She returned the mirror to the chest against the wall and faced Cecilia once more, the softness gone from her clear eyes. "There is nothing I need tell you about your duty, is there? Your father and I trust you will do nothing to bring dishonor to the family."

"I shall not," Cecilia said. Beatrice used to complain of their mother's chilly briskness but Cecilia found it bracing. Unlike her sister, she had always felt that love underlaid it.

"If you can make a good marriage, we shall be pleased, but not every maid of honor attracts a worthy suitor, nor is attraction alone a solid base for marriage."

Cecilia spread her hands. "It is in God's hands, madam." Unlike Beatrice, she was neither buxom nor beautiful and she had had a wider education than some men liked in a woman. What good were Latin and Greek in bearing children and managing households? On the other hand, she would have a good dowry and her father was a man with whom anyone would be honored to make an alliance. Save for the king's brothers, she might look as high as she pleased for a husband.

"Wednesfield will be far too quiet without you, child," her mother said, surprising her. "Kneel for my blessing."

After her mother left, Cecilia locked the coffer and put the key in the needlecase hanging from her belt. She crossed the room to the window.

The rain had stopped and in the distance, past the wall surrounding the courtyard, the clouds had lifted over the horizon, freeing a river of gold to pour from the westering sky. The ragged edges of the clouds were brilliant with gilding. Her throat closed. She did not want to leave; she never wanted to leave this place and all its beauties. This was the only place she knew; these were the only people she wanted to live amongst.

But she had her duty. Everything she owed her parents and her name demanded that she go. She squared her shoulders and turned away from the window.

Her gaze fell on the chest at the foot of the bed and she remembered the long thin box inside. A different longing crept over her. It will only hurt, she thought, and knelt beside the chest, anyway. She lifted the lid and drew the long thin box out, resting it for a moment in her lap. She should not do this. She had been a fool not to have burned them all long ago.

"If you are going to be a fool, Cecilia," she murmured, "you might as well be a thorough one." She opened the box.

It was full of John's drawings, the oldest on top. She looked at them one by one, lingering over each drawing. She was going to be homesick at Court and there would be times when she would long for Wednesfield. The castle and its people were here, captured in every season by John's gift. If she put a lock on the box, she could bring it with her. It would be like having a piece of home at Court.

She came to the series he had drawn that afternoon by the river. There was Beatrice, half glaring and half laughing. Sebastian, gloomy with longing. And Edmund: intelligent, curious, full of mischievous good humor. Beautiful, with a strong-boned masculine beauty. Her fingertips brushed close to his limned cheek and then snatched away as if stung.

Let him be there, she thought. Please, let him not be there.

She returned the drawing to the box.

Chapter Three

"Way! Way! Make way for His Grace, the Duke of Somerset!"

Edmund sauntered behind the shouting lackeys, his boredom concealed by a mask of haughtiness. Behind him, his gentleman ushers strode and jostled, full of consequence because they attended him. He longed to be elsewhere, anywhere so long as he was free of courtiers, politics and the need to protect his back from everyone around him. He had reminded Arthur he had work to do, but his brother had insisted he come to Westminster, claiming he needed Edmund by his side. Edmund obeyed reluctantly, as bound by his promise to his father as a falcon by the jesses. That old promise, made painful by his father's death six months later. He had moments when he wished he had never made it. His father's white, wasted face appeared before his mind's eye, the eyes burning and intent.

Remember your promise, Edmund!

I shall, Sire.

He shook the memory off, wanting to protest, I was too young! You asked too much of me! But there was no one to say that to, only the work to do, the fulfillment of his vow.

Someone shouted his title into the din and he and his ushers entered the king's Great Chamber. He strode to the dais and made his obeisance to the king and queen, his feathered and bejeweled cap held against his breast. Arthur looked abstracted, as if his head pained him. Wearing his smiling Court mask, Edmund bowed with a flourish while he wondered what was going on. Kati, sitting beside her husband, provided no clue. She was sparkling with happiness and health, finally past the greensick stage of pregnancy.

He kissed her offered hand. "How beautiful you are tonight, Your Majesty."

"I am an old married woman, Edmund. Test your wiles on another," she replied, turning a gratified pink at his compliment.

"Is there another? I cannot see anyone else, blinded as I am by your radiance," he said.

She gurgled with laughter. "You are outrageous!" she whispered, still blushing.

"I am perfectly serious, Kati."

"It pleases me that you use the name my family used," she remarked.

"I live to please you," he said only half jokingly, winking at her. He flirted with her because it made her laugh. If turning himself inside out had amused her, he would have done it gladly. Her kindness had helped him in innumerable ways through the years and her intelligence and wide interests made his life at Court endurable.

Idly, he glanced at the maids of honor, standing in a demure cluster to one side of Kati's throne. There was a new one, dark-haired and dark-eyed. Cecilia Coleville. His chest tightened, his heart giving a strange little jump as he stared at her, drinking in the sight of her. It had been too long; it had only been yesterday.

She turned as if she had felt his eyes on her and gave back stare for stare. Even at this distance, he saw the doubt in her eyes, the question she asked herself: could it be…?

He had seen the same look the first time when her sister Beatrice came to Court and again when Sebastian Benbury joined the Duke of York's household. Fear that Beatrice would tell what she knew had made him cold and stiff with her. She had taken it for pride; the question had left her eyes, replaced by the deference due a king's brother. Later, when Benbury had given him the same questioning stare, Edmund had drawn on his experience with Beatrice, putting on royalty the way he put on his gowns. He had learned a valuable lesson; men would accept what he believed about himself.

Now he needed to slip on princely pride once more, perhaps for the final time. Cecilia was the last person who could connect the gentleman Edmund Tudor of Pembroke-shire with the Duke of Somerset. He met Cecilia's eyes without allowing himself to truly see her, waiting for the question, the half-formed recognition, to die in her eyes.

Instead, full recognition flared in their depths. Her color deepened as she blushed, while recognition became understanding and then anger. A mad part of his mind rejoiced in her knowledge and admired the sharp wit that enabled her to see him clearly; the shrewder part of his mind was appalled. With one sentence, two at most, she could wreck him, reveal to all the world that the Duke of Somerset liked to pretend he was only a gentleman. He had to silence her before she spoke.

But he could not do it now. First he must make his bows to his brother Harry and Harry's wife, Madeleine of Angoulême, standing far enough away from the dais that Harry could collect his own little court.

Harry looked as self-satisfied as he usually did, while

Madeleine's eyelids were reddened and her mouth was puckered as if she had been sucking on a sour apple all afternoon. Harry must have a new mistress; he could not be more public with his lights-o'-love if he had a herald announce them throughout England. Edmund pitied Madeleine with his whole heart. To make her laugh, he leaned forward and whispered, "Very clever, *ma mie*. Not everyone brings a steer to Court." Madeleine followed his glance to Harry, dressed in russet and white, and her sullenness vanished as she burst into giggles. Harry turned and scowled at him. Edmund grinned in response as he lifted Madeleine's hand to kiss each of her fingers. She shot Harry a glance of triumph before giving her other hand to Edmund.

Musicians began to play and at the sound courtiers turned toward the center of the chamber, where the king led the queen out to begin the evening's dancing. The slow basse dance suited them perfectly; Arthur was too dignified and Kati too pregnant for a quick courante or lively galliard. Standing, Kati's thickened waist was plain. Though Edmund had known of her pregnancy for weeks now, relief and gratitude lightened his heart. Another heir for England; another son between him and the trap of the throne.

The next dance was a courante. He held out his hand to Madeleine, who needed a lively dance to chase away more of her unhappiness. Harry seized her hand before Edmund had a chance to take it. As her husband led her onto the floor, Madeleine shot Edmund a conspiratorial look. Provoking Harry into dancing with his wife was simple; Edmund knew no one more easily manipulated than his brother.

Duty performed, he worked his way back toward the dais and Cecilia, only to find she was no longer standing beside Kati. He turned toward the dancers and quickly found her in their midst, smiling up at her partner. The man turned his head as the dance turned in and out in a long, flowing knot. Edmund recognized Sebastian Benbury. Would Cecilia say something to him? Ask him why he had not told her who Edmund was? He watched them intently, waiting for the moment she revealed her knowledge to Benbury, but she did nothing but smile, laughing once when Benbury bent his head close to hers.

The music ended, the dancers dispersing across the room. Although Edmund told himself to wait until Cecilia returned to her place near Kati, he found himself walking toward her. All the brilliantly dressed people faded from his vision, leaving only Cecilia clear in his sight, like a single candle in a dark room.

As he reached her, she sank down in a graceful curtsy, her wine-red skirts spreading around her. She lifted her face to him as she rose and while her smile was friendly, her eyes were wary. He could not blame her.

The musicians struck up a pavane. Slow and stately, it would allow him to persuade her to silence. He extended his hand. "Join me in this dance, my lady."

"I do not know this pavane, my lord. I should not like to make a fool of myself." Her words were shy but her tone was cool and no more than polite.

"Let me guide you and you will not," he replied, his hand still stretched out.

"Then I am honored, Your Grace," she said, placing her hand in his. Warmth curled up his arm from their clasped hands.

He guided Cecilia through the dance with a light touch on her waist and a few, brief commands. She was a quick study, light on her feet and quick to turn and jump. The distance between them evaporated as she gave herself up to the pleasure of the dance, her footwork becoming more assured and her turns more graceful. When the dance brought them face-to-face, she smiled up at him as if they were alone, far from Court.

"The dance pleases you," he said.

"Yes, my lord. Your instruction is clear."

"Then you do not regret dancing."

"Oh, no, my lord."

Nor do I, he thought as the dance turned him away. The intensity of his pleasure surprised him. She is only someone I knew long ago, he told himself, but even as he thought it he knew it was untrue. *Someone I must silence.* That was not true, either.

"Perhaps you should. I am very bad company."

"I know nothing of that, Your Grace. What I do know is that you are not overfond of the truth."

He had not expected such plain speaking from her and for a moment he could not reply. "I have not lied to you. I spoke no untruth."

"Lies of omission are still lies," she said. The distance had opened up between them again; surprisingly, he wanted to bridge it. He had approached her intending simply to command her silence. When had that desire disappeared?

Thankfully, the dance came as easily as breathing to him. He did not know how he would have managed had he been forced to think of his steps. "You are right, and I beg your pardon. I—I did not think you would believe me if I told you who I am."

She looked briefly doubtful, her eyes examining him intently. Their brown was very clear, catching the candlelight in warm depths. "I do not believe you now," she said slowly.

"I assure you I tell the truth," he said. He ought to tell her to hold her tongue and have done.

She frowned at him. "Why should I believe you?"

Her continuing skepticism startled him. "Because I speak the truth," he snapped.

"As you will it, sir," she said coolly, lowering her eyes. He had offended her. He ought to be pleased; instead, he wanted to beg her forgiveness.

"I *will* nothing. I ask your honest belief in me. On my honor, I shall not mislead you again."

The dance ended, the music fading. She looked up at him thoughtfully for a long moment. "I asked you no questions five years ago. That shall not happen again."

"So be it." He took her hand and lifted it to his lips, unaccountably pleased that she had deigned to offer him what he should have commanded from the start. You are a fool, he thought severely.

"You should return to Kati. I mean, the queen," he said. His face burned at his slip of the tongue.

"Kati? I have never heard that name before," she said, curiosity apparently overcoming annoyance. He seized the chance to turn the topic to an innocuous channel.

"It was her family name at home. In Spain. I have never called her anything else."

"I cannot imagine calling the queen's grace by anything so familiar," she said.

"She is my sister-in-law and in love, so it is different for me."

"I had forgotten," she replied. "I cannot help forgetting who you are."

"Forget who I am?"

"That you are the Duke of Somerset, brother to the king. Royal, unlike common men. Though you ape the manners of a common man well enough."

"If you cut me, I shall bleed red blood like any other man. My bones break, my flesh bruises, like any other man's. I am a man, never doubt it.'' *And your beauty calls to me, as it would to any man.*

He turned to look out at the dancers, at the graceful, intricate patterns they followed. It was hard to hear the music over the din of conversation, but they had all grown up learning these dances. He hardly knew why they needed music.

"No, I do not," she said, so softly he thought he had misheard her. "But royal blood is different."

"It is not," he said thoughtfully. "I might as easily have been born to a different station. I should still have been the same man, no matter whose son I was."

"That is not possible," she said firmly.

"*You* forget my royal birth. That is not possible if something sets me apart from other men. Common men are little different than the men in this room. Take away the silk and velvet, and men are more alike than different." He had never spoken these thoughts out loud before. They could easily be interpreted as questioning the order of things, a short step shy of heresy. Or treason. He began walking and she, without his leave to go, was forced to follow.

"You are saying that if I had been a merchant's daughter, I should be the same woman?" Her high smooth brow furrowed and her eyes narrowed thoughtfully.

"Yes, that is it exactly." Almost against his will, he added, "I am glad you are not a merchant's daughter. I should not know you otherwise."

Pink crept into her cheeks again. "That is a very pretty thing to say. I see how you earned your name."

"My name?" He stopped, too surprised to keep moving.

She turned back to face him. "The queen's ladies call you the Prince of Hearts because you pretend to wear so many on your sleeve." Her grin was mischievous.

"They say I pretend?" He ought not to be offended since it was precisely the effect he had tried to achieve. He considered his annoyance and realized it was provoked by the laughter sparkling in the amber depths of her eyes. He did not care to be her jester.

"Yes, they say you dally with every woman you meet. Is it not true?" she asked.

"I have dallied with them as every other man has, but I have made no promises nor declarations. I do not mislead women about my intentions."

"That is a curious remark. I did not say you had misled anyone about your intentions, though we both know you are capable of misleading a lady about other matters. What *are* your intentions?"

When he had first learned swordplay, his tutor had relentlessly backed him into a corner with skillful feints, thrusts and jabs of his blade. Edmund had panicked, unable to defend himself or to curtail the steady assault. He had not felt so powerless since. He wanted to tell her to hush her mouth, but suspected it would reveal how shaken he was.

"My intentions are my own affair," he said in a bid to escape her examination. She was too clever by half.

Her lashes swept down, concealing her sharp eyes in a look of contrition. "You are right. Please forgive me, I was prying. If you will give me leave, I must return to the queen. She did not give me permission to dance the night away."

He had wanted her to behave like any other of the demure maids of honor but now that he had his wish, he wanted her sturdy independence back. She was turning all his notions upside down, making a mishmash of his plans. "Allow me to escort you. She will not be cross with you if she sees I have detained you." He offered her his arm.

She laid her hand on his wrist in a graceful gesture that brought his eyes to her long tapering fingers. Her skin was like ivory, smooth and warm against the dark green of his doublet sleeve. The beauty of the contrast, the pearliness of her skin, caught and held his eye.

Her fingers caressed the velvet of his sleeve and then stilled. "I beg your pardon, I should not have been so forward. But I could not resist, this is such beautiful cloth."

"I had not noticed."

"I have a great weakness for beautiful clothes. The best part of coming to Court has been the beautiful clothes, their jewels, fine materials and embroidery." She nodded at the dancers, dressed in brocade and velvet, sleeves puffed and slashed, bodices in colors from scarlet to lincoln-green trimmed in pearls and jet and gold. It was a feast for the eye, temptation for the touch.

"What has been the worst part?" he asked. It seemed a natural question, but he regretted it when he saw how it clouded her face.

"The gossip. The eyes always watching," she said, her voice quiet and flat.

"What of the eyes at Wednesfield? Surely everyone watches you there, too."

"It is not the same. They know me at home and they love me. Here, they are like wolves, waiting for you to weaken so they can pull you down." She shivered.

As they arrived at the dais, the king and queen rose, Kati laying her hand on Arthur's wrist. They were leaving. Cecilia curtsied and made to join the departing procession, but Kati stopped her, whispering in her ear. Cecilia curtsied again. Arthur paused at Edmund's side. "I must speak to you."

"I will follow you, Sire," Edmund said.

Arthur smiled faintly, a satiric gleam in his cool gray eyes. "I know you are fond of my wife, but I think not, little brother. Tomorrow morning, before Mass."

"I am yours to command, Sire," Edmund said, bowing.

Arthur chuckled. "If only that were true, jackanapes."

As soon as the doors shut behind the king and queen, the atmosphere visibly loosened, as if some faint restraint had been cast off. Edmund looked down at the woman at his side as she watched the crowd, her brows drawn delicately together over her straight nose. He wondered what thoughts filled the mind behind her lovely face and then smiled ruefully. Given his experience tonight, they were likely thoughts he would find discomfiting.

"Kati does not need you for the rest of the evening?" he asked.

"She has given leave for me to remain as long as I wish," Cecilia replied, looking up at him with a confiding air. "She is very good to me."

"She is a good woman. The king is lucky." He had never said it out loud but he was beginning to grow used to the way he spoke openly to Cecilia.

"Do you envy him?"

No one had ever asked him how he felt about anything, least of all his brother's happy marriage. Surprise held him still for a moment and then he bent his mind to answering. He should not have been caught off guard by her curiosity or her candor.

"No, I do not. Arthur deserves happiness and Kati brings it to him. I am unlikely to be so fortunate." He expected he would be like Madeleine, tied for life to someone she disliked in the interests of her country. Someday, perhaps soon, Arthur would need to make another alliance and, as had happened five years ago, Edmund's marriage would be part of the price. Edmund would set aside his personal considerations and do what needed to be done. The prompt and willing fulfillment of one's duty, not the rigid stratification of station, was what kept society from degenerating into anarchy.

"Many of us are unlikely to be so fortunate," she replied matter-of-factly.

"Then let us enjoy tonight, when we are free," he said, shaking off the faint melancholy that had gathered as he considered his probable future. "This is a courante. Do you know it?"

"Yes, I do."

"Then let us dance the night away."

She took his hand and they dove into the crowd of dancers.

Chapter Four

"Well done, Your Grace, well done! Clap in the clout! No one can beat that!" a page cried as the Duke of York's arrow thrummed in the center of the target.

The Court had gathered at the archery butts, where an informal contest had developed between the king and his two brothers. The king had wagered he could beat both his brothers in a round of three.

"The king has yet to shoot," Edmund replied placidly, leaning on his bow. Cecilia glanced away from him, afraid of her desire to gaze at him. How had she failed to see he was a prince the first time she laid eyes on him? "If we were to need another Robin Hood, I know where I would begin my search."

Cecilia shifted her weight from her aching right foot to her aching left foot, trying vainly to ease her discomfort. *If I had known my feet would hurt so, I would have retired sooner.* As it was, both her feet sported an impressive collection of blisters and there was a large, heel-shaped bruise on her left instep where a gentleman usher had stepped on it. Still, the night she had spent had been worth every pinch of pain she suffered now. Except for a round dance with the clod-footed usher and a galliard with Sebastian, she had danced with Edmund all night long. And when they had not danced, they had walked, talked, laughed and debated, discussing everything under the sun, from Martin Luther to Chaucer to Plato. Until last night, she had not known how starved she was for serious discourse. How not? She had not had a conversation like that since her tutor left. And even then she had never expressed her every thought as freely as she did when she spoke to Edmund. She could not keep a grudge against him for his deception when he proved such a clever companion.

But more than that, she was still dazzled by the glamour that had shone in every moment of the night. The warm clasp of his fingers on hers, his touch on her waist as they danced, the glinting heat of his eyes as they met and held hers for endless moments: she was still enfolded in the web of his enchantment.

The king planted his feet, nocked his arrow and sighted along its ash-wood shaft. He had removed gown and doublet; sweat made the fine cambric of his shirt cling to his broad, well-muscled shoulders. He was a fine figure of a man for all his lack of inches; Cecilia saw more than one lady-in-waiting eye him covetously.

The king released his arrow. It landed with a satisfying *thunk* so close to the other arrow that for all intents and purposes it was in the same place.

"Very pretty, my lord!" the queen cried. The king walked over to his wife and kissed her hand. From her lap he took a linen towel and wiped his face. Their patent affection for one another reminded Cecilia of her parents and was a far cry from the distance married courtiers kept between them.

"It was a neat shot, *mi esposita,*" he conceded. "Let us see what Edmund can do."

"I am not shooting against you, Sire. I yield. You are

both far better archers than I will ever be," Edmund said, bowing his head and lifting his free hand.

"Coward," the Duke of York said softly.

"No, merely a man who knows what he cannot do."

The king nodded at Edmund's bow. "If you spent as much time with this as you do clacking your tongue, you would be a fine archer. Shoot. I command you."

"I live to serve," Edmund said, making a flourishing bow.

The king grinned. "Jackanapes."

Edmund removed his gown. Holding it in his hand, he looked around as if wondering where to put it. Ignoring the hands outstretched to take it, he came to where Cecilia stood among the maids of honor and offered it to her. He smiled at her, a sunny open smile unlike the easy practiced smile he used to members of the Court.

"I should be grateful if you kept this for me, Lady Cecilia," he said. Taking three steps away, unfastening his doublet, he stopped and turned to her. Stripping the doublet off, he tossed it at her feet. "And this, if you would be so kind."

Cecilia heard the buzz of talk all around her and felt the eyes of the queen's women fixed on her, but both sensations were muffled, as if they came from far away. Her nose was filled with the scent of Edmund rising from his gown, something fresh and clean, something unique to him. She must have smelled it dancing with him all those hours last night without being aware of it. The binding of his magic deepened, her head and heart swimming giddily.

Edmund settled himself before the butts. Nocking his arrow, he lifted the bow in a smooth graceful gesture and, as the king had, sighted along the arrow's shaft. An errant breeze swirling through the crowd pressed his shirt to his body, outlining strong arms, wide shoulders, a lean waist.

Cecilia swallowed. His legs, in their hose, were long and powerful and the sunshine lit his tawny head to red-gold. Heat and hunger stirred, her sore feet forgotten. Her palms itched with the desire to touch him again, to run across those broad shoulders and down those strong arms. Look away, she thought frantically, it is sinful. She kept staring.

Edmund lowered his bow and turned. Their eyes met. She had once seen lightning arc from the sky, blasting an ancient oak to kindling in a shower of sparks. Now she knew how the oak had felt. If this was desire, no wonder the priests raged against it. She could not bear the heat of his gaze nor the yearning it awoke in her. She looked down.

She heard the rush of the arrow to the target and the *thunk* when it struck. The crowd groaned and Edmund said cheerfully, "If it were possible to say to His Majesty 'I told you so,' I might have a comment to make about that shot. As it is…"

Cecilia looked up. Fortunately for the varlets and serving maids foolishly clustered on the far side of the butts, Edmund had not missed the target but only by an inch or two.

"You are disgraceful," York said irritably.

"I beg leave to disagree. My archery is disgraceful," Edmund said. He walked over to Cecilia and lifted his doublet from the ground. "May I have my gown, Lady Cecilia?" She handed it over, afraid to meet his eyes again, afraid to feel that white-hot jolt again. He took her hand and bent over it, pressing it to his lips. He looked up and their gazes tangled. She could not have spoken a word. "I thank you for your kindness, my lady," he said softly. "Enjoy the contest."

He resumed his place on the far side of the queen, making some jest that made the queen laugh and blush. Mary

Butler, standing behind Cecilia's left shoulder, said in a very quiet voice, "Be careful of him, Lady Cecilia. You do your reputation no good being seen so often in his company."

"He bade me hold his doublet," Cecilia protested.

Mary snorted. "I did not refer to that. I spoke of last night. It is permissible to refuse to dance with him."

"But he makes me laugh."

"Will you laugh when no man in England will have you to wife? Will you laugh when you have a name as the Duke of Somerset's discarded leman?" Mary whispered urgently.

Anger tied Cecilia's heart in a hard knot. She wanted to throw Mary's sound advice back in her teeth, but she held her tongue. However unpalatable her counsel might be, Mary was right. Cecilia had not come to Court for her own pleasure; her father had secured her appointment as maid of honor to benefit the family. She was expected to use her position to attract noble suitors, to make the first steps to a good marriage. If she had sullied her good name, any marriage was beyond her reach.

"I give thanks for your kindness, my lady," she murmured.

Mary's rich chuckle purred in her ear. "Your manners are good, I will grant you that. You would really like to tell me to stop being an interfering gossip."

Cecilia smiled involuntarily. She had never heard an ill word spoken of Mary, despite her popularity among the men of the Court. She was armored against malice by a clever tongue and rock-hard common sense. "No, my lady. I am grateful for your kindness in speaking to me quietly."

"I am not such a fool as to tell you to have a care for your reputation in front of the busiest tongues in Christendom!"

"No. But not all the women here are so wise."

Mary laughed again. "I see I need not worry about you, chuck. You have a shrewd wit behind that innocent's face."

The Duke of York's next shot was several inches from the center of the target. His face darkened. Walking to the sidelines, he cuffed a page boy unlucky enough to stand in his path. The king gave him a long, considering look and prepared to shoot.

As he drew the bow, the Duke of York had a fit of coughing. The king swung his bow down and slowly eased the tension on the bowstring. Cecilia did not think York's coughing an unfortunate coincidence and to judge from the cold look on the king's face, neither did he.

When she had first come to Court and the other maids had discovered her interest in learning and music, several of them had said she might have done better for herself attending the Duchess of York. Watching York hack and cough, seeing the king's shuttered face, she was glad she was not in the York household. The duke reminded her of one of Sebastian Benbury's cousins, a stupid knave who had once tried to put his hand in her bodice and later claimed the mark from her defensive bite was a sword cut.

"I humbly beg your pardon, Sire," York croaked. "Something in my throat."

"I am sorry to hear that," the king said in a cool voice. "I will wait until the fit passes."

York gasped, a long wheezing whoop. "No, I beg you, Sire. Do not let me discommode you."

"Good Harry," the king said pleasantly, "I shall not continue until you are restored to health." Cecilia smothered a smile. How shrewd the king was, how foolish his brother. She would have been tempted to box York's ears.

York's coughing attack passed almost immediately. The

king turned back to the butts and shot. The arrow struck home in the center, jostling for space with the other two. Cecilia stood on tiptoe with delight, cheering and clapping with the rest of the crowd. *That* for your ill-timed cough, Your Grace! she thought, savoring the scowl on York's face.

"Edmund?" the king asked. "Will you shoot again?"

"I must ask not to, Sire. I will likely kill a cookboy or two, which will disorder the kitchens." Edmund spread his hands wide in a deprecating gesture.

The king chuckled.

"I cannot see how you can jest about this! The arts of war are a serious matter. English bowmen won France," York cried.

"But English bowmen could not keep France, my lord," Edmund said. He smiled ruefully. "I beg your pardon if my japery offended you. I was born to jest at serious matters and pull a long face at jests."

"If I did not know better, I should call you a changeling!" York cried.

Cecilia stiffened, wondering how Edmund would react to the insult. Her dislike of York grew. Edmund's eyes narrowed, but the pleasant smile remained on his lips.

"But you do know better," the king said sternly. "And you must remember that His Majesty, our father, was as fond as Edmund of a good jest."

A muscle throbbed in York's cheek, his mouth thinned to a white line.

"As you say, Sire," York said, with a stiff bow. "I believe it is my shot."

Cecilia gave him credit for one thing: he was a fine athlete. His third and final shot was in the center. The king must shoot his final arrow closer to the center than the

Duke's second shot to win the contest. Cecilia held her breath.

Quickly, before his brother could distract him, the king stepped forward, nocked his arrow and released it. Like his other two shots, the third arrow made room for itself in the center of the target. The courtiers burst into predictable cheers while Cecilia sighed in relief. She could not have borne it if York had won.

White-faced, York tugged the ruby he had wagered from his thumb.

"Let it not be said I do not pay my debts."

The king clapped him on the shoulder, his face lit up by his rare, sweet smile. "Harry, you are better than I am at everything but this. Do not grudge me this."

"You are the king."

"And you are the finest jouster, tennis player, hunter and musician in England, if not Christendom. You speak five, no, six languages while I can barely be understood in anything but English. You dance far into the night and awaken as fresh as a daisy. All I can do is shoot arrows."

He was a true prince, magnanimous in victory. If he was anything like his father, Cecilia could readily understand her father's great loyalty to the old king.

Mollified, York grinned. "And of course that is the one thing I wish I could do above all others!"

"That is the way of it," the king agreed. He turned to Edmund. "And you, jackanapes. Harry is right. Your lack of skill at the butts disgraces England. I command you to improve."

Edmund bowed, the blandly pleasant expression on his face impossible for Cecilia to interpret. "I live to serve."

The contest over, the rigid lines of watching courtiers broke into small chattering groups. It was a brilliantly sunny May afternoon, the kind of day when the whole world turned outdoors. The king, dressed once more in doublet and gown, offered his arm to his wife; they began to walk toward the Italian garden, trailed by their attendants. Cecilia followed, hobbling a little on her painful feet. The queen turned and said, "I cannot bear to watch you. You have my leave to sit down, Cecilia. Next time, do not dance so late."

Cecilia curtsied. "Yes, Your Majesty." Her heart tightened with affection for the queen. She had feared the queen, raised with the high manners of the Spanish Court, would be proud and harsh. Instead, Katherine was kind and thoughtful of her ladies, loving toward her husband the king, generous to the Church; in short, everything a Queen of England ought to be. Traveling the roads of England in the one move she had made with the Court, Cecilia had been astonished by the number of common people who turned out at the roadsides to cheer themselves hoarse for the queen.

She found a bench placed to one side of the path and sat, spreading her skirts widely to discourage importunate gentleman ushers. It was not enough to prevent Sebastian from sitting beside her. He pushed her skirt aside and planted his hands on his knees, looking at her with concern in his eyes.

"I must speak with you," he announced.

"I did not think you desired to rest your feet," she said mildly.

"There is much talk about you and the Duke of Somerset." He looked away, rubbing his hands along his thighs as if to wipe sweaty palms dry. "There are already wagers on how quickly he will make you his leman." He turned to face her. "How shall you attract a noble suitor if you have no honor?"

She lifted her hands to her burning cheeks, fighting the

urge to jump up and run away. How dare he! "My honor is intact. Do you think I lay with him here? Or as I danced with him in full view of every clack-jawed fool at Court?"

"Ceci—"

"Do not 'Ceci' me, Sebastian Benbury. I know what is owed my name and I know what hopes my family has of me. I do not need you to remind me."

He frowned. "I do not believe the rumors. I know you better than that. But I would do you an ill-turn if I did not tell you what I have heard." He took her hand and held it tightly. "Though kings' brothers have chosen earls' daughters before this, you must not hope for marriage from my lord of Somerset. Our king, God assoil him, will marry his brothers out of England."

She had known that, truly she had, but Sebastian's words still cut her. "I am not such a fool I did not know," she said, striving for firmness. Her voice came out a whisper. She cleared her throat. "The duke has been married before."

"I do not want to see you break your heart over a man you cannot have."

If he kept talking in this vein he would have her crying. She squeezed his hand and let it go. "You broke it long ages ago, Sebastian. And it never mended." She made herself smile at him. She did not hope to fool him, only to signal that she would talk no more of Edmund. "What of you, my friend? What maiden shall be your wife?"

He smiled as falsely as she. "One as witty as you, as fair as the queen, a maid buxom and well dowered. Can you put me in the way of such a girl?"

"They abound at Court," she said. "You have only to stretch out your hand to find one." She lied and they both knew it. Most of the women at Court were light-minded, proud and sharp-tongued; half the maids were not maids at all. Yet a goodly portion of them would marry despite their handicaps, their marriages made for the usual reasons—money and connections—with no thought to anything else. The Court was full of couples as badly joined as the Earl of Surrey and his second wife, a couple who hated one another as mortal enemies. What benefit had accrued to their families that outweighed such bitterness?

"Perhaps you and I should make a match of it. I can imagine no better wife," he said.

She looked into his eyes. "Surely you can."

He colored and looked away. "Perhaps. But if I can, what of it? She is married."

"Sebastian—"

He laid his finger across her lips, silencing her. "I pray you, do not speak another word." He lifted his finger. "I have said what I came to say and I am late returning to my lord of York." He stood and bowed. "If I may have leave to go…"

She started and then nodded. At home, Sebastian came and went as he pleased, the gap between his rank and hers largely set aside by long, friendly usage. They could not be so easy here, where a hundred eyes watched their every move and a hundred tongues were ready to cry every misdeed.

She wanted to go home. She had not lied to Edmund when she told him she hated the staring. She felt every moment that she had been judged and found wanting, that somehow, without knowing it, she violated some unspoken code.

Cecilia shuddered and crossed herself. How long must she remain here before she could run home safely?

"Why the long face, my lady?" a soft voice said in her ear. Its caress tingled in her blood, all the way down to her toes. She shivered.

"Your Grace," she said, rising and turning to face Edmund. She winced when she curtsied. Her feet had grown more sensitive while she rested.

"Please be seated," he said. She resumed her place, spreading her skirts to keep him at a distance, every warning she had ever received about protecting her name ringing in her memory. It was not enough to avoid dishonor; she had to avoid the appearance of misconduct, as well.

Edmund seemed to have no such qualms. He sat beside her, sliding underneath her skirt so it was spread over his thigh. She twitched the skirt away from him and stuffed the cloth into the narrow gap between them, building a barrier. She ought to wish him begone but she could not bring herself to that point. "I see you have some pain in your feet. It is your feet?"

"Yes, Your Grace," she said, her eyes on her hands clasped in her lap. Perhaps if she was stiff and unfriendly, he would leave on his own.

"You have been warned away from me," he said. Startled, she looked up. His expression blended amusement, annoyance and regret, his mouth curled up at one corner as if to say, What can you expect?

"Please forgive my stupidity, Your Grace, but I am afraid I do not understand," she said.

He smiled. "You have no art to deceive. You have been warned to be wary of me, for I am not free to wed as I will and therefore no man with whom to spend much time."

Nettled, she decided to be frank. "Yes, Your Grace, I have. And give me leave to add that if you had not handed me your clothing in full sight of the entire Court, I might have been spared those warnings!"

He grinned, his eyes sparkling in the bright sunshine. "Call me Edmund, as you used to do."

"I may not," she retorted.

"Did you not like dancing with me last night?" he asked plaintively.

"You are flirting with me," she said severely. He was close, too close, just as he had been in the oak tree outside Wednesfield. Only now he was a grown man, twice as fearsome.

"Only because I cannot help it. Please answer my question."

"I should think my bruised and blistered feet are answer enough," she retorted. "I can barely walk."

"I am sorry for your pain, but I would not change a moment of last night."

She put her hands up to her hot cheeks. "Please do not speak so. I do not know how to answer." Or what to think. Her thoughts were jumbled, as tossed as the mess in the old tower at Wednesfield.

He grinned again. "You might thank me for paying such a pretty compliment."

"Not if pretty compliments lead to more warnings to have a care for my name," she said, striving for lightness and failing. She sounded annoyed.

"I shall do you no harm in the eyes of the world," he said firmly.

"You and everyone else of my acquaintance have spent no little time telling me otherwise. You must forgive me if I am skeptical."

He laughed but he did not sound happy. "Caught in a trap of my own devising," he muttered. "Would you change last night?"

"No, not a breath of it. Nor today, for that matter," she said, and immediately regretted it. What was it about him that made it impossible to keep him at arm's length?

This time, his laughter was delighted. "You are not like anyone else I know."

"So you said before."

"Before?"

"When you were a mere Edmund Tudor from Pembrokeshire. Although then I had heard nothing of your usual company."

"And what sort of company do you hear is my usual sort?"

"The paid kind," she said, and blushed. How dared she be so impertinent?

Throwing his head back so that his cap fell off, he burst into laughter. The sun shone in the tawny waves of his hair, glinting on gold and copper and silver threads. Recovering his composure, he seized her hand and kissed it. "Someday, Lady Cecilia, I will tell you about my paid friends." He stood. "But not today. No, do not stand. I shall take the curtsy as a given. No more than Kati can I bear to watch you hobble."

"You are kindness itself, sir."

"You do not mean a word of it," he retorted.

"No," she said, grinning up at him. "But it sounds pretty."

Laughing again, he bent to recover his cap. Wiping the dust from its plume, he glanced at her, his eyes flashing blue before returning to his bedraggled cap. Without looking at her, his voice more serious than she had yet heard it, he said, "I was glad when I saw you beside Kati last night. But it is nothing to how happy I am today. I hope you will be with us at Court for a long time to come."

She knew she should speak some commonplace about her stay being in the queen's hands; she could not. She murmured, "As do I."

He bowed and strode away from her, following the path

his brother and sister-in-law had taken. She watched him until he was out of sight, free in her solitude to admire the breadth of his shoulders and the elegant turn of his legs in their hose. If only there were another man like him, a man of her own rank. She might find it possible to marry a man like that.

Chapter Five

Cecilia let the last notes die away, her fingers loosening on the lute's neck. She glanced at Queen Katherine, reclining against a mound of pillows on the big bed. One of the other maids of honor knelt beside the queen, combing her auburn hair and rubbing it with a piece of silk to bring out the shine.

What should she play now? Her gaze roamed the queen's bedchamber as if the hangings, the elaborate furniture or the tester over the bed had the answer written on them. Her ear caught the musical hum of the queen's ladies murmuring together and she thought it must be pleasant to be so friendly. That put her in mind of the Duke of York's "Pastime, Good Company." Dared she play that? Every time the duke and the queen were together, the queen watched him closely, her eyes guarded as if she distrusted him. Yet he wrote beautiful songs. Cecilia began the opening chords.

"Not that," the queen said immediately.

"I beg Your Majesty's pardon," Cecilia murmured contritely. Now what? Her mind was blank. As if by themselves, her fingers began a tune that had been a favorite of her mother's.

Mary Butler whispered, "That is not a lute song."

"No, my lady," Cecilia said.

"The queen plays it on the virginals!"

"Yes, my lady. I altered it so it might be played on the lute." She glanced at Mary. Interpreting her expression was not difficult: Mary's mouth had dropped open. Then she closed it and gave a gurgle of ready laughter.

"Clever chit," she said. "This sounds like something my little sister Anne would do."

The great door swung open and the queen's steward entered, bowing so deeply his nose almost touched his knees. That bow meant only one thing: the king was coming. Cecilia set down her lute and rose from the bench while the maids and ladies scrambled to their feet. The queen struggled to climb off the bed, her efforts complicated by her growing belly, but before Cecilia could move a step to assist her, the king strode into the room and she was compelled to kneel.

The king hurried to the queen's bedside to press her against the pillows. "Kati, no," he commanded.

Cecilia looked for Edmund among the men attending the king, but he was not part of the group. She swallowed her disappointment. There was no one in the world she would rather talk to. He spoke and listened to her as a woman in her own right. He helped her to see herself as Cecilia Coleville, not merely Wednesfield's daughter, or Beatrice's plain sister, or an interchangeable maid of honor. Time spent in his company flew, sped by his wit and kindness.

"You are the king," the queen protested.

"And you are as stubborn as a Spanish mule," he retorted. "God's nightgown! What must I do to you? You know the punishment for a disobedient wife..."

Cecilia, able to glimpse the queen's face, saw the hot

blush that ran into it and blushed herself. The king's hand, resting on the queen's shoulder, slid down her arm. The queen twined her fingers with his. In the back of Cecilia's mind, a shocked voice cried, *But she is with child!* while her heart ached with envy. She wanted a husband who desired her even when she was thick-waisted. Hard on the heels of that wish came the memory of the hungry expression in Thomas Manners's eyes as he watched Beatrice and longing gave way to revulsion. No, she did not want that, she thought, repressing the urge to cross herself. Mistress Emma always said to be careful of what you wish for.

"Ladies, you are dismissed," the king said. They bowed out, waiting to begin their chatter until the door shut behind them.

"Should we wait here?" Cecilia asked Mary. The king had not visited the queen at midday since Cecilia had begun attending her and Cecilia did not know what rules applied.

Mary, her lips curved in a sly, lascivious smile, said, "If you wish. I, for one, am going to see if I can pry James out of his leman's bed." James was her husband.

"'Out of his leman's bed'?" Cecilia repeated, unpleasantly surprised. It was the first she had heard that James Butler had a mistress. She whispered, "How can you do that? Take him, when he still smells of her?"

Mary curled her lip. "I should prefer by far to be the mother of an Earl of Ormonde than a woman discarded for barrenness. I will do what I must." She gave a laugh at once sorrowful and slightly malicious. "Isn't there a country saying, 'Make hay while the sun shines'?" She disappeared before Cecilia could think of a response.

Despite herself, she had quoted one too many of Mistress Emma's maxims and was now teased by the other

women for her country ways. Mary, with very little mean-
ness in her nature, was usually kind. Not so the other
women. Cecilia had not known there was as much spite in
the whole world as she had found among the queen's
ladies.

"Mistress, if you please," a piping voice said from the
vicinity of her elbow. She set the lute down and looked at
the page boy who stood beside her, his face puckered with
anxiety. "Mistress, if you would be so kind. Will you tell
me who is Lady Cecilia Coleville?"

"I am she," Cecilia said, her heart lightening unaccountably at his tense formality. *Perhaps it is because neither of us belongs here,* she thought. *Anyone else would
upbraid the poor lad.*

"I beg your pardon, my lady," he said, bowing. He held
out a letter, folded and sealed. She examined the crest im-
printed in the wax and tore the letter open. It was from
Beatrice.

To my beloved sister, Cecilia.
   Greetings. I and my good husband are stopped at
Coleville House for the next fortnight. The sight of a
loved face would gladden my heart and I would have
you visit me.

                                        Your sister,
                                        Beatrice Manners

Tucking the letter into her belt, Cecilia left the room.
She had been lonely and God had provided succor. She
needed to see Beatrice, to ask her advice and receive her
comfort. She hurried to her chamber. With a little luck,
her tirewoman would be there and she could change
quickly out of her Court velvet into something more practical for a water journey. Nor would she bring an attendant.

This was a quick jaunt upriver, not the progress of an earl's daughter.

Finding a waterman to take her upriver to Coleville House proved to be the hardest part of her trip. Most refused to take her because she was unattended, one insolent scoundrel bidding her, "Go back to the stews where you belong, jade!" The next man took her, he said, to make up for his fellow's rudeness. "No need to swear at a lady!"

No one met her at the Coleville House water stairs, but men in the distance tended the garden beds running down to the river's edge. She followed the path to the house. No steward greeted her at the door, no maids passed through the hall, but she heard the murmur of voices and the clatter of crockery through the buttery and pantry arches. She hesitated, wondering if she should go in search of the steward to have herself announced. After a moment's consideration, she dismissed the notion. She knew this house well, if not as well as she knew Wednesfield, and there was only one place Beatrice would be if she was not in the hall. She climbed the stairs leading to the solar above the hall.

The door to the solar was closed. She tapped on it as warning and pushed it open.

"Beatrice? It's Cecilia."

As the door swung open it revealed only the bench against the wall, the table in the center of the room and her parents' chairs, bereft of the cushions they brought with them when they came to London. Beatrice was not here. Cecilia took a step backward to leave when she heard a woman sigh.

She stepped forward and peered around the door.

A man and a woman stood against the wall in the corner hidden by the door, the woman's gold hair loose about her shoulders, the man's head bent so his face was pressed against the woman's breasts.

Cecilia recoiled in disgust. Beatrice and her husband!

A second, clearer glance revealed that while the woman was Beatrice, the man was not Lord Manners. His head was covered in dark curling hair and the hands pulling Beatrice close were strong and young.

"Beatrice!" she cried. She could have been anyone, discovering her sister like this.

The man straightened with a jerk. Her view no longer blocked by the breadth of his shoulders, Cecilia could see that the laces of Beatrice's bodice had been loosened; her neckline gaped at her breasts.

The man was as disordered as her sister, his doublet and gown flung on the floor at his feet and his shirt hanging free of his trunk hose. The scowl on his face made her mouth go dry. He did not lift his hands from Beatrice's waist in shame; instead, his thumb moved, stroking her almost absently. After scrutinizing Cecilia from hood to hem, he nuzzled Beatrice's neck, his eyes closed and his mouth open on her sister's skin. When he lifted his head and looked at Cecilia, his hard gray eyes glittered mockingly.

"Beatrice, alder-liefest, who is this?" he asked. His voice was deep and soft, sending a frightened chill up Cecilia's spine.

"This is my little sister, Cecilia. Who will keep her tongue," Beatrice replied. Her hands slid down his arms and released him while she stared at Cecilia with cold sky-blue eyes. "Ceci, why are you here?" No blush stained her face, she made no move to cover her near nakedness. Cecilia had the dizzying sense she had stumbled into the wrong house to confront a woman who looked exactly like Beatrice but was not her sister.

"Why am *I* here? Why is *he* here? And who is he?" she demanded. Shock had bereft her of the wits for tact.

"Allow me to present myself. Sir George Conyers, at your service." He placed a hand on his chest and inclined his head. Even as he made his mannerly gestures, she sensed his contempt. She felt the first crackling lick of anger.

"At *my* service? That is not what I see," Cecilia said tartly.

His eyes narrowed unpleasantly. "Has no one taught you to respect your betters?" he asked softly.

"My betters? Oh, indeed, sir, I have been taught well." Her stomach was churning and she feared she might be sick. Not before him, she thought fiercely. "Had you said elders…then you might have cause to complain."

"Ceci, I do not imagine you came all this way to insult my friend," Beatrice said wearily.

"Friend? He is your—"

"Silence!" Beatrice glared at her, her face at last pink. "Why are you here?" she demanded in a hard voice.

"You bade me come," Cecilia said grudgingly. She held out the letter.

"I did not imagine you would come today. It was not so easy to obtain leave to visit friends when I was at Court."

"I do not have leave. The king dismissed us. I had nowhere to go when the boy brought your note."

Beatrice looked at her for a long, thoughtful minute. Cecilia wondered if all her previous misery and all her current confusion could be read on her face. Then Beatrice looked at Conyers, releasing Cecilia from her cool scrutiny. "My love, I must ask you to go."

"What?" He released Beatrice to plant his fists on his hips. "You know how hard it is to see you! Cox my passion! I will not have this!'' Beatrice stared at him until he began to fidget. ''Beatrice, I cannot say when I will be able to return.'' A look of pain shivered across Beatrice's face, passing so quickly Cecilia was not sure she saw it.

''George. George.'' She lifted her hand to his cheek. ''My love, I must speak to her. I must. We are in danger else.'' She leaned forward and offered him her mouth. Cecilia stared, unable to take her eyes from them and the devouring ardor of their kiss. When George put his hand into the top of Beatrice's bodice, it broke the spell of her fascination and she turned away, disgusted by her curiosity. Watching them diminished her, making her no better than they.

Out of the corner of her eye, she saw George bend to retrieve his clothing. She turned to watch him. He dressed in his doublet and gown, glaring at her all the while. When he strode over to her, it took all her anger to keep from backing away. He seized her chin in a hard grip that made her gasp. ''Be warned, jade. I will not tolerate this from you again.'' She wanted to spit into his face, but did not dare. There was no knowing what a man like this might do. Besides, her business was with Beatrice. He released her and left the room, slamming the door shut.

When he was gone, Beatrice turned her back to Cecilia, revealing the gaping back of her bodice. ''Lace me up, Ceci,'' she said as coolly as if Cecilia had not discovered her with her lover. Cecilia obeyed, using the time spent setting her sister to rights to think and sort out her feelings.

Settling her hood on her head, Beatrice said, ''Out with it.''

''Out with what?'' Cecilia asked.

''I do not have the patience for this. Speak your mind, child.''

''Do not call me child,'' Cecilia said. She bit back wild

laughter. This was hardly the time to worry what Beatrice called her.

"Very well. Speak your mind. Cecilia."

"What was that man doing…here, with you?"

Beatrice's mouth curled in a faintly contemptuous smile. "Giving me pleasure."

"He will get you with child, a bastard child."

Beatrice's face hardened, as if it had become white marble.

Cecilia's heart shrank and went cold, but she pushed on. As disgusted as she was by Beatrice's behavior, she feared for her sister; there was no limit to what Manners could do to her if he found out. "What if your husband learns of this? Will he accept another man's child? What will happen to you?"

"There will be no child," Beatrice said flatly.

"How can you know that?" Cecilia cried. "How?" There was pain in her breast, pain along her arms. She wanted to embrace her sister and to shake her until she was sensible.

"How do *you* know you will have no child?" There was an ugly note in Beatrice's voice, as if they probed too close to an inflamed wound.

"I? I know because I am…" A terrible possibility occurred to her. She looked into Beatrice's eyes, turned gray by pain. "You…are you…are you?" She could not say the words.

"I am as virgin as you, little sister."

"But the blood. Your maiden's blood. On the sheets." She had wandered into a nightmare.

"The blood of my foot," Beatrice said with vicious sarcasm. "I was deflowered with my husband's eating knife. He is as incapable as a nanny goat." She turned away, her fists clenching and unclenching.

Through the buzzing stillness in her head, Cecilia asked one more question. "And Conyers...?"

"Would like nothing better than to ride me well, but I dare not allow it. I am misfortunate, a woman who could never persuade her elderly husband, plead she never so wisely, that the child in her womb is his." She turned back toward Cecilia, her mouth curved like a Turkish blade. "My husband tells me this will keep me chaste. Within the letter of the law, I am chaste. But in the spirit...George is an inventive man and there is more to bedsport than my husband dreams."

"Oh, Beatrice..." What a terrible garboil this was. Deep in her heart, under the pity and disgust, burned hatred: hatred of a man who would do this to the wife he had coveted so dearly.

"I do not want your pity, Ceci," Beatrice said sharply. "I want your silence."

"This is ruining you. You are hard."

"Life is hard. Harder than I ever knew. Now, do I have your silence? Or need I worry that my husband will imprison me because you cannot keep your tongue between your teeth?"

"Why did you marry him?" she cried. Maybe if she understood that much, the rest of this would make sense.

"Because I was a proud, greedy, ambitious fool. I thought I could lead that old man around by his lust. It says 'Pride goeth before destruction,' in the Bible. I wish I had known that before I married."

"The Bible? When did you read an English Bible? It is against the law." Was there no end to Beatrice's folly?

"Do not look like that. Do I have your silence? Ceci?"

"You must know I would do nothing to hurt you." There was a great knot of pain in her breast, throbbing like a bruise. How had they come to this disastrous point?

"I know nothing that is not explicitly stated to me. I cannot trust my judgment when it has failed me so completely in the past."

"I will do nothing to harm you. I will do nothing to help that man, your husband. But I beg you, Beatrice, have a care to yourself."

"I will, Ceci, I promise you that." She came forward and embraced Cecilia. "Now. You must go."

"But…"

"No more, Ceci. I am weary, and I do not wish to speak any more of this."

"I will pray for you." It was a weak, patronizing thing to say and the only comfort she could offer.

Beatrice sighed, blinking quickly as if against the sting of tears. "I fear it will take more than prayers to help me, but I thank you for your kind heart. Now, for the love of pity, leave me be."

Beatrice's revelations left Cecilia as hollow as a blown egg. She hardly knew what shocked her more: that Beatrice had taken a lover, that she was still a virgin, or that she had taken a lover and managed to remain a virgin. Cecilia had assumed her brother-in-law was less virile than a young man; she had never imagined him completely incapable. She stumbled toward the water stairs with no idea where to go except to put as much distance between herself and her sister as possible, as if she could leave her distressing new knowledge and her pain at Coleville House. If only she could find somewhere to hide until she regained some semblance of peace, like a wanted man fleeing to sanctuary.

Sanctuary. An image of a quiet, glimmering world rose to her mind's eye. She would go to the Abbey. And she would go unseen. From the water, no one would know where she was and if she debarked at the Abbey's water stairs, she would avoid the staring eyes of the ravenously curious courtiers.

A boat glided into sight bearing a lone passenger, a member of the gentry judging from his clothes, his bearing and the craft that bore him. The gentleman turned his head in her direction and then leaned forward to speak to the waterman.

The boat swung in toward the water stairs where she stood. She got a good look at its passenger. It was Edmund.

She blinked, certain she had been mistaken. Did he still pretend to be other than the Duke of Somerset? He must, for here he was, traveling alone, dressed in linen and wool instead of brocade and silk. The Duke of Somerset would travel in his personal barge, attended by his gentleman. The picture arose in her mind's eye—Edmund, his chin lifted disdainfully, surrounded by courtiers. She shook the image from her head. This was not that man. Intrigued, she watched his boat sidle up to the stairs.

"Well met, Mistress Cecilia!" he said pleasantly. "Where are you bound?"

"Westminster, sir," she replied, not daring to say more lest she speak wrongly. She did not know who he pretended to be.

"I am bound for Westminster myself. Join me."

She hesitated, uncertain of the propriety of his proposal. Her vow to avoid him flickered through her mind and disappeared. She could not bear to stay another moment at Coleville House. Gathering up her skirts so they would not be in her way, she scrambled into the boat and sat beside him. His thigh pressed hers, hard even through her layers of petticoats. Thankfully he did not speak as they moved downriver. Between her distress over Beatrice and her vivid awareness of the man sitting beside her, she did not think she could respond intelligently to ordinary courtesy, much less bear up her end of a conversation.

The boat swung toward a landing near the Abbey. "I go no further," Edmund said. "I shall pay your fare if you wish to continue, but I would far rather you remained with me." Cecilia glanced up at him and then at the Abbey pressing against the river's edge, the palace beyond it as she considered his offer.

"Please," he added.

She turned to meet his gaze. His eyes were very blue, something hot and fierce flaring briefly in their depths. Her stomach clenched painfully, an aching wave of longing passing from her throat to her middle. She nodded.

"Come," he said softly, and took her hand.

Chapter Six

Edmund and Cecilia walked towards Westminster Abbey in thoughtful, companionable silence. As they approached the north entrance to the Abbey church, Cecilia began to slow until finally she stopped, staring at the entrance porch, a troubled frown between her brows. Edmund waited for her to say something, but she held her tongue. Her muteness drove him into speech.

"You are distrait. Why?"

She tilted her face up to his. Her look was appraising, as if she weighed her trust in him against her secret.

"My sister Beatrice. She makes me sad," she said softly. "When I met you today, I had thought to pray for her."

He lifted her hand, pressed it to his lips, then held it against his heart. He wanted to hold her, to comfort her. The longing unsettled him, but he was growing used to the way she disturbed him. "We can pray for her now." Delicate color flooded her face. She lowered her eyes and pulled her hand away.

Annoyance wound through him. Impetuous and foolish, he had moved too fast.

Yet she did not forbid him to join her when she slipped

into the church. He followed her to a place near the high altar, where she knelt, bending her head over her folded hands. He knelt beside her and tried to pray, but neither his heart nor his mind was willing to cooperate. He snatched little glances at her, unable to look completely away, certainly unable to focus on his devotions.

Dark-haired, dark-eyed, slender as a birch tree, she conformed to no standard of beauty he knew. Beauty was golden hair, blue eyes, a voluptuous figure. Beauty was Cecilia's sister, Lady Manners. Yet Lady Manners left him cold, while Cecilia made him ache with longing.

"I cannot pray when you stare at me," Cecilia whispered severely, looking at him with a long slanting glance.

"I beg your pardon. I did not mean to stare," he said. His level tone relieved him. He had not thought he could sound so calm. "I will pray elsewhere."

He had no choice but to leave. He could not remain beside her without wanting to look at her. He wandered through the Abbey, almost deserted at this hour, until he came to the tiny chapel of Our Lady of the Pew, dug out of the heart of a pillar. Unbidden, memory returned of a time when he had overheard an anonymous couple in one of the little chapels caught in the throes of carnal delight. His mouth twisted at the memory of his youthful disgust. Unable to imagine coupling in a bed, never mind in a church? Now he could easily imagine it anyplace, anytime, with a great deal of pleasure. His recollection of the soft gasps and moans issuing from the chapel led him to wondering how Cecilia would sound. Would she gasp? Moan? Shout? Call his name?

Stop!

This line of thought was dangerous. He would never know how Cecilia sounded when aroused. He would never arouse her. She would marry someone wholly appropriate and…

Like Thomas Manners?

His skin crawled. An old toad like Manners to enjoy Cecilia's body, kiss, caress her? His fists clenched. No! he thought furiously. I will not have it!

He forced himself to be sensible, logical. There were few old toads left alive and all were married. To young women. Who were not pregnant and therefore less likely to die, leaving a decrepit widower free for Cecilia. On the other hand, there were any number of young men of the right rank who were free to marry. Good men, who would cherish her as she deserved. Good men, who might actually love Cecilia.

His fists clenched again.

Why did this idea make him feel worse?

Virile men, who would find delight in her flesh. Honorable men, who would have the right to touch and caress and kiss her as they pleased. Experienced men, who might give her pleasure. Lucky men, who would know whether she gasped or moaned or shouted or called out her lover's name.

"Edmund?"

She stood framed by the doorway. Golden light licked across the velvety flesh exposed by her square neckline, a shadow hinting at the valley between her breasts. Candlelight shone in her eyes, making them appear enormous.

She stepped forward. "Is something amiss, Edmund?"

"Amiss?" He hardly knew what he said. A wicked voice in the back of his head murmured, *Closer, come closer.*

She moved nearer. "Yes, amiss. You do not answer."

He stretched out a hand and touched the ivory curve of her cheek with his knuckles, hardly aware of what he did.

She was soft, softer than he had imagined. He opened his hand and cupped her cheek, brushing it with his thumb. She stood quietly under his touch, her soft dark gaze fixed on his eyes. Slowly, as if in a dream, he reached out his other hand and, slipping it around her waist, drew her to him.

She was soft and warm in his arms. His body responded instantly and yet he felt no urgency. Only the same dream-like sense of certainty. Slowly, never taking his eyes from hers, he bent his head and kissed her.

Her lips were sweet and passive, their touch not enough. He needed her response. He tightened his arms, nibbling her lower lip, caressing the corners of her mouth with his tongue, stroking her throat and the line of her jaw with his thumb. *Yield to me, Ceci.* Her lips parted with a gasp and her tongue met his. The rough brush sent shivering pleasure up his spine and made his arms tighten, drawing her still closer. The kiss deepened as she pressed herself against him, arching into his arms.

His head spun. It had never been like this.

"Ceci, Ceci."

He rained kisses on her upturned face, returning helplessly to her lips. He trailed kisses to her neck, sucking gently on the tender spot below her ear. She moaned softly, her fingers in his hair drawing him closer. He shuddered in response. His mouth moved along her collarbone, drifting obliquely toward that tempting shadow as if it had a will of its own.

"We should not," she whispered raggedly, putting her hands on his shoulders.

He tightened his arms again, gathering her close, hungry for the feel of her against him. She was sweet in his arms, sweeter than he had dreamed possible. He could not let her go, he could not let this end.

"I cannot." she gasped. She pushed on his shoulders, no match for his strength.

His lips brushed the edge of her neckline, his tongue tasting her tender flesh. He felt her tremble in response. He knew it was wrong but he could not stop.

She took his face in her hands and lifted him away, staring fiercely into his eyes.

"Edmund, we must stop! We cannot go on."

His arms loosened and she pushed herself free, so abruptly she staggered. He put out a hand to steady her, but she moved beyond his reach.

"When you caress me so, I cannot deny you," she said in a trembling voice. "I beg of you, for my soul, do not touch me."

"Ceci…" What could he say? That he desired her? That alone must be apparent. That he… What else did he feel, besides desire? He shied away from the thought.

"Please," she said. "Do not be angry with me."

"Angry with you? It is you who should be angry with me. I never intended to… I swore no harm would come to you."

She looked away, biting her lip. When she took a deep, shaking breath, her breasts swelled in her neckline. He stared unwillingly for a long moment before forcing himself to look elsewhere. He could not stay in this chapel where the very stones seemed to speak of carnal hunger and satiation while frustrated desire throbbed sullenly in his veins and other, unnamed emotions made him a stranger to himself. If he did not escape, he would take her in his arms again, and if he did that, God help them both. He did not think he would stop.

"Come with me," he said abruptly. "Please."

He half expected her to use this opportunity to escape him but when he glanced back, he saw she followed. He did not know if she was very brave or very foolish; he only knew he was glad.

He strode to Henry VII's chapel as if driven by the devil. He hoped desire would die in the place his father and grandmother rested. He laughed bitterly to himself. If it did not die there, it was not going to die.

In the chapel he crossed the floor to a choir stall and flung down its seat. "Sit down," he commanded, too tense for courtesy. White-faced, her arms wrapped around her waist, she obeyed. He pulled down the seat in the stall beside her, sat down and buried his face in his hands.

His brain went blindly 'round and 'round like a horse turning a grindstone. She wanted him; she refused him. He wanted her; he could not have her. She was right; he was wrong. You need a woman, he told himself and then wondered why the thought made him feel slightly sick. Propping his chin on his fist, he turned his head to look at her, sitting stiffly in the stall beside him with her eyes unfocused and her mouth in a thin, unhappy line.

Blessed Virgin, she was beautiful! Yet if he examined her features one by one, her beauty dissolved into mere prettiness. Why did he desire her so much? It was not simply that she was unattainable—he had hungered in the past for women who were out of reach. No, there was something different about this woman, something that made her infinitely desirable to him even as he wanted above all to protect her and keep her safe. He could not have her without endangering her, that was the rub.

As if she felt his gaze, she turned to him. Her eyes were very clear. It always amazed him how clear such dark eyes could be. He could not read her expression and foreboding gathered in his heart.

"Earlier, before we…I came here to pray for my sister because she is sinning. Dangerously. Stupidly," she said.

He knew she did not make this confession idly. It must relate both to what had happened and what she needed him to understand. He ached to comfort her but he suspected if he tried, she would run away. He sat very still, his hands open on his knees. "She has taken a lover." She paused. He could see her throat working and could imagine what the admission cost her. "Even as I love my sister, I despise her for her dishonor."

"She is married to a very old man. It must be hard for her." He spoke very gently, kindness the only consolation he could offer.

"I know." Her voice wavered. She stopped and gripped her skirt. "I understand why she does it." She smiled wryly. "I even understood before...before you kissed me. Her lover...her lover is comely and virile. As different from her husband as a man can be." She swallowed, took a deep breath and let it out slowly. "Thomas Manners is a wretched man. I love and honor my parents, but I think they made a terrible mistake letting Beatrice marry him."

"He is not their choice."

"No. He approached them. Beatrice is beautiful and with her dowry, a prize for any man. Lord Manners promised her wealth and a life at Court. Beatrice begged my parents not to refuse him. They should not have listened to her. She is a great fool."

"And?"

"How can I despise her for her sin and yet commit the same sin?" Her cry was despairing.

"It would not be the same sin." It was hard not to reach out to take her hand and hold it.

"Sophism," she whispered. "Carnal knowledge of a man not one's husband, however you look at it."

"Ah, Ceci." He put his face in his hands again, as if

he could hide from the knowledge she held up to him. *If only we could be mad together.*

"I am sorry," she whispered.

"Why? Why apologize to me?" he asked as gently as he could.

"I should not have kissed you," she said, her voice full of self-reproach.

"I kissed you," he said, turning to look at her.

"True," she said with a hint of her usual smile, "but I kissed you back. I do not think we would have…I was afraid we…oh, dear."

"I want you," he said soberly. "I have never wanted a woman in my life as much as I want you." She blushed, her face and bosom turning visibly pink even in the uncertain light. He wondered how far down her blush extended… He jerked his mind away. He could not even sit quietly in a church with her without his imagination flinging up carnal images. What was wrong with him? He compelled his unruly mind to focus on the matter at hand. "But I cannot marry you and you cannot be my mistress. You are right to have a care to your honor."

She jumped to her feet and commenced pacing to and fro like the lions in the Tower of London. "Let us talk of something else. Anything. Tell me why you are clothed as a gentleman and not a prince."

It took a moment to let go of desire and denial, and then another to gather coherent answers to her questions. "The day after the Prince of Wales was knighted, when I was twelve years old, I met a man named Tam Watson in the Abbey church. He was part of the crew tearing down the stage. I didn't want him to know who I was, so I told him only my name. As I did the first time we met."

"Edmund, Duke of Somerset, becomes plain Edmund

Tudor for the first time?'' She lifted her head from the path she trod to shoot him a shrewd glance.

"Precisely. Every time the Court came to Westminster, I sought Tam out. When I was sixteen, I think, he told me about a priest who was shielding a murderer. The murderer walked free, unless the priest heard king's men were planning a visit to the sanctuary. Then the priest made sure the murderer got back to the abbey and safety. The monks knew nothing of this priest's actions. They would never have sanctioned it. When I heard about it, I knew I had to tell my brother the king. When it was all over and the murderer had been arrested, the king asked me what else I had heard. He gave me leave to continue to act the part of Edmund Tudor. Now I am Edmund Tudor throughout England.''

Her brows drew together thoughtfully. "Does this Tam not realize who you truly are?''

"I suspect he does.''

"Then why continue to pretend?''

He had wrestled with that question when he first realized Tam knew. In his desire to cease pretending, he had nearly spoken, until he realized that in an inexplicable way, the lie he told in pretending to be Edmund Tudor allowed him to be more truly himself. It was one of the paradoxes of his situation.

"If I go to him as the Duke of Somerset, he will need to honor me as the king's brother. He will guard his tongue and a friendship I treasure will be destroyed.''

He watched her while she puzzled it out. Aside from his brother and sister-in-law, she was the only person in the wide world who knew him as both men. Her knowledge of this was all of a piece with the rest she knew. He could keep no secrets from her, as soon as he was with her he revealed everything.

And it was as he wanted it to be. The truth was he wanted no lies between them. Being able to be honest with her meant more than anything else in the world. She had become his touchstone.

"Since that German monk, Luther, defied the pope, men of goodwill have been asking how Christ's church could have become such a haven to greedy, corrupt worldly men. I fear for England if that question is not answered well," he said.

"Shall we become dissenters? Heretics?" she asked.

"Heaven forfend!" he said.

She had asked the vital question, putting into words the thing that drove him out to peer into the hearts of his fellow Englishmen again and again and again. If men threw off the spiritual authority of the pope, what would become of the temporal authority of kings? And without kings, what would become of the world? Anarchy, madness, war? He crossed himself involuntarily, frightened by the dark tenor of his thoughts. He had promised his father he would do everything in his power, give everything he had, including his life, to keep Arthur's throne safe. Nothing asked of him was too much.

"Then there is no peace to be found anywhere," she whispered wearily.

"There is peace in heaven."

"And I am in the world. Peace in the cloister?"

"I cannot see you as a nun," he said, recoiling from the image her words evoked.

A rueful smile tugged at the corners of her mouth, laughter glimmering in the depths of her eyes. "No, nor I." She sighed. "I must go back to the palace."

"I cannot escort you."

"I did not ask it of you," she said.

What would happen to them now? He did not want to

lose her friendship or her regard, but he could not blame her if she did not trust him.

"Lady," he began.

Her chin lifted. "Am I no longer Cecilia?" His heart lightened to see the return of her independent spirit.

"Cecilia. It would please me if you would count me among your friends."

"What of your poor name? Your doxies and dissipations? And your laziness?" she asked lightly.

"Perhaps you might show me the error of my ways?"

"Perhaps." She sobered. "I shall always count you among my friends, if I may ask the same of you."

Drawn closer almost against his will, he took her hand. This time, when he pressed it to his breast, she did not pull it away. He looked into her eyes, losing himself in their clear, dark depths. If only, he thought. "I wish I truly was Edmund Tudor and you my sweetheart, Ceci," he whispered. He lifted her hand and held her palm against his face. For a moment, for a brief, unholy moment, he gave himself up to dreaming he might have her. Reluctantly, he recalled his duty. "But I am not, nor are you. If you cannot be my sweetheart, then I shall be glad to call you friend."

Her thumb caressed his cheek. He turned his head to place a soft kiss in the center of her palm and then stepped away from her. She sank into a deep curtsy, bending her head in deference to his royal rank. As much as the gesture stung, he was grateful to her for helping to build the wall of formality that would keep them within acceptable bounds.

"I beg your leave to depart, Your Grace."

"You have it, my lady."

Chapter Seven

Cecilia bent her head over her hand of playing cards without seeing them. All around her, on the fringes of her awareness, courtiers chatted and laughed, filling the anteroom with their noise. She and Sebastian were not the only people playing cards; tables had been set up all around the room and the rattle of dice and the clink of coins threaded through the roar of voices.

She thought of Edmund: Edmund laughing, Edmund dancing, Edmund trying in vain to win the game of chess they played. In the last fortnight, she had spent as much time as she could with him, without being conspicuous, and it was not enough. He had not laid another unwarranted finger on her, but the touch of his hand as he partnered her in the dance, the laughter in his eyes as he teased her, and the shape of his mouth as he spoke to her, kept the memory of his kisses and her response alive. An echoing ache rolled over her, making her breath catch and a prickle of faint sweat sting her face. It was the same every time she remembered, the longing, the burning wave of desire. She had been able to think of nothing else for days.

"…Conyers?" Sebastian said.

Cecilia started and looked across the table at Sebastian.

"I beg your pardon! My thoughts had gone woolgathering. What of Conyers?"

"I asked if you have met Sir George Conyers," Sebastian repeated with exaggerated patience.

She grimaced. She had seen Sir George as he performed his duties and had gone out of her way to avoid him. As a maid of honor, she was expected to be pleasant to all, something she feared she could not do in Sir George's case.

"I have spoken to him on occasion," she admitted. "Why do you ask?"

"From the way he is staring at you, I think he may wish to extend his acquaintance."

Cecilia lowered her head over her cards.

"I wish him to depart," she muttered, flicking a quick glance at Sebastian.

Sebastian examined his cards. "You do not care for him?"

"No, I do not." She wished Sebastian would cease his questions. Talking about Conyers made her think of Beatrice with her bodice loose, her face hard as white marble. It was an image Cecilia longed to forget.

"What has he done to earn your animosity?" Sebastian asked curiously.

Cecilia folded her cards.

"I mistrust him without knowing why. Does that satisfy you?" She flung her cards down. "Here, let us deal out the cards again and begin a new game."

"We have not played the first one out! I was sure I might win this time!"

"I freely concede the game to you, dear Sebastian. Deal afresh."

Sebastian laid his cards on the table, faceup. A quick glance at them showed her she would have beaten him handily and for a bitter moment she regretted conceding the game. In their long friendship, she had never forfeited a game to Sebastian, whether it was chess, Primero or dice.

Sweeping up the cards and shuffling them, she gathered her wits. She had yielded the game to him to distract him from George Conyers, lest she be driven into one of her weak, useless lies. She had no choice but to sacrifice her pride.

The reminder braced her. She handed the cards to Sebastian.

As he dealt a fresh hand, he said, ''It is not like you to give up so easily.''

''I had made some poor discards and lost my way. I did not think I could win and did not care to play it out,'' she said easily, examining her new cards.

''Your mind is much occupied if that is the case.''

Her heart began to pound. Had Sebastian heard a rumor about Beatrice and Conyers? What if he began to question her? She would surely give Beatrice away. And if Sebastian knew, it was only a matter of time before Lord Manners knew.

''My mind occupied? By what, pray tell?'' she asked as easily as she could. Sebastian glanced up, his eyes as blue as cornflowers between his thick golden lashes. Distractedly, she noticed that in his own very male way he was as beautiful as Beatrice, but his beauty did not warm her.

''By my lord of Somerset.'' Quick heat beat in her face and, for a brief moment, it was as if Edmund's long body was pressed to hers. Edmund was behaving as she wished him to, with courtesy and discretion. Why was she so discontented? ''Do not deny it. I see your blush.''

Setting Edmund aside, she thought quickly. She was weary of being warned not to spend too much time with Edmund, but if chiding her distracted Sebastian from

George Conyers, she was willing to bow her head and listen.

"He is comely," she admitted.

"Do not let him turn your head. Look at the maids Harry of York has ruined. The Earl of Shrewsbury has a daughter who will never marry because she bore York a bastard. Do not travel her path."

"We have talked of this before, Sebastian. Somerset has never insulted a girl of gentle family, never mind a nobleman's daughter. I do not know why you fear for me."

"So said the first girl York dishonored. I should not like to see you learn to your cost that you may not trust Somerset's former habits."

She met his eyes squarely, unable to let that remark pass without protest. "Sebastian, I did not lie when I told you before that I know what I owe my family and myself. I shall be careful."

"It is not simply the sin you must avoid, Ceci. The appearance of sin is as ruinous." He was somber and paternal, the gravity sitting oddly on his usually cheerful countenance.

"I know," she said sharply, more sharply than she intended. She sighed. "I beg your pardon. I know you have only my benefit in mind."

"I am not the only one to speak of this to you, am I?"

"No. Mary Butler also warned me."

"Then I beg your pardon. You ought to tell me to tend my own affairs." He looked down at his cards, faint color tingeing his cheeks.

She stretched out her hand and covered his. "But you spoke for love, and for that I could not deny you." She pressed his hand and released it.

"That heart of yours is too tender," he said sternly. "How shall you survive this nest of vipers?"

"I am not so kind to the serpents," she replied, arranging her cards. "In whose number, I might add, you cannot be counted."

"I have known you too long to try to beguile you."

"That is wise. There is no trick of yours I have not seen."

"I beg leave to doubt that." He looked over her shoulder, his eyes narrowing. "Have a care. Conyers is coming this way."

Cecilia's heart sank, a quick, nauseating plummet. She could not escape him now. *I ought to let Beatrice save herself,* she thought irritably.

"Lady Cecilia, how pleasant to see you," Conyers said easily. As he bowed, the candlelight glittered in the jewels of his slashed sleeves. A quick glance through her lashes showed her a handsome, smiling face and eyes as hard as iron.

"Sir George," she said as pleasantly as she could. "Sebastian, may I present Sir George Conyers? Lord Sebastian Benbury is a near neighbor of my family's, Sir George."

"I am honored, my lord," Conyers said, with another bow for Sebastian.

"The pleasure is all mine," Sebastian said. Cecilia met his eyes and read his dilemma. She had made it clear she did not care for Conyers's company but good manners would force Sebastian to ask him to join them. She nodded as imperceptibly as she could, hoping Sebastian would understand her. It was too late to avoid Conyers, since she was not prepared to snub him. "Please join us. We are playing Primero," Sebastian said. Cecilia sighed, relieved. That was the great blessing of old friends: no explanations.

"I am honored," Conyers repeated, sliding onto the settle beside Cecilia.

Cecilia handed her cards back to Sebastian. She wanted

to start a new game, rather than finish this one under Conyers's eye.

"Will you deal, Sir George?" Sebastian asked, sliding the pack across the tabletop.

"Gladly."

Conyers dealt the cards with quick, almost nervous movements of his graceful hands. They examined and arranged their cards in silence, Conyers and Cecilia turned on the settle to protect their hands from view.

"How goes Lady Manners?" Conyers asked idly, his eyes on his hand.

Cecilia had expected some question about her sister and replied easily enough. "She is well, sir."

"I did not know you knew Lady Manners, Sir George," Sebastian said stiffly. "She has not mentioned you to me."

"I am a friend of her husband's. I am sure she has not told you about all her new friends." Conyers's teeth gleamed faintly between his firm red lips.

"Beatrice and I are old friends. We have no secrets from each other," Sebastian said.

"I should not be so sure of that," Conyers murmured.

"Oh? What are you implying, sir?" Sebastian asked.

Cecilia thought they were like a pair of dogs, circling one another, preparing to fight over a bitch in heat. A bucket of cold water was enough to stop the dogs. What would stop these two?

"I imply nothing, my lord. Lady Manners and I have been friends since her marriage to Lord Manners. You said you were unaware of our friendship and that she has no secrets from you. These statements are incompatible," Conyers said with an air of humility that bordered on insulting.

"Perhaps, sir, you are not as great a friend to my sister as you believe," Cecilia said quietly.

"You know better than that, Lady Cecilia," Conyers said softly.

"Do I?" As much as Conyers daunted her, she could not help opposing him. She disliked men who assumed she was a fool. "I am not sure I take your meaning."

"You understand me well enough, my lady. You have seen us. Did we not seem great friends?"

"Appearances can be deceiving. It bears remembering here at Court." She arranged the cards in her hand. Across the table, Sebastian folded and spread his cards, watching her as she baited Conyers.

"And the implication is…"

"Why, there is no implication. The king throws his arm around Sir Charles Brandon and the world thinks they are bosom friends. The next day the king cannot remember his name. It is easy to be deceived when one does not see all."

"But some things cannot be mistaken," Conyers said.

"I doubt me that." Cecilia threw down a card, trying to look engrossed in her hand. Her mouth dry, her heart quivering in her throat, she could not see her cards. But if she did not look at her cards, she would be forced to look at Conyers.

"Shall I remind you of our meeting, Lady Cecilia?" Conyers asked. She knew he meant to scare her with the recollection of his painful grip on her chin but what came to mind was how angry he had made her. The memory was as heartening as a cup of mulled wine on a winter's afternoon. She lifted her eyes and smiled sweetly at him.

"My dear Sir George, you could repeat our entire conversation and change nothing of my view. I remember everything that passed between us quite clearly."

"Everything?"

"Oh, every word, gesture and tone," she said. "I also remember what was said when you departed."

"Tell me."

"I cannot. You must ask Lady Manners. I am sure she will be glad to tell the tale of our conversation. Since you are such great friends." The sudden darkening of Conyers's face confirmed her guess that Beatrice had refused to tell him anything. She repressed a satisfied smile. He was not so fearsome now that she felt she had the upper hand.

"But you are here," Conyers said.

"I do not care to bore Lord Benbury with women's talk, sir. It is your discard."

They played out the hand in silence. Cecilia won, playing with a fierce concentration that smothered conversation. Conyers flung down his losing hand and stood, jolting Cecilia on the settle as he shoved it back. Digging in his purse, he counted out his loss and flung it on the table, the coins bouncing with a discordant clatter.

"There. We are even, Lady Cecilia. Until we play again." He bowed and stalked away, disappearing into the surging crowd of increasingly drunk courtiers.

"What is he to Beatrice, Ceci?" Sebastian said in a low, hard voice. "And do not try to lie to me. You are no good at it."

"That is a question you must ask Beatrice, Sebastian." She might protect Beatrice from Conyers, but not from her own folly. Maybe the shock of Sebastian's hurt and anger—for Cecilia had no doubt of his hurt and anger—would compel Beatrice to give up this dangerous game she was playing.

Chapter Eight

Cecilia stopped outside the door to the suite of rooms given over to the maids of honor. Sick of chattering gossips, tired of staring eyes, she could not enter. She needed solitude, a quiet place to calm herself after her difficult evening.

She thought furiously. Not far from where she stood was a curtained oriel. Tonight it would be peaceful to stand beside the window, watching the cold moonlight pearling the surface of the river. She turned toward the alcove.

The corridors were dim, torches guttering or burnt out. She hurried through the shadows, the darkness and silence both soothing and unnerving. Arriving at the window alcove, she took a quick glance down the corridor to be sure no one saw her before she dove between the drawn curtains.

"Unh!"

She blundered into someone solid and warm, dressed in velvet and fur. Hands shot out and gripped her arms. She caught a whiff of canary wine underlaid with a scent she had come to know well, a scent unique to one man.

"Find another hiding place, mistress," Edmund hissed. "This one is taken." His face, broken into planes of white and black, was almost unrecognizable in the stark moon-light.

"I should prefer not to."

"Ceci?" he whispered, his hands relaxing.

"Yes."

"Thank God." His hands slid down her arms, his fingers winding through hers as easily as if he had done it all their lives. "Are you hiding, too?"

"No." Their glances caught and held. His eyes were dark in the uncertain light. He stepped closer, until he was nearer than he had been since kissing her. Her breath would not come evenly. "Yes. I do not know." She could not see him, standing so close she could almost hear the beating of his heart.

"I think you are hiding," he murmured. She could hear the smile in his voice. "But from whom?"

"No one," she said. The other maids of honor were far away, as distant as legendary Muscovy. "What of you?"

"I come here to watch the river. And to keep my distance from the lickspittle lackeys who follow my every step."

She turned her head and looked through the thick glass. "Oh," she breathed, entranced. The world outside was a blue-white blur, the river flickering on the horizon. The wavy glass gave the smeared scene a strange beauty, discomforting and otherworldly.

"You see it, too," he said.

She tilted her head to look at him and found him smiling at her, the corner of his mouth quirked upward. She could not read the quality of his smile in the flat blue light, but his hands were gentle and his body held none of the restless tension that made him so ebullient in public.

"The light and the windowpanes and the river," he said. "You see it, too."

She nodded and looked out the window again.

"You never answered my question," he said.

"My reason to hide?"

"Mmm."

She thought about her answer, considering and discarding half-truths and meaningless commonplaces. "I did not want to listen to the maids of honor spreading tales," she said. "None is my friend, they all whisper about me behind my back, and some of them say things to my face. I could not face that." She could not endure another evening of half-spoken gibes about her education, her music, her aloofness.

"Ah, Ceci," he sighed. "Does Kati know of this?"

"No." This was not the queen's battle to fight. "And she shall not, unless you tell her. Promise me you will not."

He was silent for a long time, so long that she began to think of arguments to persuade him to her view. "Very well, if that is what you want." He hesitated. "I do not like to see you unhappy."

"And you do not." She grinned up at him. "They are nothing more than honking, hissing geese. I do not listen to any of them."

"But I do not like it," he said.

His melancholy surprised her. "It is the way of the world."

He opened his mouth as if to reply but closed it without speaking. He put his arm around her shoulder and drew her against him. The edge of her hood struck his chest, the blow jarring her neck. Sighing irritably, she reached up and pulled the hood off, rubbing her scalp where its gold wire trimming had dug in. She set it on the window frame and turned into Edmund's warm embrace.

It was peaceful here, in his arms. He was tall and

straight, beautifully made. The arms that held her so gently
were heavy with muscles and strength but what she felt
was comfort, warmth. It was not like one of Sebastian's
hugs—she was far too aware of the body that held her for
that—but she felt safe nevertheless. Perhaps her fever for
him was breaking and they could return to the simple
friendship they had begun as children. She told herself it
would be best for both of them if that were so and tried
to ignore the desolation that followed. His arms tightened
and she lifted her head, looking into his eyes. Something
in their depths caught her, something that frightened and
exhilarated her at once. She began to tremble.

Never taking his gaze from hers, he leaned over and
brushed her temple with his lips, his breath warm against
her skin. "It is not safe to be here," he whispered.

"For which of us?" She was achingly aware of him,
his arms holding her, his mouth delicately brushing her
brow, his tall strong body pressing hers.

"Both." His mouth moved along her hairline and her
thoughts spun in her head.

"We should leave." She spoke almost at random, barely
aware of what she said. Peace fled, replaced by longing.
The sound of his linen shirt rustling as he shifted tingled
along her skin.

"I cannot." He sounded as dazed as she felt, his warm
mouth nibbling her cheek.

"Nor can I." She turned her head and kissed him. His
lips were soft and full, his mouth sweet and dark with the
taste of wine. His tongue caressed the corners of her mouth
before slipping between her lips. His chin, rough with a
day's whiskers, rubbed hers; the rasp, so very male, gave
her gooseflesh.

She parted her lips, letting the kiss deepen. His tongue
in her mouth felt as if it were stroking her body, her soft

linen shift chafing her suddenly sensitive nipples. She shifted so that the swell of his thigh pressed the apex of her legs and a hot quivering jolt shot from her groin to her breast and made her head swim. It was as if her desire had been hidden all along, waiting for his touch to reveal it. She had not known, not even the kiss in the Abbey had shown her, how quickly her passion for him could flare to life.

"Oh, Ceci," he whispered, his lips nibbling the corners of her mouth, his hands lifting to cradle her face. "You are so beautiful...."

She opened her eyes and stared into his, clear as water in the blue moonlight. His thumbs stroked her eyebrows, tracing a line from the corners of her eyes to her hairline and along her jaw. She half closed her eyes against the ache his touch awoke in her.

His fingers traced her lips. She kissed them one by one. "Am I? Am I beautiful to you?"

"Oh, yes," he said, and tilted her head for another deep, yearning kiss. She gripped his shoulders, determined to kiss as well as be kissed. His hands swept down her arms to her waist and then up to her breasts, lightly tracing their shape, fingertips jolting her as they touched her nipples through the suddenly thin velvet of her bodice. She gasped and then moaned, her knees wobbling weakly.

Gently, so gently she barely felt it, he eased her sleeves down. His fingers were warm on her naked shoulders, caressing, exploring, tracing the edge of her neckline. She swallowed, hardly able to breath, her sight blurring. When his mouth and tongue followed his fingers her head spun and she thought she might swoon. She clutched his doublet to hold her up, afraid she was going to fall.

"Edmund!" she whispered. She was hungry for something she could not name; only he could satisfy her.

His kiss turned fierce, demanding, bruising her lips and fueling her excitement. He bent his neck, returning his attention to her neckline and the tops of her breasts. He half lifted her, so they were pressed groin to groin.

She did not care that it was dangerous, ruinous sin. A sweet, gasping tension built, fueled by the touch of his lips and hands. She was burning hot, aware only of the touch of his long fingers, his mouth, the pressure of his long body.

"Please, oh, please," she cried softly, hardly knowing what she begged for.

"Not here," he said thickly.

"What?" she said breathlessly, and then understood him.

"Not. Here."

He bent his head and kissed her again. Her head, which had begun to clear in the brief instant they spoke, clouded. She lifted her knee, trying instinctively to bring his groin into closer contact with hers. He shifted his weight and ground his hips against her. She tore her mouth from his, panting, her whole body afire. He surged against her again. A soft moan tore from her throat.

"Ceci," he whispered harshly. "Ceci."

He sank to his knees, drawing her with him, his mouth and tongue and hands everywhere. She was dazed, aware only of him and the fiery pleasure he had awakened. Still caressing her, murmuring her name, he reached for her skirt and slid his hand underneath. She felt the touch of his skin on hers to the marrow of her bones. Blindly, she rubbed herself against him, desperate to feel him, the silky skin of his neck faintly salty under her tongue. He gasped, shuddering, his hands, one under her skirt and the other above it, pressing her closer. She cried his name, wanting him with an animal fierceness that allowed no room for thought, never mind silence.

"Edmund. Oh Edmund!"

He froze. Slowly, his hands lifted from her body and smoothed her skirt down.

"We cannot do this," he whispered.

She ignored his words, determined not to hear them. She tightened her hold on him, her face buried in the curve between his shoulder and neck.

He grasped her shoulders and shook her gently. "Ceci, we cannot."

She clutched his sleeves, unable to believe he had halted them. The beat of her heart slowly faded as her blood cooled.

"I cannot tumble you in the floor rushes as if—" He swallowed. "This isn't right."

She flinched at the harshness of his words. "What have I done?" she whispered. She was not sure if she referred to the way she had yielded to his embraces or if she asked how she had offended him.

"Nothing," he said. "I have wronged you. I should not have kissed you."

"I did not struggle." She could not let him take the blame, not when she had desired him as much, if not more, than he had desired her. "I should have, but I did not."

He smoothed her hair back from her brow and then traced the shape of her face with gentle fingers. She quivered as he caressed her shoulders, his thumbs brushing along her collarbone. He confused her, first saying, "No," and then touching her with such seductive sweetness. She raised her eyes to his. Some of her confusion must have shown in her expression because he snatched his hands away as if her skin scalded them.

He scrambled to his feet. "I cannot stay here. If I stay, I will keep touching you. I am sorry, Ceci."

And then he was gone, the curtains swaying with the swiftness of his passage.

Bewildered, she knelt where he had left her. She knew she ought to be ashamed of herself and of her wanton behavior but, prod as she might, shame would not come. She was dazed, subtly bruised, and uneasy about Edmund's abrupt departure, but not ashamed.

Why?

She remembered the feel of his body pressing hers, and she weakened, heat sweeping her, making her almost as dizzy as she had been when in his arms.

God help me, I still want him.

She wanted to lie down with Edmund, to offer him her body and to take his. Her concern for her honor, her pride in her virtue, meant nothing in the face of her lust. And her scorn of Beatrice. Was it because Beatrice's behavior cut too close to the bone? She did not know.

And still Cecilia felt no shame. Something within her refused to admit that she had done wrong tonight. She had never felt so right as she did in his arms, his mouth on hers. As dark and red with carnality as it had been, it had also been like coming home. We belong, she thought.

But what if he does not feel it, too? The thought brushed her with ice. He could not feel otherwise. Or could he? She knew nothing of love, nothing of men. If men were not capable of pretending love to bring them a quick tumble, then why were maids like her always being warned to beware? Could Edmund be one such as that?

No, she thought. If he had been bent on seduction, he would be with her now, laying her down on the floor rushes and taking his ease. God knew she would not have stopped him.

What did she want? Heat coursed from her throat to her groin. She sat back on her haunches, swallowing against a suddenly dry mouth. Edmund. What else?

Chapter Nine

Edmund lifted his hand against the glaring sunlight, his eyes throbbing and the flagstones of the water stairs unsteady under his feet. His mouth was sour and sticky and the inside of his head felt as if it were drying out and shrinking.

He braced his hands on his thighs and pushed himself upward, clammy sweat breaking out on his brow. After leaving Cecilia last night, he had gone in search of wine, as much of it as he could hold. Harrowed by their fitful lovemaking and the knowledge he had come within a hairsbreadth of dishonoring her despite his best intentions, he had had no choice but to drink himself into oblivion.

He had known then that he could not stay at Richmond, seeing Cecilia every day. Though it was wrong to spend so much time with her, he would not stay away from her. Without the king's leave to go, he sent a boy running to have his barge brought to the water stairs. He was going back to London, to his little house in Southwark where he could be miserable in peace. If need be, he would abase himself later; now he could not risk refusal.

His barge slid up to the water stairs. He stumbled

aboard, flinging himself onto the padded bench beneath the awning.

"Close those accursed blinds." A manservant hastened to obey him. He closed his eyes, as much to shut out the sight of the riverbank rocking gently as to hide from the sunlight burning as it struck the water. His stomach rolled greasily. He clamped his lips shut and fixed his concentration on keeping his gorge down.

"Southwark," he said. They had better understand him. He was too miserable to have a firm grip on his temper and would strike anyone who crossed him. The barge was shoved away from the stairs, the water rustling silkily. The coxswain barked a command, the oars were lowered with a head-splitting rattle and the barge surged forward.

He sank into blackness that was not sleep, his thoughts shifting in sluggish misery. He thought of his father, remembering the late king as he always did when unhappy. His father's death had torn a gaping hole through the center of his life, a hole nothing had ever filled.

Arthur had tried his best to be a father to him, and Edmund would always be grateful for his kindness and affection. But Arthur was not their father. He never ruffled Edmund's hair and stroked it smooth. He never mangled a harp trying to play it, laughing all the while. His face never lit up when Edmund came into the room.

The only thing of his father that remained was the promise he had extracted from Edmund, the vow to support Arthur, come what may. If Edmund broke or betrayed that promise, the cord binding him to his father would be cut and he would be cast adrift.

Cecilia had no place in his life unless he intended to marry her, and he could not marry her and keep the promise. No one had ever explicitly told him he could not marry an Englishwoman, but no one had ever explicitly told him not to stab himself, either. Some things did not need to be said. Arthur had signed one treaty that had Edmund's marriage as part of its provisions and, after Edmund's eight-year-old bride had died on her way to England, had come close to doing it again on half a dozen subsequent occasions. Edmund, like his brothers and sisters before him, was a pawn in the royal game of making marriages. He was no more free than anyone else to follow his heart.

He sighed, the delicate edifice of his life beginning to crumble. It was easy to tell himself to stay away from Cecilia, but it made no difference. She drew him to her, against his will and judgment. He suspected it was against hers, as well. What was the cord that bound them? A linty sweetmeat shared with a bold little girl in the autumn dusk? Or was it the smile she had offered in thanks, the first response he had ever received that had nothing to do with his rank and everything to do with himself?

As they neared London he was distantly aware of an increase in river traffic: the raucous shouts of the waterman, the hollow bang as two boats collided and the rhythmic cries of costermongers carrying across the water on the breeze. Sooner than he wanted, the barge nudged against the jetty and a low voice said, "We are arrived, Your Grace."

"I know, you fool!" he said, fighting the inexplicable urge to weep. He was sicker than he had dreamed. He dragged himself off the barge and sent it back to Richmond. Trying to gather his wits and courage, he paused for a moment. His soul seemed only lightly tethered to his unhappy body, as if it might go floating away at any moment. He forced himself to start walking, praying that no one accosted him on the short journey. He did not have the strength to defend himself.

The stench rising from the gutters, a hideous mixture of

excrement and rotting meat, made him stop three times along the way to retch uselessly.

He stopped in his tracks. His house. At last. It had taken hours to make the five-minute journey. His feet did not want to move, his legs were as heavy as lead. He wanted to sleep right here, standing in the stinking street. He forced himself to go on, bribing himself with the promise he could rest once he was within.

It was the longest ten yards of his life, but with a desperate, sweaty effort, he made it. He pushed at the door. It would not open. He stared at it, baffled. He was tired, so tired it hurt. He wanted to sleep. Why wouldn't the door open? Barred. It was early yet. He beat on the door, desperate to enter. What was taking so long? He felt as if he pounded his own head.

The door flung open. Piers, his servant, stood in the doorway, a gown flung over his nightshirt, a cudgel in his hand. "Who the—! My lord! I beg your pardon!"

"What the devil took you so long!" Edmund snarled, shoving past him. "I should not have to wait to enter my own house!"

"No, my lord."

The door shut behind him, the bar booming as it dropped into place. "Must you make so much noise?"

"The headache, my lord?" Piers asked sympathetically.

"No!"

His heart was lodged in his temple, throbbing unmercifully. Bed, he needed a bed. He stumbled toward the stairs and crawled upward.

"Piers? Who is it? Piers!" Piers's wife, Joan, poked her head out of the door to Piers's bedchamber. Her hair was tangled, her fine skin creased with a coverlet mark. Edmund turned and glared at Piers, climbing the stairs behind him.

"You are a damned fool for lying with her. You are a priest, for mercy's sake."

"Yes, my lord."

"You will be found out."

"Yes, my lord."

"A pox on you," Edmund said wearily. "Good morrow, Dame Joan." There was no point in trying to provoke a man who would only agree with anything he said. And did he truly want to quarrel with Piers? No. What he wanted was rest.

He entered his bedchamber, the longing for sleep almost unendurable. Dame Joan had hung new curtains from the tester, a strong, soothing blue. He staggered across the room and fell onto the bed. The mattress was deep and soft, the pillows like clouds. He stretched out, kicking his shoes off. Oh, Blessed Virgin, this was what he had wanted. His stomach stopped churning, the pulse in his temple dying down. All the crackling tension in his muscles dissolved in relief as his eyes closed.

When he woke, it was late afternoon. He rose, walked to the window and opened the shutter on the distant hum of the street, muted on this side of the house. His headache was gone, his abused stomach grumbling with hunger. The door opened to reveal Piers, carrying a tray of food. The ability to anticipate Edmund's needs was not the least of Piers's gifts.

"I have cheese, ale and a meat pie, my lord. I thought you might be hungry."

"Bless you," Edmund said. Piers set the tray on the table by the window and reached out to close the shutter. "Leave it. It is too early for candlelight, and I should like to think I saw something of the day."

The meat pie was fresh, its light pastry Dame Joan's

handiwork. He would recognize her touch even in Cathay. The cheese was strong, the ale cool and heartening. When he had finished his meal, he thought he might be able to face the world. Or at least the part of it he needed to face.

He changed his clothing from princely velvet and sable to a more gentlemanly wool and squirrel. Piers, assisting him, cast a considering eye over his choices.

"Black Margery?" he asked.

"Yes. I hope to return with a guest," Edmund replied, experimenting with the tilt of his cap in the silver mirror Piers held up.

"Like that, is it?"

"Nothing certain, but a wise man is a prepared one."

"Aye, my lord."

Edmund pulled the mirror down to look sternly at Piers. "It might have been someone from the Abbey this morning."

"I know, my lord."

"Joan must sleep on the third floor."

"My lord, you do not know what it is like to want to sleep with the woman you love. Not to lie with her, but to have her beside you when you go to sleep and find her there again when you wake," Piers pleaded.

His words conjured up Cecilia's face. To lie down with her at night and wake with her at dawn.... Edmund crushed his longing, hardening his heart against himself. He knew what his obligations were, he understood what was possible and what was not. Only a fool ate out his heart for what he could not have.

"That cannot matter. The penalties are harsh for a married priest. They are still harsher for the woman who marries him. You endanger Joan."

"Aye, my lord," Piers said miserably.

"For what it is worth, I do know," Edmund added softly.

"My lord?"

"Forget I spoke. I must go." Thrusting a sharp little knife into his belt, he left the room. Dame Joan waited for him at the bottom of the stairs, twisting her apron in her hands, a worried look in her eyes.

"Take care, my lord. It isn't safe in those streets."

Edmund had to laugh. Here was a woman who risked everything short of death to sleep with her man, cautioning him to be careful. "Dame Joan, I am no green boy."

"I am a woman. It is given to me to worry."

She was right to worry, right to say the streets were unsafe. The wicked little knife at his belt was there for a reason. But he expected no trouble. Black Margery's house wasn't far, just around the corner, and his dress, while gentlemanly, was not rich. And even if some fool cut his purse, what of it? There was nothing in it.

Black Margery met him at the door, greeting him with a flinty look and a smacking kiss. "It's been some time since we've seen you here, Edmund." She was a pretty, middle-aged woman whose mane of dark hair had given her the name "Black."

Unable to resist the silk, Edmund wound one of her curls around his finger. "A month or two, Margery."

She lifted his hand away from her hair, her hard green eyes gleaming shrewdly. "None of that, my lad. What brings you to me on this fine summer night?"

"Can you not guess?"

"Well, 'tisn't for me, I know that," she said sharply.

He put his arms around her, enjoying her soft, comfortable curves. "It's more than I know." Her brisk affection eased his raw heart, his body whispering that it would be a simple matter to slip back into her bed. Looking down into her face, he knew that if he made the least little push to win her, they would spend the night in mutual pleasure. He let her go. "You see too much."

She patted his face, the slap stinging although it was meant affectionately. "I am old enough to have seen too much. And you are too young to want a beldam like me."

"There is no one like you, Margery, young or old," he said, surprised by the language she used and the bitterness of her tone.

"Well, I shall be closing down soon enough. I am getting too old for this game, whatever you say, Master Sauce. I bought me a bit of land outside the city. I am going to retire to Hampstead and grow herbs and become an old herb woman."

"I didn't know you knew anything about herbs," he said, diverted.

"There's much you don't know about me, lad. Now. Why are you here?"

"I need a girl—"

She planted her fists on her hips. "Well, I don't offer boys!"

She startled an unwilling laugh out of him. "Margery!"

"It was a foolish thing to say," she replied with lifted eyebrows.

He looked back at Margery. "I need a girl to live at my house for two months, give or take a sennight."

She snorted, shaking her head. "That again!"

"Yes. She must be able to hold her tongue and do exactly as she is told."

Her eyes narrowed in the look that meant she prepared herself for serious bargaining. "It will cost you."

"I expected that," he replied. "This is not charity."

"You've too much gold to need my charity."

"I am sure I will have less of it when we are done."

"I expect so. Come into my chamber. We'll discuss this over a cup of wine. I have a nice canary...." She tucked her arm into his.

The phrase brought to vivid life his debauch the night before. "No wine for me, I pray you. But let us go discuss our business quietly."

They climbed the stairs to her private chamber, a pleasant room furnished with a narrow bed, a padded bench and a table and chairs. After pouring herself a mug of wine, she seated herself at the table and pulled forward one of the ledgers piled high, opening it and thumbing through the pages. Edmund sat on the padded bench and leaned his head against the bare wall.

"I've a girl that will do nicely. She's grown weary of the work and it's showing, so a few weeks without a rider may do her some good." She tapped a finger against her cheek thoughtfully, her lips moving as she calculated. "Twenty pounds for two months."

"For a girl who is no longer working well? Six is more like it."

Margery choked. "You shall beggar us both! Eighteen."

"I shall have the feeding and the clothing of her for two months. And no doubt you will find a new girl to take her place. Nine." He folded his arms over his chest and closed his eyes in an attitude of boredom.

"New girls are not so easy to find. And even when found, must be trained. Sixteen is a fair price."

"You sell virgins at auction, Margery. A new girl is extra money. But, since I love you so well, I will offer you twelve."

"Fifteen. Not a shilling less."

He opened his eyes. "Thirteen pounds, ten shillings and she can keep her clothes."

She closed the ledger. "Done!" She raised her glass of

wine to him and drank deeply. "Who taught you to bargain so well?"

"Why do you ask?" He hardly cared why she wanted to know. He needed time to compose an answer that would not give too much away.

"You are plainly noble yet you dicker like a merchant. It's a puzzle, and now that I am getting out of the business I can indulge my curiosity." She eased back in her chair, her cup resting on her belly, and watched him intently.

He made himself grin at her. "I have spent too much time with caitiffs and cutpurses, my love. Only a clothhead could fail to learn a thing or two in company like that."

Margery stared at him for a long moment, her eyes narrowed, as if she weighed the likelihood he spoke the truth. Yet he knew her well enough to be sure she did not believe him, because belief was not part of her character. He met the look as blandly as he could.

She sighed. "Too bad you could not come with me when I bought my land. I think I was cheated."

He grinned at her improbable remark. "I beg leave to doubt that."

"Stranger things have happened." She set her cup down and stood. "I expect you'll like to see your new leman." He gathered himself to rise but she pushed him back. The smell of her heavy scent mingling with the tang of the wine and the honey of the beeswax candles released a flood of erotic memories. Margery had known things and shown him things.... He swallowed, willing himself to forget. It had been a long time ago, when he had been a stripling of seventeen. "No, do not get up. I will fetch the chit and send her in. And remember. She's yours now. If you want to have a little taste of her, why, the bed's right there and no questions asked." She disappeared through the door.

"I thought she was weary of the work!" Edmund shouted in protest.

Margery poked her head back into the room. "You are too sweet a dish to pass up, my lad. She is weary of fat merchants." She disappeared again, swinging the door shut.

Edmund eased back against the wall, smiling softly at his memories. He admired Margery's strength, her lack of self-pity, the way she refused to let her way of life wear her down. If she was thinking of quitting the business, it meant it was more than time. He would miss her teasing, miss her sharp-tongued kindness, miss the way she accepted him on his terms. Friends like her were rare and all the more valuable for their scarcity.

His thoughts swung to Cecilia, the longing to be with her gnawing at him. He wanted her, wanted to be with her. He sighed. There was no point in continuing with this line of thought. Duty held him to a course that did not include her.

The girl would help. Margery had spoken truly when she said the girl was his to use as he wished. Not that he intended to press her if she was unwilling. Never that. But he might not scruple to charm her out of reluctance.... It might distract him from Cecilia.

There was a scratch at the door.

"Enter," he called. The latch lifted and the girl slipped in. Edmund's breath caught.

She was tall and slender as a sapling, with dark hair rippling red in the candlelight and great dark eyes that watched him warily. Her resemblance to Cecilia made his heart stop. One side of his mind whispered that she was ideal, so much like Cecilia that if he narrowed his eyes he could pretend it was Ceci he lay with. Through her, he could let his fever burn its course and afterward return to his sensible life. The other half of his mind warned that it would never do, that all this trollop could do was remind him of what he could not have.

"Dame Margery sent me to you, sir." Her flat Londoner's voice shattered the spell of her looks. He suddenly saw her rough skin, the faint lines at the corners of her eyes and the narrowness of her mouth. She looked nothing like Cecilia.

"What is your name?"

"Cecily."

God must be punishing him. He closed his eyes and cast a brief plea for mercy heavenward.

Opening his eyes, he said gently, "Send Margery to me."

"Sir, I beg you…" She plucked at her red skirt, the corners of her painted mouth quivering. "Do not."

"What did Margery tell you?"

"That I must obey you in all things. That you would take me to your house, where I need service only you."

His heart went out to her, so plainly unhappy. He considered his options. He could refuse to take her, on the unspoken grounds of her appearance and name. If he did that, she would weigh heavily on his conscience. Or he could bring her to the house, a strange shadow of the woman he wanted. If he did that, would she be a constant reminder of what he wanted to forget?

His eyes ran over her body. Whatever he did, he would not touch her. Not from any moral qualms but because the wicked side of his mind had got it wrong. This shadow-Cecilia could not even arouse him. He already resented her for not being the right Cecilia. He sighed. How damnably fate twisted him, bending his will, forcing him into directions he did not want to go.

"Very well. I shall not send for Margery. Nor will you

service me as you service the men who come here. You will assist my steward, obeying him in all things.''

''But she said you would buy me...'' She stopped, as if she realized how impertinent she was.

''Clothes. Yes, that is what I promised her. It is part of our bargain. I shall dress you for two months.'' He could not call her Cecily. ''Is Cecily your real name?''

''No, sir.''

''Then your real name is?''

''Marguerite, sir. Dame Margery said the men won't like to lay with a Frenchie, so she made me change it to something more English-like.''

''I shall call you Marguerite.''

''My old dad called me Daisy. For the flower, the marguerite.''

''Would you like to be called Daisy?''

''Very much, sir.''

''Very well, Daisy. Come with me.''

Chapter Ten

"I cannot believe Somerset," Mary Butler said.

Cecilia sat on a padded bench tuning her lute in the queen's chamber, Mary beside her sorting silks for needlework by color.

"What of him?" Quick heat tingled in Cecilia's face. Had anyone spied them? Was her good name already ruined? She concentrated on keeping her voice neutral.

"He left Court this morning without so much as a fare-thee-well. The king is furious."

Cecilia's fingers tightened involuntarily on the lute strings, jangling them. Thank God, her head was turned away. She could not have kept her shock from showing.

"Does anyone know why?" she managed to ask.

"No, but it is a fearsome scandal nevertheless."

Her fingers danced over the lute strings, testing their tone while she listened halfheartedly. It sounded well enough, but with her thoughts so disordered, could she tell if it jangled tunelessly? She glanced at Mary to see if she had noticed anything amiss and found Mary eyeing her speculatively.

"What? Have I a smudge on my nose?"

"No. But I thought you might know something of Somerset's abrupt departure," Mary said slowly.

"No, I knew nothing of it until you mentioned it." And it shocked me, too, she thought.

"You and His Grace have been much together these last weeks. I thought he might have confided in you."

"We are not so close as that. He knew me as a child and has a kindness for me. There is nothing more to our friendship." She ruthlessly thrust aside the memory of his mouth on her breasts.

"That is not what I hear."

"You can hear anything you like, if you listen long enough." She wished Mary would stop probing. She returned to her lute. An old air formed itself out of the strings and she began to hum.

"You are so discreet you make me think you have something to hide."

Cecilia laid her hand across the lute's strings and looked up at her. What did she have to do to still Mary's persistent tongue? And for how long could she keep her countenance?

"Mary, you and Sebastian Benbury have spent much breath telling me to beware the Duke of Somerset. I have listened to your wise counsel and know nothing of him or his actions. My ignorance you take for coyness and suspect me. I may as well sin as not for all the difference it makes."

"Cecilia!" Mary looked honestly shocked.

"It was a jest, Mary," Cecilia said wearily.

"Not a funny one." Mary snapped, her color high. She gathered up her silks and hastened to join a group of the queen's ladies on the far side of the chamber.

Cecilia sighed, annoyed with herself for offending Mary and annoyed with Mary for being so easily offended. She had no doubt that when Mary smoothed her ruffled feathers, she would make peace, but for now the wisest course Cecilia could pursue was to leave her be.

In one way, Mary's abrupt departure was a blessing: it left Cecilia free to think without worrying about what her face gave away. She played her lute to discourage conversation, while she puzzled over Edmund's abrupt departure. Why had he left so suddenly? Had something she had done last night driven him away? Do not be so vain, she told herself. His behavior can have nothing to do with you.

I shall miss him.

He was the only man in the world who could follow her thoughts wherever they led, the only man who never betrayed by so much as a flicker of a look that he thought her education peculiar and she unwomanly for not hiding it better. There was nothing she could not say to him.

She shivered, the world suddenly a much colder place.

Ten days later Cecilia wandered disconsolately through the knot garden, scowling at the fragrant herbs in their beds. She missed Edmund. With no word from him in days, rumor had run wild. The king intended to arrest him, try him, put him to death; every story she heard was more lurid than the last, and all, as far she could see, without any foundation whatsoever.

''Ceci!''

A man called to her from the gate.

Edmund! Her head shot up, the corners of her mouth lifting happily until she recognized Sebastian.

He walked toward her, a troubled frown on his face, his mouth set in a particularly grim line. Disappointment that he was not Edmund vanished, swamped in annoyance. What now? How much more would she have to endure?

"Ceci, I must speak to you," Sebastian said abruptly, coming to stand before her.

Something in his flat tone sent a chill rippling across the back of her neck. "Speak then."

"I have heard from a friend that the Duke of Somerset has taken a mistress."

The sun stopped in its orbit, the breeze died, the world stilled. A mist of darkness passed before her eyes and then cleared, the sun spinning onward, the breeze cooling her hot cheeks, the world restored to her.

"No," she said.

"My friend is usually reliable in matters like this, Ceci. I did not want you to hear it from anyone else."

"It is not true." She did not know how or why she knew the tale for a lie, but she trusted the instinct that said Edmund would not behave so.

"I know it is not easy to believe ill of someone you love…"

"Love?" she cried, shocked, and looked up into his face.

Violet shadows circled his eyes, flattening their brilliant blue, and there was a discouraged twist to his mouth. He was not speaking of her. He meant himself.

He must have found out about Conyers. She laid a hand on his arm. She had always known that Edmund was beyond her reach, but Sebastian had grown up believing that he and Beatrice would be wed someday. "Oh, Sebastian." There was nothing more she could say, nothing that would not shame him.

"You knew about it," he said through stiff lips.

Was he angry with her? Her cheeks tingled. "I found out by accident. Beatrice swore me to secrecy."

"You should have told me! God's sweet toes, Ceci, what did you think would happen?"

"I told you to ask her. I could do no more." She took his hand in hers and squeezed it, willing him to understand, willing him to let his anger go. "She is my sister and I love her, no matter what she does."

He jerked his hand away as if he was too angry to be held.

"You could have told me."

On what grounds? And to what end? She took a deep breath, knowing her next question must hurt him. "And what would you have done?"

"I do not know. I have no right…" His voice faded and he frowned as if his thoughts had become disordered.

She did not want to speak. "No, you do not." He paled and his mouth flattened in a shallow, downward curve. She flinched. She had not meant for her words to cut so deeply, yet he had needed to hear them.

"I believed in Beatrice just as you believe in Somerset, and with better cause." She suspected he meant to wound her in payment for wounding him, but his words stung nevertheless. "If my good Beatrice can become a whore, what is Somerset capable of? Do not be as blind a fool as I was, Ceci. Let this madness go."

"Beatrice is not a whore and Edmund does not have a mistress." Tension knotted her arms and shoulders as her patience ebbed. "You are cruel to say so."

"A pox on Beatrice, a pox on Somerset and a pox on you!" He took a deep, shuddering breath, his face red and his eyes blazing blue in contrast. "I will have done with this!"

"A pox on you!" Her temper broke free. "You are a pap-lapping cullion, crying after what he cannot have! Beatrice is another man's wife and none of your affair. Or mine."

The red rage bled from his face, leaving his mouth in a

thin line and his eyes cold. He looked nothing like the Sebastian she had known all her life. Her heart twisted, half in fear and half in loss. "I wish you joy of your illusions."

He turned on his heel and strode away, his short gown swinging, his boots crunching on the path.

For a moment all she could do was stare at his back as he left, her mouth hanging open. She shut it with a snap. All her anger had been swallowed up in surprise; he had never walked away in the middle of a quarrel in their lives. "Sebastian!"

He kept walking, betraying by not so much as a twitch that he heard her.

"Sebastian, please come back!" she cried. They could not part like this, after such bitter anger.

He disappeared around a hedge. She lifted up her skirts to chase him but then dropped them. If he did not wish to turn back and make peace, she would not pursue him. If it had been a common quarrel, the kind they had been having for most of her life, she could trust that he would return within the hour to beg her pardon. But this had been different, cutting closer to the heart, scratching things best left undisturbed.

Sighing, she turned and resumed her stroll along the herb beds, searching for calm and absorbing, however reluctantly, Sebastian's news. Could Edmund have taken a mistress? Mistress Emma had once told her that a man, aroused by one woman, might spend his passion on another. Was Edmund such a man? Was he purging himself of the lust they had churned up in the window alcove? And if he was, could she blame him? She told herself that his actions were not her affair, that he insulted her by going from her arms to someone else's.

You are lying to yourself.

If Edmund had taken a mistress, it would tear her in two.

Please, Blessed Virgin, make it not so. I cannot bear it if it is true.

The following week crept by on weary feet. The rumor was repeated again and again, embroidered and embellished as it traveled, so that Cecilia heard it a hundred, unhappy times. She grew skilled at smiling while her heart suffered, a hot, bruised lump beneath her breastbone.

Almost as soon as the rumors began swirling, Cecilia found herself running the queen's more difficult errands, as if the queen knew that demanding work was what Cecilia needed. A week after Sebastian had spoken to her, Cecilia encountered Sir George Conyers in a quiet passageway as she returned to the queen's chambers after delivering a message to the king.

He lounged against the wall as if lying in wait for her. Her heart sank and her stomach ached for a moment with fear. She was all alone in the corridor, entirely at his mercy.

Something, courage or foolhardiness, stiffened her spine. What could he do to her in such a busy place? Her best defense was to nod pleasantly as she went by and to keep moving.

He stepped into the center of the corridor and blocked her way.

"Lady Cecilia." His smooth, deep voice sent a chill crawling up her spine.

"Sir George," she said pleasantly, and tried to move past him.

"Oh, no, my proud Lady Cecilia," he said, gripping her arm. "You and I must speak."

"The queen awaits me, sir." She lifted her chin. "I may not tarry."

"We shall not be long. I intend to have it out with you."

"To what end, sir?" What did he want? How badly did he want her to remain? She made as if to pull her arm out of his grip. His hand tightened, the fingers digging into her flesh. She would have bruises, despite the thickness of her sleeves. So, he wanted badly for her to remain. She narrowed her eyes, angry and intrigued at once.

"Unhand me, sir, or I shall scream to bring the angels from heaven, not to mention the queen's ushers." She refused to let his glare intimidate her. His fingers released her arm. She resisted the urge to rub the place he had gripped.

"You are not as clever as you think, my lady. I will see your sister again."

Cecilia raised her eyebrows disdainfully, her mind consumed by giddy suspicion. Did he mean Beatrice had refused to see him? He must. And he blamed her. She wanted to laugh out loud, but she contented herself with saying, "I have no notion of what you mean."

He scowled at her. "Do not be coy. It does not become you. You have convinced your sister not to see me. I want you to convince her otherwise."

"Why should I do that, Sir George? I have no desire to see my sister come to harm, as she must if she persists in her relationship with you." That had the virtue of being true, although Conyers made her so angry it was possible she might be able to lie to him.

"Because I will make it very unpleasant for you if you do not," he replied.

Cecilia sighed, annoyed. She resented being waylaid for such a mess of bluster and bombast, especially when it ended in an empty threat. He could do little to make her life more unpleasant than it already was.

"I cannot imagine how you could do that, Sir George, so I find it difficult to take your threat seriously."

"Perhaps Lord Thomas Manners might like to hear me out," Conyers suggested softly.

"Perhaps," Cecilia said, breathing deeply as she fought the longing to slap him. To be a man and give this braggart a taste of steel! "But then neither of us would see Beatrice again. I cannot see how it would benefit you to speak to my brother-in-law."

"Oh, I should miss Beatrice, but I would have the memory of harming you to console me," he said coolly.

"Does my sister know how little you love her?" Cecilia asked, the question wrenched out of her.

His smile gleamed smugly. "I doubt she does, and I should counsel you not to tell her. I do not think she will believe you."

"But she might, Sir George. Shall we find out?"

It was a blind shot, made in desperation. Unexpectedly, it struck home. His face darkened and he snarled through clenched teeth, "You are a wicked, presumptuous chit!"

"I? Presumptuous? I think it is you who has over-reached himself," Cecilia said, too angry to remember the bruises on her arm, too angry to worry about Beatrice. "How you can dare to accost me in this fashion...I have not yet interfered in your relationship with my sister and until this meeting had no desire to do so. You have changed my mind, sir, indeed you have! I think I shall make my way to Coleville House this very afternoon to lay everything, everything, before my sister. I think she will find your threat to speak to her husband most...illuminating, shall we say?"

He seized her arms, the blood in his handsome face

turning it purple. He looked angry enough to do murder. The fury began to drain out of her, leached away by fear as he shook her. "I wish you were my wife so I might beat you until you bled."

"That is against the law." Why did she always say these foolish things when she was afraid? Irritation with herself fanned her fear back into anger. "Unhand me!"

His fingers dug harder into her arms. She winced involuntarily. "I shall make you pay, lady, on my honor I promise that."

"You frighten me, sir, promising on something you do not have," she said breathlessly, fighting the desire to struggle in his hands. The pain was coiling 'round and 'round, getting harder and tighter, making it difficult to think. She did not know how long she could remain angry, how long before she began to beg him to let her go.

"You are a sharp-tongued jade."

Her arms ached where his fingers gripped them but she refused to pull at them. "And you, sir, are a mannerless whoreson."

He lifted a hand as if to strike her across the face. She stared at his half-clenched fist in horrified fascination; no one had ever raised a hand to her like this. She wondered if she would watch it with the same calm detachment as it came hurtling down.

"Unhand her, Conyers."

They both turned as guiltily as lovers caught in a tryst. Edmund stood just beyond them in the corridor. There was no mistaking the sound of his voice or the set of his shoulders, but in the shadowy corridor, his face was invisible.

"I said, unhand her. I should not have to tell you twice," Edmund said. His voice was very cold and stern; for the first time, he sounded like a prince in her hearing. Slowly, Conyers's fist lowered as he shoved her away, staring at Edmund. She stepped back out of Conyers's range, daring to show her fear only now that rescue had come. "You have my leave to go."

Conyers shot one last, venomous look at her before hurrying down the corridor. He made a quick bow to Edmund and attempted to scurry around him. Edmund seized the shoulder of Conyers's short gown and swung him around so they were face-to-face.

"If I should hear by the faintest whisper of rumor that you have been causing this lady unease, I shall visit you and, on my honor, you will not enjoy it," Edmund said very softly. "Do we understand each other?"

"Yes, my lord," Conyers said, his eyes lowered.

"Good," Edmund said, and flung him loose. Conyers bounced off the corridor wall and stumbled away.

Cecilia stood where she was, so undone by the sight of Edmund she could not move. Now that he had routed Conyers she knew he must leave, but until he did she would let him fill her mind's eye.

He began walking toward her. Her heart, which had held itself calm all through her confrontation with Conyers, began to pound. All the pain of the last week faded into a half-remembered nightmare now that he was here. There was nothing on earth or in heaven she wanted more than to see him. Except perhaps to touch him.

Light fell across his face. He looked weary, with blue shadows underneath his eyes and the corners of his mouth turned down unhappily. She wanted to take him into her arms, to kiss and soothe him. He stopped three feet away, his eyes fixed on her as if he, too, meant to see as much as he could while he could.

"Ceci," he whispered.

"Oh, Edmund." Her throat closed; she could say no more.

"Did he hurt you?"

His gentleness was crueler than indifference. The longing to reach out and touch him sliced through her. She spoke past the ache. "No. He meant to frighten me, no more." And succeeded, she thought, pressing her hands together to still their trembling.

"Why should he care to?" he asked softly, his hands curling into fists.

"He thinks I have persuaded my sister not to see him."

His face cleared, as if light shone suddenly upon it, but his shoulders remained stiff with anger. "He is the one."

"Yes, God rot him." She could not help cursing Conyers, though he was no worse in his arrogance and self-absorption than most of the other men at Court.

"I must go. The king has summoned me." He remained where he was, his gaze never leaving her face.

"Rumor says he is greatly offended by the way you left. Do not let me detain you."

"That rumor lies," he said. "As does the other."

"The other?" she asked, stalling foolishly. She could not speak of his mistress or the worse rumors, her only defense spurious ignorance.

"Of a woman, living with me. Of my new mistress." His voice was low and his eyes shadowed as if he feared she would disbelieve him.

"I have not heard that one." A little voice in the back of her head jeered at her. She ought to tell the truth and be done with it. She was so poor a liar that only a fool would not know how much his actions meant to her.

"Then how have I angered you? Tell me, I beg of you." He had not moved yet he seemed closer; he did not touch her but she felt his yearning.

"You have not offended me," she said slowly.

"Something constrains you, Ceci. If it is not anger, what

is it?'' His hand lifted as if he reached out to her and then dropped to his side. He looked past her, the weariness deepening in his face.

Pride abandoned her. "I heard you had taken a new mistress, and I thought…'' She faltered. To say what she felt was presumption.

"That I left you and went to her?'' His gaze returned to her face, his brows lifted in surprise.

"How could I not?'' She saw then that her certainty he had not taken a mistress had only been hope. In her deepest heart, she had believed the rumor.

"You do not trust me.'' He looked down at the floor, holding himself stiffly, as if waiting for another, harder blow.

"Should I? Can I? I know so little of men, so little of you. How can I trust you when everyone warns me you are not to be trusted?'' There was the truth, with a vengeance. Let her see what he made of it.

His face tightened. "You are right. There is no reason for you to trust me and every reason not to.''

She could not confess the way her heart defended him. It revealed too much, more than she was willing to tell.

"Believe me as you will, but she is not my mistress.'' He stepped with one stride across the distance separating them. Her heart flew into her throat, where it fluttered like beating wings.

"You have… You never…'' she stammered, her cheeks stinging with heat.

"Not once, I swear it on my father's soul.'' He seized her hand and lifted it to his mouth, pressing a quick kiss into its palm. When he released it, she closed her fingers to hold the kiss. "I must go, the king waits. Stay here. I shall return as soon as I may.''

Every ounce of wit cried that she must be on her way.

"I shall be here.''

Chapter Eleven

It was one of the king's pages who came.

"His Grace, the Duke of Somerset, bids me ask you to return to the queen," he said, his young voice cracking on the last word. Cecilia bit her lip, amusement at the sound warring with embarrassment at being caught loitering in a corridor, waiting for a man like a lack-witted dairymaid. At least the page blushed, not she.

She returned to the queen's chambers. Thankfully, no one asked outright why her errand had taken so long. She ignored the narrow-eyed sneer from one woman and disregarded the two who bent their heads together, whispering and casting covert looks in her direction. They had taken her in dislike so everything she did was food for speculation and harsh glances. She took her place against the wall and picked up her needlework, her heart muffled in darkness.

Sometime later, the doors opened and the queen's steward announced, "His Grace, the Duke of Somerset."

Edmund swept into the room, looking neither right nor left. He knelt before the queen and murmured something to her, his voice pitched too low to carry. Cecilia caught one of the other maids of honor staring first at Edmund,

then at her. She met the maid's knowing look with a disdainful lift of her eyebrows, repressing a weary sigh. These
skirmishes wore her down.

The queen stood. "Remain seated. I must speak privately to Somerset. No, no, Maria, do not join us." This
last was directed toward her lady-in-waiting, Maria de Sa-
linas, who had come from Spain with her and knew all her
secrets. It must be a serious affair if Maria was not to be
privy to their discussion.

The queen and Edmund left the room, the doors shutting
firmly behind them.

Cecilia ignored the buzz of talk that rose around her,
her unseeing eyes directed at her needlework. She had
come to Court with high hopes, careful plans. How had
things gone so awry? *Nothing is as easy as I thought it
was.* She picked up her needle and resumed stitching.

"Lady Cecilia, the queen bids you attend her." One of
the queen's pages stood beside her, awakening her from
her dream. She set her embroidery aside, rose from her
stool against the wall and followed him into the queen's
inner chamber.

Edmund sat beside the queen. In the tight silence, the
door latch snapped sharply as it closed. All Cecilia's
senses were alert as she curtsied. Details stood out vividly:
the glittering dust motes in the sunbeam pouring through
the window; the moon-serene glow of the pearls in the
queen's headdress; the rich russet of the fox fur trimming
Edmund's gown. Edmund's clean scent, the queen's attar
of roses and the green smell of newly laid rushes filled her
nose while her fingertips delighted in the rough texture of
her brocade skirt, smooth and rough at once. Sinking into
the sunbeam as she curtsied, she passed through a current

of warmth, like the currents of cold trickling through the sun-warmed pools in the river at home.

The queen said, "You may rise, child." Cecilia stood. The queen, with a languid gesture of her white hand, gestured to a stool. "Be seated."

Cecilia sat, settling her skirts, and waited for someone to speak.

"My lord of Somerset has told me that you are aware of...that you know who Sir Edmund Tudor is." The queen watched Cecilia intently.

"I am, Your Majesty."

"And you know that he travels on the king's business, at the king's command?"

Still those sharp eyes examined her. Looking for what? Cecilia took a deep breath, hoping to slow her racing pulse. "I do."

Cecilia glanced at Edmund, looking for guidance. His eyes were fixed on her, their depths shadowed in his somber face. Yet he looked happier than he had in the corridor, as if whatever oppressed him had been eased.

"There are reports that heresy flourishes in Buckinghamshire. His Grace is bidden to investigate these reports." The queen paused and looked at Cecilia expectantly.

Cecilia rose to the bait. "Please pardon me if I am impertinent, but should not the Church investigate these charges?" Why was a layman, any layman, looking into reports of heresy?

"The king does not trust what he hears, Lady Cecilia. Before he turns the matter over to the bishops, he wishes to be certain there is meat to the allegations." Edmund broke the silence. "From what I understand, it does not need a churchman to know if the reports are true. A Turk could recognize these heresies as contrary to the Church."

That explained Edmund's part, but not hers. "And me? Why do you tell me this?"

"I need you to go to Buckinghamshire with me."

Shock struck her as soundly as a fist. "Go with you?" she echoed. "But why?" Her ears burned and she looked down submissively. "I beg your pardon. I am insolent."

"Understandably," the queen said gently. "You are a noble maiden, accustomed to the protection of your station in life. You know enough of His Grace's habits to understand you must leave protection and nobility behind."

Edmund said, "My excuse for traveling through Buckinghamshire is that I am bringing my wife to visit her cousins in Suffolk. I will need a wife if I am to be believed. You are the only woman in England who can do this. I trust you, and you can pass as Lady Tudor."

"I should not consent to this if my lord husband did not require it for the weal of the realm," the queen said.

Cecilia swallowed. The queen, in her gentleness and honor, could not understand the effect of her request. To travel with Edmund, far from the prying eyes of the Court, was temptation, sweet temptation. She wanted to say, Yes, yes, I will follow him to the ends of the earth.

"If the king asks, I have no choice." She kept her gaze on her hands, afraid that the queen would clearly read her greed for Edmund in her eyes.

"In this you do have a choice, Lady Cecilia. You risk your reputation by taking up this work, a risk I will not command you to take. You must understand that before you accept," the queen said.

"If the king asks, I have no choice," Cecilia repeated quietly, raising her eyes. Her answer was partly a lie, but only partly. Whatever the demands of her heart and her unruly flesh, duty and family honor also played a part in her decision. She had not been raised to shirk her obligations, especially not her obligation to her sovereign. Her father had been among the first to swear his oath of fealty at both King Henry's and King Arthur's coronations; certainly he was the last man on earth to break it. "My father fought with King Henry of blessed memory on Bosworth field with no thought of honor or reputation or earthly reward. He fought for his king with his hands, his sword and his skill. If needful, he would have given his life. I am a woman and cannot offer a sword to defend His Majesty, but I would give him my life. My reputation seems a small thing in comparison."

"A noble speech," the queen said dryly, "but a woman with a stained reputation will not marry, cannot serve me, and brings dishonor to her family. You must be sure of what you do."

The queen knew nothing of her parents, of their old-fashioned, intensely personal notions of honor. Cecilia leaned forward on her stool, determined to make the queen understand.

"If I give less than everything to the king, that will bring dishonor on my family, as nothing else that touches the king's well-being will. Everything I have, everything my family has, we owe to King Henry the Seventh. How could I give less to King Henry's son?"

Queen Katherine smiled. "You should have been born a man, *Cecilita,*" she said. "I should give a gold mark to see you in armor."

"And I will pay you two not to don it," Edmund said quickly. "It is unwomanly."

"You never saw my mother, Queen Isabella, God assoil her," the queen countered. "She was a great warrior."

"But Lady Cecilia is not," Edmund said, a crease appearing between his brows.

"She has the honor of a man. Do not argue with me, *mi hermano*. You cannot win."

A grin lit Edmund's face. "No, not when I must obey you in all things, O My Queen." He turned to Cecilia, the smile fading. "On my honor, I will treat you with all due respect."

That is not what I want. "I had no doubt of it, Your Grace. I should not have consented otherwise."

"Then it is settled," the queen said, sitting back in her chair.

"How will she leave Court?"

"For once your flirting has been useful," the Queen said. "You turned her head and when you abandoned us to return to your wicked ways, she was shocked. She has asked permission to pray and meditate until she can return to my service with a clean conscience and I have bidden her to Bermondsey. From Bermondsey she will travel to a smaller priory, preferably one outside London. You will meet her there and go on your way." She turned to Cecilia. "You will suffer somewhat from the tongues of my ladies. I know they are not as kind as befits good Christians, but it will only be for a short time, and when you return I will show you great favor."

Cecilia murmured, "And they will abuse me in jealousy."

"That is so, but it is the lesser of several evils," the queen replied with a shrewd look. "It takes a thick skin and a stout heart to survive at Court."

"I have both," Cecilia said. She was not sure she had either, but that was a truth the queen would not want to hear. Besides, the future must take care of itself. God had granted her heart's secret wish and who was she to question the workings of Providence?

"Excellent." The queen folded her hands in her lap.

Mistress Emma did the same thing when she was pleased with Cecilia; the gesture brought on a rush of homesickness. It passed quickly, replaced with a tingling excitement. She was ready to run to Bermondsey at this instant. With an effort, she schooled herself to patience. There was much to do before she departed. The queen said, "Aside from my favor when you return, I should like to make a gift to you. Shall I give you the monopoly on sweet wines imported next year?"

She offered a rich gift. Everyone who bought sweet wine would have to pay Cecilia a duty. Since sweet wine was the only kind the English bought, the monopoly on it would make her rich, with money of her own. Until her parents claimed it. Or her husband. Nor was it what she wanted.

"You are kindness itself, Your Majesty. No gift is needed. I am honored to be able to serve you and the king."

"A very pretty speech. But there must be something you want."

Cecilia fingered the brocade of her skirt. Did she dare ask? She raised her eyes. The queen was watching her carefully, the expression in her eyes a mixture of affection and wariness. The blend of warmth and coldness impelled her to speak, to answer the kindness and allay the suspicion.

"Please, send for my brother John in Rome. Bid him return to England, perhaps to paint Your Majesty's portrait." Her palms were sticky with sweat and her hands trembled. What if the queen refused? Her request demanded the queen's time, something in shorter supply than money. She might be left with neither money nor brother.

"Your brother is a painter?" the queen asked with a surprised lift of her eyebrows. Cecilia cursed her thoughtlessness, remembering that the family had tried to keep John's activities and whereabouts a secret. Nothing John did shamed her, but she was the only Coleville who felt that way.

"And a good one, I'll warrant," Edmund said easily, filling the gap of silence with his evident admiration. "When did he go to Rome?"

Cecilia shot him a grateful glance. "He left for Germany five years ago and has never come home."

"And that is all you want? You could ask for a great deal more and I should probably grant it. This is a very small thing." The queen's face lost its disdainful look, as if Edmund's approval had persuaded her that an earl's son painting in Rome did not warrant censure.

"There is nothing you could give me that would bring me as much pleasure," Cecilia replied. Her heart lifted like a lark leaping sunward. How could John refuse a summons from the Queen of England? He would come home, home at long last.

"Very well. I will send for him this very day. When you leave, do not linger in the antechamber. I have just spoken very sternly to you about your misbehavior before giving your leave to go to Bermondsey."

Cecilia reined in her excitement, schooling her face to discreet calm. She could not reveal her jubilation. Edmund had not taken a mistress. And she would have days and days of his company, far from the sharp eyes and busy tongues of the Court.

"Yes, Your Majesty."

Chapter Twelve

Sebastian cornered her in the tennis court the next morning. Drawing her from the knot of ladies watching a tight match between the Duke of York and Sir Charles Brandon, he said, "The story is everywhere that you have asked the queen to go Bermondsey because of your flirtation with the Duke of Somerset. I warned you. I warned you he would break your heart."

Unexpectedly, her temper flared. They had not spoken since their quarrel; he overstepped his bounds, demanding such a thing of her after the way they had parted. But she bit her tongue, choking back the words that leaped up her throat; the deception would be best served if she seemed depressed and penitent, a woman prepared to do much soul searching, and upbraiding Sebastian for unwarranted interference was neither heartsick nor regretful.

"True," she murmured colorlessly. "I should be a happier woman today if I had listened to you."

Sebastian stared at her, plainly uncertain how to respond to such a mild reply. "The queen will not reconsider?"

"I dare not ask." She was surprised by how easy it was to lie when she did it for someone else's benefit. "She is exceedingly wroth."

He frowned, chewing his lips. "What will Lady Wednesfield do to you when she hears?"

Her heart jumped against her ribs. She had never considered what her mother would have to say about this. She gripped her courage and made herself smile at Sebastian, hoping he would be reassured. "It is not as bad as it could be. The queen did say I could return to her once I have done my penance."

"I had not heard that." He looked down at his hat, turning it around and around. "I shall tell them you have gone to pray for Beatrice, that her barrenness may be ended. In fact, I shall spread that story in answer to the rumors."

"You will not shame Beatrice so!" She could not allow her sister to be sacrificed for her.

Sebastian's mouth compressed, his eyes glittering. "I shall not say anything everyone does not know, Ceci. Let your sister suffer on your behalf. You have suffered enough on hers."

Later that week, the queen stopped Cecilia as they left the chapel after morning Mass to ask if she had spread Sebastian's counter-rumor. Cecilia reported her conversation with her friend, adding, "I dared not contradict him, lest he ask questions."

"No, no, this is for the best. The muddier the waters, the less likely you will be caught out." She fingered her rosary meditatively. "I understand from the Duke of Somerset that Sir George Conyers bears you some ill-will."

Cecilia smothered her start of surprise. "Yes, Your Majesty."

"I am sure you have wondered at Conyers's absence from Court." The queen spoke neutrally, offering no clues as to the direction she intended to go.

Cecilia looked down at her hands, weighing expediency against curiosity, politeness against candor. "I have been glad of it, without questioning it, Your Majesty."

"He has been a good and loyal servant to my husband for some time. I thought it time to reward him. He has been given the opportunity to conduct some business for the king in Lincoln."

Cecilia glanced up and met the queen's sardonic gaze. "Your Majesty is too kind."

The Queen smiled blandly.

The day of her departure from Court arrived. All her belongings had been sent to Bermondsey, where she would stay the night. In the morning, she would travel north to a small priory where she would wait for Edmund as his wife, Cecilia Tudor. She quivered with impatience, longing to go. She ought to be afraid, traveling alone with Edmund far from the prying eyes of Court. Yet her heart was as light as swan's down, light enough to float out of her breast. She refused to think what it meant.

Climbing into the boat to take the river journey, she took a long, last look at the palace. Would she come back to Court? Would she ever again see the royal servants, clad in their green-and-white Tudor livery? And if she never returned to Court, would she miss it? She did not think so. The only thing worth having in the length and breadth of England was Edmund. If she could not have him, what did the rest matter?

"Mistress, your husband has arrived." Cecilia lifted her head. The priory's lone novice stood at her shoulder.

"Thank you, Sister." She rose from her knees, straightening her dark red skirts, smoothing her bodice over her stays, soothing her nervous stomach. *It begins now.* Slipping her rosary into the pouch hanging from her belt, she followed the nun from the chapel. "Pray tell him I shall join him presently."

She returned to the small grimy cell that had been hers to put on her riding cloak and retrieve the bundle of oddments she had not want packed with her clothes. Leaving the tiny chamber without a backward glance, she passed quickly through the outbuildings, hurrying toward the gate to the outside world.

Pausing in the archway of the gate, she watched Edmund pace up and down the path, slapping his gloves against his palm. When he saw her, he stopped in midstride, staring at her. He dropped his gloves.

"Cecilia."

She stepped forward and then stopped, as if uneasiness were a contagion.

He bent to retrieve his gloves. When he straightened, his face had lit in a happy smile. "I am glad to see you."

"And I am glad to see you." The gate shut with a bang behind her. She closed the distance between them.

He stretched out a hand for her bundle. "Let me take this."

"Thank you. I should be grateful."

He took the bundle and tried to tuck it under his arm. She heard the muffled thump as the box of John's drawings struck his ribs. He winced and held the bundle away from his body.

"What have you got in there?" he asked. "The priory's entire library?"

She stared at Edmund, trying to think what to say, feeling her face burn. She feared if she told him what was in the box, he would want to see the drawings. She was not ready to let him know that she had saved the sketch of him drawn when they were sixteen.

"No," she said after what seemed long minutes had crept by. "A book of my own. And a box. With things in it."

"Things?"

"My things."

"I see."

Her tongue was dead in her mouth, her fount of chatter bone-dry. She had never felt so awkward in her life, not even when she had been a coltish twelve-year-old, her arms and legs only partially under her control.

Edmund tucked his hand into the crook of her elbow and led her toward the horses. The touch of his hand reassured and unsettled her at once. She gave herself a mental shake. This was no time to turn foolish; they would be in each other's company, pretending an intimacy that didn't exist, for some time to come. She must keep her wits about her.

The sturdy dappled gray mare she had ridden to the priory stood patiently under a tree beside Edmund's roan gelding. A stranger, dressed in drab servant's clothing and mounted on a third horse, held their reins, as well as the reins of a packhorse.

"Cecilia, allow me to present Piers," Edmund said. "Piers, this is my...er, wife, Cecilia." A warm ache twisted through her stomach at his words. That pull of desire, so familiar to her now, helped steady her.

"Yes, master." He was older than Edmund by a good fifteen years. Gray dulled the darkness of his curly hair and a fine web of lines spread from the corners of his eyes. His bearing was not altogether that of a servant, nor were his eyes, bright with intelligence and humor, completely deferential. And yet he did not seem proud.

She held out her hand. "Piers. How pleased I am to meet you." He took her hand, his palm rough and dry against her own, and then stared down at their clasped hands as if wondering how they came to be joined.

"And I am happy to meet you, mistress."

"Let me help you mount, Ceci." Edmund placed his hands on her waist.

"I can mount on my own," she said. His proximity quickened her senses and tightened her nerves.

"But I should take no pleasure in it if you did," he said, and lifted her into the saddle. He mounted while she settled herself, calming her racing pulse. He urged the roan onto the road and they were off.

As they passed out of the priory lane onto the main road, a pair of men-at-arms joined their party. It was not nearly the retinue her father would take, but perfectly appropriate for Sir Edmund Tudor.

"Who is Piers?" she asked as the priory disappeared from sight.

"He keeps my house in Southwark," Edmund replied.

"You trust him?"

"With my life."

It had been a foolish question, worthy of a short answer. Of course he trusted Piers with his life. He would not have brought him else.

"And I can trust him with your name, as well. He is utterly loyal."

"Loyalty can be bought," Cecilia said.

"Only if it is on the market," Edmund said. "Piers's is not."

"How can you know that? Only God knows what is in a man's heart."

"That is true. On the other hand, I know things of Piers he would not want revealed, so we are even. He keeps my secrets and I keep his," Edmund replied.

They rode on in silence through the warm, overcast afternoon. They passed a villein driving an oxcart and a small, grimy girl herding geese, and then saw no one else. The road was broad and well maintained, the underbrush cut back a good hundred yards. No need to worry about ambushes, at least not here.

Edmund's roan grew restive at the jogging pace, tossing its head and sidling.

"Let me see if I can run his fidgets out," he said, after fighting the roan back onto the road for the third time. "Piers, attend Mistress Cecilia."

They had ridden a good mile by the time Edmund returned. His fair hair was tangled, his cap lost, his eyes brilliant blue with delight. The roan, quiet now and obedient to the touch of Edmund's heels and hands, looked as pleased as his rider.

"Now we shall be well," Edmund said cheerfully. "What a run we had! And jumps! He may not look like much, but Farrago can leap like a hare."

"Farrago?" she asked, surprised. "Isn't that Latin for…"

"Mixed fodder, yes." He patted the roan's neck affectionately. "That is what he is, a mixed bag. I ought to be used to your erudition by now, Ceci, but you still surprise me."

"The company you keep speaks no Latin?" she asked lightly.

"The company I keep…you are the only company I keep," he said quietly.

Silence stretched between them, tight as a drumhead. Edmund broke it, saying, "I am glad you are here, Ceci."

"So am I. I had rather be far from London and the Court." Riding through the sweet green countryside, far from the bitter, amoral Court, was like waking from a nightmare to find herself in her own bed, with her mother leaning over her to offer comfort.

"You would rather live and work in the country than spend time at Court," he said thoughtfully.

"Should I not? At least in the country I am useful. At Court, I do nothing but chatter and dance and worry about my dresses," she said. Intimate exposure to the busy, useful nuns at Bermondsey had made her wonder if she might not prefer that life to marriage.

"You are bored."

She looked at him, meeting his blue-gray gaze. Here was a man, above all others, who would understand how she felt. "I am."

"As am I. Every minute of every day I spend at Court I am afraid I will run mad."

"Then why do you stay?"

He blinked in surprise. "I must."

"Why must you?"

His throat worked. "A promise." Farrago sidled, betraying Edmund's uneasiness. "Leave it be, Cecilia, I beg of you."

"As you will it." She smiled at him to show him she took no offense and to mask her curiosity. What had he promised, and to whom?

They stopped at noon to rest the horses and to eat the bread, cheese and ale provided them at the priory. Piers took the horses to cool and water them, leaving Edmund and Cecilia to sit in comfort underneath an oak tree, the men-at-arms within view if not earshot.

After they ate, Edmund stretched out on his side and closed his eyes as if to nap. Cecilia looked at him for a long, puzzled moment and then sat back against the bole of the oak. The stillness of the afternoon, the soft gurgle of the stream, the heat and her full stomach wove a web of weariness, so that her eyelids grew heavy, so heavy she could not keep them up. She dozed.

Her head rolled. She jerked awake. Piers and one of the men-at-arms sat underneath another tree, eating; the other man-at-arms also napped. She rubbed her eyes and yawned and then looked down at Edmund, asleep beside her. His mouth was relaxed and slightly open, his spiky lashes gilded crescents against his sun-browned cheeks. Tenderness wringing her heart, she longed to smooth his hair away from his brow, but she dared not. All she could do was watch him, as she did until at last his eyes fluttered open. He saw her and smiled, the expression in his face simple happiness. She smiled in answer, unable to resist.

"How long did I sleep?" he murmured.

"I do not know. I dozed myself," she said.

He turned and half rose, propping himself on his elbow. He looked around, rubbed his eyes and looked again. "I should say I slept no more than an hour." He smiled. "There is still time to sleep. And your lap the perfect place to rest my head." His blue eyes sparkled in the dappled leaf shadow, sunlight spangling across his tawny hair.

On impulse she lifted her arms away from her sides. "It is indeed the perfect place, dread lord," she said. Do you dare? she thought and grinned. She was divided between her hope that he would take up her gauntlet and her fear that he would not.

His smile faded, but he crept forward and found a comfortable spot among the tree roots, laying his head, as she had invited him to, in her lap. He closed his eyes. She lowered her arms to her sides but that felt awkward so she laid one hand on his chest. He covered it with his own. She put her head back against the tree bole.

"It must have been like this in Eden," he murmured. "Before the Fall."

"Mmm." She considered, not for the first time, the potential danger of their trip. What would happen if they were found out? Would they be harmed? "Edmund?"

"Hmm?"

"Are we in danger?"

His eyes opened. "From whom?"

"I do not know." His question puzzled her. How should she know from whom they might be in danger?

"Aside from the usual danger to any traveler?" he asked.

"Yes."

"Not that I know of," he said.

"What will happen if we are suspected?"

Edmund sighed and took her hand to lay it across his eyes as if they pained him. "Not very much for good or ill will happen to us," he said wearily. "We shall not find what we came to find and then the king will be compelled to make a decision based on information he does not trust. He will either have to ignore what he knows, in which case heresy may flourish where it is now only a seed. Or he will have to leave this in the hands of the bishops, who will perhaps root out heresy where it does not exist and increase men's doubts. That is why we must not fail in this."

She digested what he had told her. This had seemed a game to him, but now she saw he was in earnest. Why? Why was a royal duke engaged in this game of pretending to be other than he was, if not for his own pleasure? How could he bear to be treated as a mere gentleman, with none of the deference due him?

There was only one way to find out. She must ask, despite knowing the answer might be related to his vow, the vow he had commanded her not to question.

"Why must you do this work, Edmund? Why cannot someone else?"

She sat very still, waiting for his answer, praying she had not offended him. For a long time he did not move or answer.

"I promised my father that I would always support my brother the king, no matter what form my help must take, no matter what befell. And then he died," he whispered at last, his voice harsh, as if the words clotted in his throat. Under her hand she felt the tears slip from his eyes. His throat worked and he pressed her hand against his eyes, his tears leaking between her fingers. Her throat ached, her eyes stinging. Edmund sighed and then went on in a stronger voice. "The best thing I can give the king is information he can trust. The only way I can trust the information is if I collect it myself, or collect it from men who do not know me and so speak frankly to me."

"I see." She wanted to speak to his grief but feared to shatter his trust in her. All she could do was yield to the old impulse to stroke his thick hair back from his brow.

He lifted her hand from his eyes and pressed it against his mouth and then returned it to its first place on his breast. He looked up into her eyes, his own wary.

"Do not pity me."

"How could I? You are not pitiable," she said calmly. "But I cannot help grieving for your grief."

"It is old," he said with would-be casualness. She did not reply; it did not warrant an answer since he must know she no more believed it than he did. He smiled, one corner of his mouth lifting like sun breaking through black clouds. "I am a fool. It is old but it still stings as you well know."

She smiled back, knowing it must be tender and full of love but unable to restrain herself.

"I do."

Chapter Thirteen

Eight days later, Piers came out of the largest inn in Aylesbury, replacing his shapeless cap on his head.

"They have one room left, sir, which I took. The lady cannot ride farther and we shall not find a better inn for miles," he said quietly as he approached Cecilia and Edmund where they waited, still mounted, in the inn yard.

Edmund nodded. "I know it is not what we wanted, but I shall have to share the room with you," he said softly to Cecilia, refusing to meet her eyes.

"Very well." Pulses throbbed in her wrists and abdomen, images of heat and languorous pleasure. She could not have said another coherent word if her life depended on it.

He looked up, staring at her for a long moment, as if trying to puzzle out the meaning behind her placidity. She met his look calmly, her every thought focused on keeping her emotions from her face. She would not reveal them. Not here. Not now.

"Then that's settled." He looked away, freeing her from the constraint of his eyes.

"It was settled before," she said lightly. "Let us go within."

The bowing innkeeper brought them to their room, plainly the best he had to offer. The furnishings—chairs, chest and bed—were new, as were the jewel-bright wall hangings and the mulberry damask bedcurtains. The sweet smell of herbs mixed with the new-laid rushes filled the air.

"I hope this pleases, my lord," the innkeeper said, watching Edmund anxiously.

Piers answered. "It is well enough for my lord. My lady cannot dine in the common room with every drover in Buckinghamshire, so I shall expect dinner served to her here."

"Very good, sir. If that will be all…"

"For now," Piers replied.

The innkeeper bowed himself out, bobbing like a cork.

Cecilia sat in one of the chairs and contemplated the bed with its three wool-stuffed mattresses while Piers bustled about, settling their belongings. Edmund crossed the room to the tiny window and opened it, leaning on the frame. Cecilia let her gaze follow him. His shoulders filled the window and the late afternoon sunlight turned his tawny hair red-gold.

"You should dine with Lady Cecilia here tonight, my lord," Piers said to Edmund. "It is market day and the common room is no place for you, either. It is certain every farmer and drover in the county is below."

"Getting drunk," Edmund finished, still gazing outside. "You must stay here, too."

Piers shook his head. "No, sir. Drunken tongues wag. I may well learn something of value." He shook the pouch at his belt so it jingled. "I have a penny or two to buy ale with."

"So long as it is not your drunken tongue wagging," Edmund said, turning to Piers.

"I have a granite head, sir, unlike some I could name."

Edmund's eyes narrowed while ruddy color stained his cheeks under their sun-browning. The byplay and Edmund's embarrassed reaction to it piqued Cecilia's curiosity and she shifted her gaze to her hands so they would not discover she listened.

"Perhaps I shall come with you, to keep an eye on you," Edmund said.

"Someone must remain with Lady Cecilia."

"You do it. I shall spend the evening in the common room."

"And silence them all? I think not, sir. Stay here and protect Lady Cecilia and I will go below and hear what can be heard."

"Oh, very well," Edmund rumbled.

Out of the corner of her eye, Cecilia saw Piers kneel at Edmund's feet. "As you will it, my lord," he said with such exaggerated humility that she had to bite her lip to keep from laughing.

Edmund sighed. "Piers. Get up and do not mock me."

"Your wish is my command, sir."

"I only wish it were. Go on, you knave. Go about your business and stop trying to make me a better man than I am."

Piers rose to his feet. "I leave that to God, my lord. If you will excuse me."

"Go, go."

Cecilia looked up when the door shut behind Piers. Edmund smiled ruefully at her. "No one obeys me."

"You do not demand it," she said. "I do not think you would enjoy it if anyone did."

"You know me too well. How is that?" He walked away from the window, taking the chair beside hers.

"I have known you long," she said. "Do I know you so well?"

"Indeed you do. None better."

She was silent, unable to think of a single response.

He reached out and took her hand, his thumb rubbing her palm. She felt every brush of his skin in her lower abdomen, where she melted and burned. A hollowness like hunger emptied her but she did not think food was what she craved. Her glance flicked to his firm mouth, to the corner that quirked upward as if he was always ready to smile. She wanted to taste that friendly, intriguing corner and press her lips to his until they parted. And that was not all. Memories of their encounter in the oriel, the vivid recollection of his mouth and hands on her naked skin stirred her. She wanted that, and more. Much more.

The demanding carnality of her thoughts took her breath away. Who was this woman in her skin, shamelessly imagining such things? It was her true self, the Cecilia who had nearly yielded to him in the window alcove, the Cecilia who loved him. The other Cecilia, the demure Lady Cecilia, was a mask she wore, as if her life was a play. Mistress Emma's tales of romance and rogues had not made her understand passion the way the simplest touch of Edmund's hand did.

She looked away. Whatever the truth of her heart, she hungered for the impossible. She could never make love to him because she must bring a maidenhead to her marriage bed.

If I marry. If I take the veil, I need prove nothing.

For a moment, she hesitated, hardly daring to think further. Her mind kept spinning, moving past her doubts. Could she do it? Could she spend her life as a celibate nun?

Why not? Life in a monastery promised scholarship,

work for body and mind and soul. If she did not become a nun, she must become a wife: living under her husband's thumb, her body his to use as he wished; bearing his children year after year until it wore her out or killed her; learning in abeyance, her wit suspect.

She wanted Edmund. She wanted to know him, his body as well as his soul. She wanted him to be the first and only man to know her body, to touch and kiss her mouth, her breasts, her most intimate places. Him and no other. She would not lie to herself anymore.

She looked at him again. His beauty caught in her throat.

Her past and future slipped away, drawing with them everything her mother and Mistress Emma had tried to drill into her head about sin and honor. She was left only with her need for him, a need she would no longer deny. She would lie with him, seducing him if necessary. She did not think it would come to that.

A faint voice in the back of her head protested that it was sin. I shall do penance for it, she thought in response, and gladly.

With that, her long confusion lifted, lightening her heart. She knew what she was going to do, her path lay clearly before her.

"Why do you smile?" he asked, his eyes narrowing suspiciously, a faint answering smile curling in that tempting corner of his mouth. She wanted to rise and kiss him, but dared not, not when Piers might interrupt them at any moment.

"I shall tell you, but not now," she said quietly. "Tonight. After we dine."

Edmund picked up his mug of wine and sat back in his chair. Cecilia sat opposite him, nibbling on a piece of marchpane, her eyes half closed in an expression of concentrated delight. After the servitors had cleared the remains of their dinner, she had removed her hood, letting a thick, half-unwoven plait of dark hair hang over her shoulder. His fingers itched to loosen her hair, to run through its silky length. He shifted in his chair, suddenly uncomfortable. Had there ever been a time when the sight of her did not send desire surging through his veins?

The pink tip of her tongue flicked out and licked a crumb of marchpane from her lips. The sight made his loins tighten. How was he going to share that bed with her and not touch her? For that matter, for how much longer could he sit with her and not kiss her?

Get up. Get up and go downstairs, Piers be damned.

He remained where he was.

Her lashes lifted and she looked at him, returning stare for stare. Heat flashed the length of his body. He reached up to unlace his doublet, hoping it would cool him. This, from a mere glance?

Her eyes followed the movement of his hands.

"Ceci..." His voice died in his throat.

Her gaze still locked with his, she licked her fingers one by one. He imagined her licking him with the same delicacy and clenched his hands against the pulse of desire that shook him. He waited, rooted in his chair, unable to move. She rose to her feet and crossed the gap between the chairs in two steps. Because he wanted to touch her, because he could not sit another minute without touching her, he reached out and took her by the waist, his thumbs caressing her and feeling for the stiffness and ribs of her stays.

She was not wearing them.

Oh, sweet Mary.

Beneath the practical linsey-woolsey of her bodice, she

wore nothing, save perhaps a shift. No armor to protect her from wandering amorous hands.

Almost in a dream, he drew her onto his lap. He ignored the faint voice of his conscience whispering that his behavior was stupid and dangerous. He wanted to hold her too much to listen. For a long moment, she sat passively in his lap, staring at him with fathomless dark eyes. He was at a standstill, caught between desire and his promise not to harm her.

She was not so constrained. Cupping his face in her hands, she leaned forward and kissed him. Her lips pressed one corner of his mouth and then her tongue traced the outline of his lips. Heat, red and violent, crashed over him and paralyzed him.

She straightened. He had a momentary glimpse of her face, its serenity clouded by doubt before he slid his hand up to the back of her head, burying his fingers in her thick hair and drawing her back to him. He kissed her deeply, lips and tongue tasting, teasing. Her lips parted and her tongue met his, her feverish response stoking his own fire. When he caressed her from arm to abdomen to breast, she tore her mouth away from his and cried out. The soft sound licked fire along his spine.

He ought to stop but she was so warm, so sweet in his arms, that he could not let go. He wanted more, to take the fullest advantage of this while it lasted. He tilted her head back to kiss the skin beside her ear and gently nibble the lobe. Her hands clutched his arms and then slid inside his shirt. His arms tightened.

Her lips found his throat and she followed his every move, even to the faint tug of lips on earlobe. He shifted in the chair, trying to ease his aroused discomfort. The chair arm dug into his back. The bed would be more comfortable…. Another voice in the back of his head warned that the bed was dangerous, but he quelled it. He had no intention of seducing Cecilia. They had not gone too far to stop; their play was too sweet to end just yet. He stood, lifting her in his arms, and carried her to the bed.

Sense cleared a path through the red-hot haze in his head as he sank down beside her. This was Ceci, not some doxy he could swive without a second thought. He had been fooling himself to think he could go any further and still stop. Making the greatest effort of his life, he began to rise from the bed. Cecilia caught the edge of his doublet and held him.

"Ceci..."

She rose on one elbow and leaned forward to kiss him, her lips demanding and hungry. This was not the kiss of a demure virgin playing with fire; it was the kiss of a woman who knew what she wanted. His response swamped his sense and he yielded to her kiss, following her as she sank back against the pillows.

He thought, Just a moment more, and then I will stop. But her kisses confused him, the way her lips nibbled him, the stroke of her tongue against his.

She reached inside his doublet and shirt to stroke his ribs and the muscles of his chest. "You are so warm," she whispered.

He was hot, burning with a desire so fierce he did not think he would ever cool. "You are beautiful," he murmured, and caressed her cheek, marveling at its velvety smoothness.

"You are," she said, and turned her head to kiss the hollow of his throat.

"Ah, Ceci," he sighed, and ran his hand up her arm. The tips of his fingers brushed the outside swell of her breast and she gasped.

He reached behind her, feeling for the laces of her bodice. She pushed him away and sat, turning her back to him. "Unlace me."

He obeyed her. This was so far beyond the scope of his imaginings that for a brief instant, he thought he was dreaming. By the time he recollected himself and realized this was really happening, and that it was up to him to stop it, she had pulled her bodice off and flung it on the floor. She turned to him, her nipples showing rosy dark through the sheer linen of her shift. *This cannot be happening*. Blushing, she took his hand and placed it on her breast. His fingers curled around the swell and stroked it. Her lids lowered and her lips parted as she caught her breath.

He was sweltering in his heavy doublet. He thought, It can do no harm to remove it, and shrugged out of it. He would stop in just a moment, once he had had his fill of caressing her. He reached up and tugged her shift off her shoulder. She pushed it further down so it pooled at her waist, leaving her naked to his gaze. He raised himself on his elbow and caressed her with his mouth.

"Oh, sweet Edmund," she gasped. She was hot, burning with desire, furious with it. She wanted his hands on her naked skin, his naked skin under her hands; she wanted their mouths fused, tongues mingling, she wanted to caress every inch of him. What she had was not enough, not nearly enough. She did not think she could have enough of him. She was afraid and excited at once, gone too far to pull back now, hurtling blindly into the unknown, led by her senses and her love and her lust.

"Love me," she whispered. "I beg of you. Love me."

He groaned, his hands on her hips tightening. He lifted his head, staring up at her with eyes clouded by doubt. She stroked his hair back from his brow.

"Ceci," he began, but she would not let him finish.

"I want you, no one else. Please, do not deny me."

"This is wrong," he said, but he sounded uncertain.

"No, no, it is not."

She bent to kiss him, to persuade him with lips and tongue, twisting so that she stretched out on top of him. Her breasts were crushed against him, tingling at the warm dry brush of skin against skin. She almost drowned in the wave of desire that swept her.

His hands stroked down her back to her hips, pressing her tightly against him. She kissed his neck, licked along the length of his collarbone, ran her hands along his ribs. A groan burst out of him.

"Ceci, no, do not. I will not be able to stop..."

"I do not want you to stop," she said, and kissed him.

His resistance broke. He found and undid the closure of her heavy skirt, pushing it down her hips. She lifted her hips to help him, kicking the skirt onto the floor. Her petticoat followed immediately after. He rolled, carrying her with him, so that she was half underneath him. He threw his leg over hers and ran his hand from her shoulder to her hip.

"Are you sure?" he asked. He knew deep in his heart that he should not even consider taking what she offered, but more than anything he wanted to be the first. He needed to be the first, to set his seal on her flesh. And he promised himself he would make it right.

"Yes, yes," she whispered. "Please." She was afraid, desperately afraid, but for once fear did not make her angry. It made her bold. She reached up and pushed his shirt off his shoulders to encourage him.

Trembling in his haste, he stripped off his shirt and breeches. He hesitated before removing his hose.

"I want to see you," she whispered.

"Not yet," he said.

He eased her shift past her hips. He stroked her, shoulder to breast to hip. She sighed and turned her face into the pillow. He bent to her nipple and kissed it, feeling it pucker as he nuzzled it. "Ah!" She twisted away and then returned. He shifted and kissed her neck below her ear while sliding his hand lightly toward the apex of her thighs. More than anything else, he wanted to bring her pleasure. That he must hurt her, he knew and regretted. Before then, he wanted to bring her to joy.

The familiarity of his touch, the alien presence, jolted her into shyness. She clenched her thighs involuntarily and then relaxed them. This was what she wanted, to allow him the freedom of her body.

"There?" he whispered, and touched her again. Tears stung her eyes. She nodded, drawing a sobbing breath as pressure grew, her hips rolling as the beat of delight grew stronger, more tightly wound. She clutched the coverlet, the pillow under her head, his shoulder. Just over the crest, just over the crest she would find satisfaction and release, just over the crest . . .

A red-hot thrum built in her belly, bearing down on her. He touched her once more and the storm overtook her. She broke open, spasms shuddering through her, burning red behind her eyelids and wringing gasping cries from her. She came back to herself to find she was weak and wrung out, trembling in the aftermath of her pleasure. She had not known anything like that existed.

With a great effort, she moved her head to look at Edmund. He smiled at her with a look of such happiness that her heart turned over. How could he be so happy when she knew he could not be satisfied?

"I want to please you," she said. It was the only gift she could offer in return.

"You—" he kissed her shoulder "—have." His fingers

traced idle circles on her hip. Strength began to seep back into her limbs, heavy with languor.

"No," she said. "I want to make you feel what I felt."

His mouth moved along her arm. "You do."

"Edmund." He looked up at her. "I want to see you," she murmured. "I want you to be naked."

If she had touched him, she could not have moved him more than her words did. Obedient to her gentle command, he eased out of his hose. He had not trembled like this since the first time he lay with a woman, all those years ago. "There," he said. "I am naked before you."

She let her gaze travel the length of his beautiful body. Broad, strong shoulders and wide chest, where a faint dusting of golden hair blurred the lines of his muscles. That hair had been silky beneath her hands, almost as beautiful to the touch as it was to the sight. Flat stomach, muscle curling over his hipbones. Strong thighs, veiled like his chest with gold hair. And in the center, the evidence of his arousal. Used as she was to women's bodies, she was startled by how alike and how different he was. Curiosity and avidity drove out shyness. She reached out and touched him. She glanced at Edmund's face. It was rigid, as if he resisted great pain.

"Am I hurting you?" she asked.

"No," he said shortly.

She caressed him, touching him as he had touched her. "Ceci, stop, please," he said. She lifted her head and looked at him.

"I have hurt you," she said.

"No, no, you have not. It feels…it feels too good." His face was ruddy, as if he blushed.

He could wait no longer. He pulled her to lie beside him, stroking her body until she gasped and clutched his arm. He moved swiftly, parting her knees and stretching full-length atop her. He gave her a moment to adjust to his weight, to grow used to the sensation of a man between her legs. Everything had happened too swiftly his first time and the speed had terrified him. He did not want that for her.

"I am going to hurt you, Ceci, I cannot help it."

"I know."

"Are you ready?"

Her answer was to pull his head down and kiss him, her tongue sliding between his teeth in a kiss both carnal and loving.

He set himself to thinking about salt taxes, wine monopolies, anything but the sensations radiating from his loins. He stroked her and felt her hips roll in response. He could wait no more.

She gasped and flinched at the sudden hot pain. He kissed her eyes and mouth, tenderly stroking her face and breasts and arms.

"My love, my heart, my dearest one," he whispered, brushing her hair back from her brow. She had never been more beautiful to him, so beautiful he wanted to taste every inch of her. Still, he waited, waited for the pain to ease, fighting his body's rush to fulfillment. As hungry as he was for the pleasure, he did not want this to end. She was so sweet, his Ceci, his alone.

But he could hold back only so long. Unable to stop himself, goaded by her sweetness and warmth, he began to move. As the lightning of his climax crashed over him, he spilled his soul into her in unending waves. It had never been like this, never in his life. "Ceci," he moaned, "Ceci."

As the surge subsided, he lowered his head and kissed her, the caress of his lips gentle. He pressed his forehead against her neck. "I love you, Ceci. Sweet Mary, I love you."

Chapter Fourteen

The words came out of the center of his being. Hearing them, he knew them for the truest he had ever spoken. He had come home.

Her arms around him tightened briefly and then her hand came up to stroke his hair in a tender gesture that made his heart ache. "I have always loved you," she whispered. "From the moment you handed me that sucket, I have loved you."

Her words were sweet, sweeter than he had thought words could be. He lifted himself and looked at her. "As long as that?" In the golden candlelight, her eyes were dark, unreadable. He could lose himself in their depths for eternity.

He bent and kissed her, his mouth conveying his love as clearly as his words had. He wanted her more than ever, as if possessing her had done nothing but deepen his desire. There was no urgency to his hunger, only the sense that it would never be wholly sated.

He withdrew from her as gently as he could and rolled over onto his back, pulling her with him. She cuddled close, her head on his shoulder, fitting perfectly in his arms. He shifted to look down at her. Her eyes were closed, her lashes dark against her pale cheeks. His heart clenched with tenderness. *My little love,* he thought. *My beloved.* He turned his head and grinned ruefully at the tester. How easily the endearments came to him. He rubbed her arm, just to feel the silk of her skin against his palm.

This is happiness, he thought. *I will never know anything like this again.*

Why not? a voice at the back of his head demanded.

Because I will never love anyone as I love her.

It is only coupling, the voice sneered.

It is more, much more.

What of your wife, when you take one?

My wife? She is my wife.

He had to marry her. Not to save her from dishonor but because he could not imagine marrying anyone else. She belonged to him—and he to her, as if he had been moving toward this moment his whole life.

The part of him dedicated to the memory of his father rose up in protest. *What of Arthur? What of your vow?*

He frowned, pressing his lips together. He could not keep his vow as he understood it and still marry Ceci. He had always been a pawn in the games Arthur played with the other kings and princes across Europe, a prize to be offered to sweeten this or that diplomatic bargain. If he married her—when he married her—it would remove a valuable piece from the board.

He looked down at Ceci, her soft breath tickling his shoulder as she slept against him in perfect trust. He could not leave her. Arthur had other pawns to use, two sons and three daughters; most of Edmund's value lay in the work he did gathering information. There would be a scandal— how could there not be, a royal duke marrying for love?—

but it would blow over, as noisy as a thunderstorm and no more damaging.

Memories of his father flashed through his mind, bringing with them an echo of the old pain. In some corner of his heart, he would always be a nine-year-old boy, weeping in grief. But his life had gone on, flowing past that moment, and he had to make his decision as a man, not as a boy.

I am sorry, Papa, he thought, I cannot give up everything for Arthur. I cannot give up this woman.

Cecilia woke slowly, languorous with well-being. It must be dawn or nearly so; a blade of red-gold light slid between the edges of the bedcurtains where they did not quite meet. During the night, while she slept more deeply than ever before, someone had drawn the curtains, cocooning her in dimness and warmth. Cocooning her? Cocooning them.

She turned her head on the pillow and looked at Edmund lying beside her, his arm flung over his head, his lips parted as he breathed softly in sleep. How beautiful he was. Her heart twisted in her breast, love aching like sorrow. *Let me lie here with him forever.* Her prayer was folly, its answer no. They would part when he returned her to St. Agatha's. He would resume his life as the Duke of Somerset and she would go back to the queen's service until she left it for the nunnery.

She smothered a gasp at the thought. How was she going to live without him when he was woven into the fabric of her being? Turning on her side, she watched him sleep. Let her have something to hold on to in the long, cold nights alone, some recollection of this short, sweet time. Let her fix in her memory the way he looked at this moment, the lines of his face limned in gold, the warmth of his body brushing hers under the coverlet. Even if her memory were perfect, recollection would fade; nothing she could do would hold time still.

Sweet Mary, I cannot give him up.

But she would have to. She was not well born enough to marry him, not when the king kept trying to betroth him to the royal maidens of Europe, but she was too well born to be kept as his mistress.

She pressed her face into the pillow, fighting tears as the pain in her heart surged up once more. She should give him up now, before she grew to love him too well. Parting from him would hurt enough as it was; must she deepen the pain by deepening her love? Honesty forced her to recognize that she would not be wise. She would hold on to him for as long as she could, knowing the world would come between them soon enough.

Yet she had no regrets. Oh, there would be confession, repentance and penance soon enough; however she felt about it, she had committed a sin and she did not want its stain on her soul. But if she had it all to do again, she would still choose for him to make love to her.

She laid her hand on his. Without waking, he laced his fingers with hers, then turned on his side with his back to her. He still held her hand, cradling it against his chest. She fitted herself against his back and closed her eyes. With sleep might come peace.

When she woke again, she found Edmund beside her, his head propped on his hand, sleepy eyes softly blue. She smiled at him, because she could not help herself, and was rewarded with a kiss, deep and tender. "My heart," he whispered against her lips.

He gathered her close, his warm skin brushing gently against her own. She rested her cheek in the hollow of his shoulder, alive to every inch of his body, from the hand idly stroking her arm to the ankle under her foot. The only strangeness in lying naked with him was in how right it felt. She wanted to remain there forever.

His hand swept down her arm and circled her wrist, lifting her hand to his mouth. He held her palm against his lips, pressing kisses into it and her fingers. Then he held her hand up, looking at it. "So tiny," he said, "and so beautiful." He turned his head to look down at her face. "Like you." Heat rushed into her face. He shifted, turning on his side and easing her onto her pillow. He stroked her face with the back of his hand, brushing his thumb over her mouth, a little smile in the corner of his mouth. He looked at her as if memorizing her. "I want to see you."

"I am here."

"No. All of you."

Before she could stop him, he flung the coverlet back, exposing her. Her hands lifted to cover her nakedness but the avid delight in Edmund's eyes relaxed her. He found pleasure in what he saw, whatever she thought of her charms. "'Thou art fair, my love; behold, thou art fair,'" he quoted in Latin, his voice rough.

"'His banner over me was love,'" she answered, the words springing to her mind, the fruit of forbidden reading in her youth, when her tutor had been foolish enough to leave a Latin Bible where she could find it. "'Stay me with flagons, comfort me with apples: for I am sick of love.'"

He lifted his head and looked into her eyes, a gleam of appreciation bright in his. "Only you," he said. "Only you among all the women of the earth would know that as I do."

He turned back to her body, his expression a complex blend of humility and desire. Something swelled and broke in her breast, sharp tears stinging her eyes. He reached out and brushed his knuckles along her ribs, feathering his fingertips along the swell of her hips, murmuring, "'The joints of thy thighs are like jewels.'"

All the words of praise he left unspoken sang softly in her memory, shaking her to the depths of her soul. She felt them in the touch of his mouth and hands.

He then bent and with warm lips caressed her breasts and belly, his beard stubble a delicate rasp on her skin. "'Thy navel is like a round goblet that wanteth not liquor: thy belly is like an heap of wheat set about with lilies. Thy two breasts are like two young roes that are twins.'"

He lay beside her, so much love in his eyes that it was hard to meet them. "'Thou hast ravished my heart, my sister, my spouse: thou hast ravished my heart with one of thine eyes.'"

His hand touched her cheek as lightly as swansdown. "'How fair and how pleasant art thou, O love, for delights!'"

She pulled his head down and kissed him, longing to offer beauty for beauty. Only one thing would do, one place to find her words.

She pressed him back against the pillows and knelt at his side.

"'His eyes are as the eyes of doves by rivers of waters, washed with milk and fitly set.'" She cupped his face in her hands and kissed his eyes, one by one, those eyes that spoke such love to her, love that mere words could never tell.

"'His cheeks are as a bed of spices, as sweet as sweet flowers: his lips like lilies, dropping sweet smelling myrrh.'" His mouth was gentle and hot at once; desire kindled, robbing her of breath. She swallowed, trying to gather her fleeing Latin; the long strong body lying patiently on the bed consumed her.

She forced the words to return to her. "'His hands are as gold rings set with the beryl: his belly is as bright ivory overlaid with sapphires.'" She swept her hand across the flat expanse of his chest and belly, his hair silky under her palm. She looked at him, seeing him entire, seeing how she moved him. Her breath caught, her body melting.

"'His legs are as pillars of marble, set upon sockets of gold.'" She ran her hand from knee to groin, touching him to know him, finding joy in his gasp of pleasure. "'His countenance is as Lebanon, excellent as the cedars.'"

She trailed her hand back up his body, delighting in the softness of his skin and fine golden hair. "'His mouth…'" She kissed him until his lips parted, wanting to be lost in the depths of his mouth. "'…is most sweet: yea he is altogether lovely. This is my beloved…'"

His arms came around her and pulled her across him until she lay beside him on the bed. He bent to her, his mouth gentle, until she arched against him, compelled to abandonment by the force of her longing. He groaned and pulled her tight against him, his mouth devouring her. Tears sprang into her eyes. Arousing him aroused her; she had not expected that.

Her desire, now she knew what awaited her, was sharper and quicker to kindle, glowing fiercely from belly to breast. She turned into his arms, hungry for him.

He joined them all at once, his sigh almost a moan. She felt no pain, only the indescribable satisfaction of sharing one flesh. He nuzzled her neck, the heat of his mouth making her head spin.

"I don't know what to do," she whispered, hardly aware of what she said.

"What do you want to do?" he asked, rubbing his nose against hers and kissing the corners of her mouth, sucking gently on her lower lip.

She brushed her fingers over his mouth. "I should like to lie here for the rest of our lives, just as we are."

"Not I," he said, grinning wickedly. He slid his arm under her waist and, holding her hips tightly against his, rolled in one swift movement onto his back. "This is how I should like to spend the rest of our lives."

For a moment, she was at a loss, shy at being in such an exposed position.

He slid his hands up her back and over her shoulders to her breasts, caressing them. His face was absorbed, ardent, his eyes blue as flames between their spiky lashes. Her head spun, the intensity of his gaze as he watched her somehow adding to her fiery pleasure. She bent to kiss him. Lips and tongue mingled in long slow kisses that drove thought from her mind. His hands were warm on her back, her thighs, her breasts, touching lightly, kneading.

As they came together, stars burst against her closed eyelids, pleasure shattering her so she did not know where she ended and he began. Falling back to earth, she lay down on his broad chest, her face pressed against his neck.

He wrapped his arms around her and held her close. "Sweet Mary," he whispered into her hair. "You will kill me."

This time, she woke alone, white-gold light cutting into the gloom of the bed. She lay for a long time staring at the dusty tester, thinking nothing, content.

Beyond the curtains, water gurgled and splashed. The door opened and shut. Piers murmured something, so softly she could not understand him.

"I am clean enough," Edmund replied. "No, hand me that. Have them empty the tub and refill it. Mistress Cecilia will want a bath when she rises."

Cecilia's face burned, so hot she thought it might melt like candle wax. Piers had to know she and Edmund had shared this bed, had to know what they had done in it. How could she face him? She knew Edmund trusted him and because of that, she believed Piers would not spread the tale of her behavior, but in the meantime, what would she read in his eyes? She had forgotten Piers.

Regrets? the voice in the back of her head asked.

No.

Edmund put his head through the curtains, grinning at her. "Time to rise, beautiful slugabed. Your bath awaits."

"It is ready?" she faltered. She had thought she had time to gather wits and composure.

His grin faded. He pushed through the curtains and sat on the bed, wrapped in a length of linen gray with damp hair. His hair stuck up in curly spikes, dark as honey.

"Tell me, Ceci."

The way their physical intimacy belied their other closeness surprised her. She had done things with this man, was willing to do things, she had only imagined a short time before. He had kissed and caressed every secret place of her body. Why now was it difficult to speak to him?

"Ceci. What is it?" He took her hand in comfort.

For a moment she thought to deny her fear, but something in the openness of his expression loosened her tongue and made it possible for her to speak.

"Piers. I am afraid."

"Of Piers? How shall he harm you? No whisper of this will escape him, I swear it." He spoke gently, like the Edmund she knew. Some of the strange new constraint dissolved.

He lifted her into his arms, cradling her in his lap as if he could protect her from the world. She buried her face in his neck, savoring the feel of him and learning anew the comfort of his body.

He held her in silence, his arms strong and warm, his heart beating calmly beneath her ear. Her misgivings and the rest of her constraint melted. She lifted her head and smiled at him. "You look like a hedgehog."

He rubbed his chin against her cheek, scraping her with his bristles. "And I feel like one, too."

The latch rattled and the door banged against the wall. Edmund peered through the gap in the curtains and said, "Your bath is here." He bent over her, resuming his game, tickling her with his unshaven beard.

"Stop," she whispered, giggling, twisting away from him as best she could. He held her in his lap, growling against her throat.

The door banged and Edmund stood, lifting her in his arms. She pressed herself against him, as if she could hide her nakedness, relaxing when she saw the room was now empty. She was not normally modest before maidservants, but she had never faced them flushed from passion, either. Edmund walked to the wooden tub standing by the lit brazier and lowered her into the steaming water, his linen towel slipping as he bent over. Cecilia traced the line of golden hair running from his navel to where it disappeared into the towel, grinning up at him. He snatched her hand away and bit her fingertip.

"Do not, or I shall be forced to join you," he said sternly, ruining the effect by kissing her fingers one by one.

As she bathed, Edmund dressed in the plain woolen clothes he had worn throughout their journey. She watched him through half-closed eyes, admiring the turn of his calves, the strong muscles of his thighs, his firm buttocks. She had always thought the sight of a naked man would make her feel shy; instead it gave her nothing but pleasure to see Edmund whole.

Dressed, he looked like a gentleman, nothing more, yet she saw the prince shining through, like the sun imperfectly hidden by a gray cloud.

"When you are washed and dressed, meet me at the inn door. We shall go to the fair," he said, standing by the tub, watching her while she soaped her arms, his eyes following her every movement.

"Do you think we shall hear something of value?" she asked, lowering her arms and sluicing warm water over her shoulders and breasts.

"Er...no. It is a fine day, and I thought...I thought we might walk out and see the fairing," he said, flushing. His gaze followed her hands as they swept over her breasts. His gaze fixed, he swallowed and then looked away, but not before she had seen the flare of desire in the blue depths of his eyes. She sank until the cloudy water reached her neck. She had meant to tease him but had underestimated the impact on her. Another glance like that and she would be out of the bath and into his arms.

She had thought that if she lay with him once, she would be cured of her sickness, that desire, satisfied, would die. She had been naive. Every kiss, every touch, fed the fire they should have quenched.

"I should like that," she said.

He left shortly afterward, kissing the top of her head quickly, as if he were afraid to do more. Once he was gone, there was no reason to linger; she hurried through the rest of her ablutions and left the tub.

As she dried herself, the memory of his hands on her hips, of the tightness of his face in the shadowy confines of the bed, sent a wave of heat over her. She gasped and let it pass, but she could not help wondering how she was going to be able to survive the cloistered life.

She dressed herself in clothes that did not need the assistance of another pair of hands: her sleeves were sewn to the bodice, which also laced up the front; the waistband of the skirt fastened on the side with a neat tie, easily reached with a little twist of her upper body. It was the work of a moment to pull up stockings, tie her garters and slip her feet into her shoes. Tying the lappets of her cap underneath her plaited hair, she left the room.

She had hardly taken four steps when the knot on one of her garters loosened and her stocking slid down her leg. She hated the feeling of loose stockings, the way they flopped around her ankle, brushing her skin with the delicate touch of an ant's foot. Sighing, she crouched to retie the offending garter.

It was dim in the corner where she knelt. She was only vaguely aware of men in the corridor beyond her but something about their soft voices caught her attention, perhaps the furtiveness of their murmured conversation. Unnamed instinct held her still. She only dared to look up when she heard them begin to walk away, one set of footsteps thudding down the stairs, the other scuffling toward the other end of the corridor.

On the floor, half against the wall, was a square of white with the dark blob of a wax seal affixed to it. Looking swiftly around to be sure no one observed her, she walked down the hall and retrieved the letter, hiding it in a fold of her skirt. She went back to their room and bolted the door behind her.

Chapter Fifteen

Edmund stepped through the open inn door. He had satisfied himself that the grooms were doing all that was proper in caring for his horses; now all he wanted to do was collect Cecilia and go to Aylesbury Fair. She was not waiting for him and a quick glance in the common room showed she was not there, either. She must still be dressing.

To while away the time, he opened the purse hanging from his belt and pulled out a handful of pennies and farthings. Did he have enough to buy her a gift, something to remind her of this journey? If she chose something small, such as lute strings or a length of ribbon....Both were discreet and within his means; neither seemed like enough. He put his money away. Lute strings or ribbons were the kinds of gifts you gave a woman you flirted with, not the kind of gift you gave the woman you wanted to marry.

A shadow crossed his mind, a chill at the thought of claiming her. He wanted her, wanted her with him until he died, but something inside protested at the repudiation of his vow to support his brother. He ignored it. He had made his choice gladly; it was too late for second thoughts.

Footsteps boomed on the stairs, the tread too heavy to be Cecilia's. Yet he still looked up, smiling at his own eagerness. She made him as giddy as a page boy, sick over his first love.

A stout tradesman came down the stairs, a soft cap pulled low on his forehead and his gaze fixed on his feet as they thumped on the stair treads. Tugging his forelock without looking up, he pushed past Edmund and went out the door. Something, some niggling disquiet, pricked Edmund. Left to himself, he would follow the man, but he was trapped here, waiting for Cecilia. He paced from the foot of the stairs to the open inn door and back again. What was taking her so long?

A door banged in the distance. There was a patter of footsteps overhead and then Cecilia hurried down the stairs. Her face was as pale as a pearl in the soft shadows of the stairwell. Edmund's heart jerked, his unease deepening. When she reached him, she gripped his arm and said in an undertone, "Let us leave this place now." He led her through the door into the sunny inn yard.

"What is it?" he said quietly. "You are nearly green."

"Wait. Wait until we are further away."

Her voice was low and hard, her body vibrating with excitement. Why? He held his tongue until they were well into the streets of the town.

"Tell me, Ceci. What have you learned?"

"As I left our room, my garter came undone. I bent to tie it and I think they could not see me in the darkness. They met and spoke but—"

"Who?"

"Let me finish. I could not hear them, they spoke too softly, and that made me wonder what they were about. I cannot say why, but I distrusted them both. When they parted, the fat one dressed like a carter dropped this." She reached into her bodice and pulled out a letter. "I went into our room to look at it. As soon as I saw the seal, I had to read it. Here."

She thrust the letter into his hands. She had taken great care in opening it; the seal was intact, hanging from the flap like a great drop of blood. He examined the seal carefully but the shallow imprint of wings and arch was unfamiliar. He lifted the flap.

He recognized the handwriting instantly, all the air rushing from his lungs as if he had been struck. Trembling with disbelief, he read the brief message: the exhortation to be faithful even in the face of persecution, the promises of support. He could not believe what he read and so read the letter a second time. The words did not change, nor did the elegant handwriting. With shaking hands he folded the letter and handed it back to Cecilia who thrust it back into her bodice.

Oh, God, oh, Sweet Savior, it cannot be true. It cannot.

His brother Harry, who had been so adamant that they root out the burgeoning cancer of heresy, had written a dangerous letter, urging other dissenters to stand by their beliefs. Bile rose to his throat. What was Harry doing?

"You are pale," Cecilia said. "This is more than finding a heretical letter. Tell me."

"I know that handwriting," Edmund said hoarsely.

Cecilia's eyes narrowed. "Whose?" she asked softly. She pulled the letter out of her bodice again and looked at the seal. "York," she whispered.

"How did you know?" he demanded, startled.

"The seal—it is the old seal of the dukes of York. And the signature. Harry," she said.

"The old seal?"

She held the letter so he could see the seal and its markings. Her finger following the wings of the bird, she said, "The falcon."

Now he saw what the arch was. "And the fetterlock."

"If I can see it, anyone can. If this is the Harry we believe it to be, he has been foolish, using the old seal," she said, replacing the letter in her bodice and grimacing as if one of its corners had scratched her. Her calm steadied him, allaying his queasiness and his nagging sense that the bottom had dropped out of the world. And she was right about Harry's stupidity.

He began to walk again. If they were moving, they were less likely to be overheard. "It is my Harry," he said slowly. "I should know his hand anywhere."

"We agree, then, that the letter was written by your brother. I do not think it is the first."

He thought for a moment, remembering the tone of the text, the way its author wrote as if he spoke directly to his audience. She was right. "Very well. He has written other letters. Ceci, he is the one urging Arthur to stamp this out. Why would he light a fire and then draw notice to it?"

"A man might start a fire and then give the alarm if he wanted to make a name for alertness. Or if he wished to destroy an enemy without being suspected of ill-will."

"Why would Harry wish to be known as such a devout son of the Church?" It made no sense. What could the Church give Harry that would justify such lengths?

"It might not be that. He may wish to destroy someone," Cecilia said, linking her arm with his and smiling up at him. "Smile, my love. If we do not look happy, no one will take us for sweethearts." Only the intent look in her eyes, revealing the clockwork of her thoughts, gave her seriousness away.

My love. The endearment warmed and heartened him. He was grateful for her companionship, for the way she understood what he did and how he did it, for the intelligence that helped him untangle the knots he faced. He kissed her swiftly, because her mouth seemed to beg for it, and bent his mind to the puzzle before them.

"Why would he wish to destroy merchants and artisans in Buckinghamshire?"

"No, not the heretics themselves. Who else would be harmed by this?"

He considered the possibilities but each seemed more absurd than the last. Cecilia crowded close to him to avoid bumping into a stout woman with a basket over her arm. The brief pressure of her body reminded him that here was someone with whom he could test his ideas. He had grown used to working by himself; how long would it take to become accustomed to her assistance?

"The Bishop of Lincoln? The Duke of Buckingham? Who?"

She chewed her lip. "I have not seen sign that York bears ill-will toward either man, so I cannot say it is personal. Would he have other reasons for bringing one of them down?"

She asked the questions that cut straight to the heart of the matter. He tightened his arm to press her hand against his ribs, and considered the possibilities opened up by her remark.

"I cannot imagine what Lincoln could have done to earn Harry's enmity. Buckingham's worst sin is that he is my cousin and descended from Edward the Third. It might, if he were mad, give him the idea he has a claim on the throne."

"Does he think he has a claim? Could York be trying to bring him down for that?"

"By fomenting heresy? It is too uncertain. It would be far easier, if he knew anything, to tell the king."

"But—" She fell silent. He looked down at her to see why she had cut herself short. She was chewing her lip again and a frown had gathered between her brows.

"What were you going to say? You can ask me anything. Surely you know that."

"It was not a question." She hesitated. "I do not think York is as loyal to the king as you are."

He had taken Harry's resentment of Arthur for granted for so long that it had never occurred to him that someone else would see it. "I know he is not. But I cannot believe he would attempt to bring Buckingham down using heresy."

"What if York is encouraging heresy because it creates unrest? I have been thinking that the plan is to disgrace Buckingham, or perhaps the Bishop of Lincoln directly. But perhaps York is more subtle than that."

Edmund shook his head. Harry was as subtle as cannon fire. "I cannot see that. He is not that clever."

She stopped and turned to face him, her brows raised skeptically, her eyes bright with intelligence. "Is he not? He has written letters encouraging heresy and disloyalty while demanding the king hunt down his correspondents. And no one suspects him of double-dealing. Tell me truly, is that not the work of a clever man?" She pulled the letter out of her neckline and shook it under his nose. "This tells me there is more to Harry than you are willing to see." She shoved the letter back into her bodice.

"I have known him all my life, Ceci. I cannot believe he is capable of this."

Her expression softened. Laying her hand on his, she said, "Sometimes, we cannot see those closest to us with any clarity. I thought I knew my sister. I was wrong. Perhaps you are wrong about your brother." Stepping closer,

she clasped his hand. "The king is a clever man and so
are you. Is it so strange that York should be clever, too?"

He chuckled ruefully. "I do not feel very clever." He
rolled his head across his shoulders to loosen the tightness
in his neck. "Very well. Let us assume the worst of
Harry." He sighed. "I wish we had more information. This
is like trying to find your way on a dark night with a single
candle." He began to walk, drawing her with him, absorbed in his unhappy thoughts. Despite what he had told
Cecilia, he could not believe the worst of his brother. He
did not love and admire Harry the way he did Arthur, but
he was still fond of him. Fond enough to dread the punishment for treason, if indeed treason was Harry's game.

They arrived at the ground set aside for the fair and
began wandering the narrow lanes between the booths,
shoving their way through the dense crowd. Men and
women of nearly every degree filled every inch of space,
some roving between the booths, others pausing to examine the goods displayed. The babble of voices, from pie
men crying their wares to merchants dickering with cus-
tomers, thundered in all directions. Behind him, a woman
shouted "Cutpurse!" and the crowd turned in her direction, momentarily diverted. Edmund touched the mouth of
his purse and then smiled ruefully at himself. Ahead, the
crowd cried "Ooh!" and "Aah!" at the antics of a troupe
of tumblers.

Cecilia looked up at Edmund, her face glowing with
delight, every sign of worry gone. "This is like Wednesfield Fair!"

"Country girl," he said, tapping the tip of her nose.

She wrinkled it and grinned at him. "Assuredly."

The breeze picked up, dissipating the cloud of dust and
smoke that hung over the crowd, and wafted the rich
brown smell of meat pies to him. His stomach grumbled,

loudly enough to make Cecilia look up at him, her eyes sparkling with laughter.

"I am hungry, too. Shall we find the pie man?" she asked.

He shook his purse, making the coins jingle with the pleasant music of wealth. "I can purchase whatever your heart desires," he said, grinning down at her. Craning his neck, he spied smoke rising from a booth on the edge of the crowd. He grasped her upper arm and pushed her in the booth's direction. "This way."

The pie man had set up a small oven from which he produced a never-ending stream of pies. He had also laid in several small kegs of ale. Dickering with the ease of long practice, Edmund purchased meat pies and horn cups of ale, enough for him and Cecilia. They strolled to a hedgerow beyond the fairground where they sat in the shade to eat their hot pies and drink the strong, fresh ale.

Licking the last crumbs of the pie from his fingers, he leaned back on his elbow and watched Cecilia as she ate. She held the pie up to her mouth and scooped out the filling with her tongue, then nibbled at the crust as delicately as a mouse. He had to check his impulse to laugh at her childlike absorption in her meal.

He looked away, at the small town of the fair cowering under Aylesbury's walls, at the other people sheltering in the shade of the hedgerow. The turf under him smelled green and brown, of grass and rich earth; the sun's heat released the sharp scent of the hedge. With his stomach full and Cecilia beside him, some of the bleakness in his heart faded. There must be a good reason for Harry to have written that letter; they simply had not thought of it yet.

"I have been thinking," Cecilia said. He glanced at her in time to see her licking crumbs and gravy from her lips. There was a smudge on her cheek that she had missed.

Reaching out, he wiped it off with his finger and then, unthinkingly, offered her his fingertip. Her eyes began to dance with mischief. Leaning forward, she took his fingertip in her mouth and sucked gently on it. Heat flared in her eyes. Aroused and a little shocked, he snatched his finger away, wanting nothing more than to drag her into the hedge and toss up her skirt. From the look in her eye, she would go willingly. He looked away, hoping it would cool him.

"You have been thinking," he said after a moment.

"Yes."

Her voice was husky and sent tendrils of heat curling through a body he had barely subdued. He closed his eyes and dug his fingers into the turf. The more he possessed her, the more he wanted her; everything she gave was not nearly enough.

"You have been thinking," he repeated. He could not think.

"About Harry and the letter." Harry? Harry who? he wondered for one dazed moment, then his head cleared and with the rush of memory, his body cooled. "Can you not go to the king with what we have?"

He turned his head and looked at her. She sat with her arms wrapped around her upraised legs, her chin resting on her knees. Only the color in her cheeks betrayed that she had been as moved as he.

"We have nothing," he said.

"That letter is proof that there is heresy here, although it is not a strong spark, and that your brother is fanning it."

It was a good theory, but he wanted to believe her too badly to trust his judgment. "The letter proves there are nameless heretics in Buckinghamshire to whom my brother writes, that is all."

She turned her head and looked out on the fairground as he had. "I cannot help thinking that if heresy was flourishing, it would not need your brother's encouragement."

The breeze, which had been ruffling the leaves of grass and whispering in the hedges, turned. The world went still, the indistinct roar of the fair quieter than the glassy silence surrounding them. For a brief moment, quick as lightning, he thought he understood what was going on. Then it was gone, leaving as residue the knowledge that Cecilia had been right: they had to return to the king.

He sat up and reached for her hand. He turned it over and spread her fingers wide, examining the fine whorls of her skin and the broad creases crisscrossing her pink palm. He touched the thread-thin blue vein at the base of her third finger while he faced a truth he had known from the moment he read Harry's letter.

When they returned to Court, he would not be able to claim her immediately. Working through whatever Harry was up to would take Arthur's time and energy. It might end with a royal duke being tried for treason, though Edmund could not believe it would come to that. Whatever befell them, Edmund refused to add to Arthur's burden by asking leave to marry as he willed. It was bad enough he intended to take a valuable piece off the diplomatic board.

He lifted her hand to his mouth and pressed her palm to his lips. "You are right. We must lay this before the king." He stood without releasing her hand and pulled her to her feet.

"Shall we leave now?" she asked.

He looked at the sky and at the shadows creeping out from underneath the hedgerow. It was well past midday. They could hardly make a good start before darkness forced them off the road. "No, tomorrow is soon enough."

"Very well. Shall we return to the inn?"

"Not yet. I wanted to buy you a gift."

Her face lit. "A gift! There is no need."

"I have need," he said. "What would please you?"

The flicker of hungry thought came and went in a flash, but he saw enough to feel the familiar rush of desire. Hard afterward came the equally familiar squeeze of tenderness. How had he lived without her? And how was he going to survive their coming separation?

"Let me give you something, please, Ceci." He had never asked to give before and he groped for the words. He wished he could still ask her to marry him now, but he could not treat Arthur that way, not when Arthur had Harry's actions to sift through. "It will not be the same when we go back and I want you to have something to remember me by."

She stepped close to him and gripped his hand with both hers. "Do you think I will forget you?"

He touched her cheek, hungry for the feel of her but mindful of the eyes all around. "No." He stopped, bereft of words. "It would make me happy if you had something of me with you."

She smiled with heartrending tenderness. "I do. Let us go to the inn and I shall show you."

They turned back to the inn, hurrying now where they had lingered before. In their room, she paused and said, "This means more to me than anything you could buy me at the fair." She knelt by her bundle and pulled out a long flat box. Opening it, she searched through sheets of paper and parchment, laying them on the floor beside her as she lifted them out of the box. He could see they were drawings, although he was too far away to see any details. Finally, she found something that pleased her, a drawing she examined with more care than she had yet shown.

"Here," she said, and handed him the sheet of paper.

He had not seen it in years but he remembered it instantly, the memory bringing back with it that long-ago day at Wednesfield in a way its companion sketch, hanging on the wall in the house in Southwark, did not. The beginning of the road that led here, to this inn, this love.

"Do you remember?"

He nodded. "I never forgot."

"Nor did I." She came to stand beside him, leaning against him so she could look at the sketch, as well. "You do not look the same and yet you do. I shall have this to remind me and it is better than anything you could buy."

He put his arm around her, holding her tightly against him, his mouth pressed to her forehead. Her generosity, her strength: both astonished and moved him. He had never done anything in his life to deserve the gifts she had given him and he could not do the one thing that would make this right. *In time. In time I will make it right.* But his confidence was seeping away and he began to wonder how long it would take to sort out the mess Harry was in. Would she wait for him? And did he have the right to ask it of her?

Chapter Sixteen

"What possessed you to behave like a fool, Cecilia? Your father did not obtain this post for your idle entertainment. You were given opportunities which you have heedlessly thrown away," her mother cried, pacing from one side of the solar at Coleville House to the other, the train of her gown lashing like a cat's tail. Cecilia sighed and fixed her gaze on a flower, flattened amid the floor rushes. Her mother could go on for hours in this vein without once repeating herself.

Her parents had come to London while she was away. She had found a small bundle of messages on her arrival at Bermondsey, all pointing toward the same thing: her parents requested her presence at their London residence and had obtained the queen's gracious permission to keep her with them for as long as they chose.

"This is what comes of overeducating women," her father said. She heard his heavy tread as it crossed the room and the clink of pewter as he poured more ale into his mug. "Beatrice knows how to sew a straight seam, she can manage a household and she always looks neat as a pin. We never had this kind of trouble with her."

"No, we did not. Instead, she chose to marry a man old

enough to remember when Henry the Sixth was king. And she made a mess of her marriage. Do not throw Beatrice in Cecilia's face, Michael. Things are not so bad as that.''

Cecilia glanced up. Her father, standing on the far side of the room where her mother could not see his face, winked at her. By pretending to compare her to Beatrice, he compelled her mother to be more just than she might be, given her anger. Thank God her father was on her side. If both of them were angry with her, she had no hope.

"They are bad enough, Philippa," her father said. He held out his free hand, the thumb cocked as if he had begun counting on his fingers. "Banished from Court—"

"Not banished. Sent away to consider her sins," her mother said, taking another turn about the room.

"Might as well be banished," her father said, closing his spread fingers into a fist. "She must come home, there is no other hope." He took a long pull on his mug of ale.

"She is not dismissed from the queen's service," her mother said. She rounded on Cecilia. "Or are you?"

Cecilia lowered her eyes. Would her mother be angered or mollified by a show of spirit? There was no way to know beforehand.

"No, madam, I am bidden to return when you dismiss me," she said.

"Look at me, Cecilia. It is too late to pretend demureness," her mother said irritably.

Cecilia looked into her mother's pale blue eyes. Despite the fine web of wrinkles surrounding them, they were a young woman's eyes, snapping and bright. Cecilia quailed a little at the anger in their depths.

"I had hoped for better from you." Her mother's mouth turned down wearily.

"I am sorry," Cecilia whispered. She could withstand her mother's fury, not her disappointment. She thought quickly. She had promised not to tell where she had gone, but surely there was no harm in telling her parents why she had gone? "I was not banished for flirting. I was not even banished. It is a story we made up to explain why I was away from Court for those weeks."

"What tale is this?" her father demanded. He put his mug down on the table with a thump, his dark eyes bright and hard, as if he did not dare trust her.

"I left Court at the queen's request. I was not at Bermondsey, but I may not say where I was, again at the queen's request."

"Humph," her father grunted.

"Michael, Cecilia is not stupid enough to make up a lie like that," her mother said. "Nor is she given to lying in a general way."

"No, she is neither stupid nor a habitual liar. But this story may not be checked. So if it is a lie, it is a good one."

"At any rate, she has kept her wits," her mother said practically. Her father guffawed abruptly, as if jolted into laughter. The tightness in Cecilia's chest eased. This refrain was older than she: her mother's shrewdness, her father's delight in it.

"I should like to think she has kept her honor. But it seems I must settle for wits."

"Have you kept your honor, Cecilia?" her mother asked suddenly, blue eyes shrewd.

"I have," Cecilia said. She had done nothing dishonorable, nothing at all. Edmund rose in her memory, the brief recollection of his weight in her arms, but she thrust the memory away. She would never stop missing him if she did not stop thinking of him.

Her mother's eyes narrowed. "We did not come to London to ask you about where you have spent the last several weeks. In fact, we only learned of your behavior when we arrived and asked after you. We wish to discuss something else with you, Cecilia.''

''Something else?'' The anger and reproaches were not the heart of the matter? What had happened while she was away?

''We would like to talk to you about your marriage.''

For a moment she thought the floor had given way. And then she thought she had misunderstood. ''M-my marriage?'' Her head felt as if it were full of mist.

''Sebastian Benbury has asked your father to consider a match between the two of you. He has pointed out many advantages to such a match, not least of which is the fact that there is affection and esteem between the two of you. Your father and I have come to London to assure ourselves that you have not made any promises to anyone else before we proceed.''

No, no promises but the gift of my honor, Cecilia thought. There was another thought pushing at her, some knowledge she did not dare face.

''I have spoken no word that could be interpreted as a promise,'' Cecilia said. ''I am no beauty, and my dowry has not been enough to tempt anyone.''

''Then there is no impediment. You are free to marry Sebastian.''

Her thoughts whirled through her head like autumn leaves caught in a gale. *Edmund!... Sebastian is not so ill...I cannot do this, I cannot.*

I have no choice. I have no hope.

She had never believed in her plan to enter a convent; she had never thought beyond the moment when she had chosen to seduce Edmund. Anger at her own self-willed blindness crashed over her. You are fool, she raged, her heart skipping beats.

And Edmund? What must he believe when he heard this news? Would he hate her? Or would he be relieved? She hardly knew which thought hurt most.

"Cecilia, what ails you?" The sound of her mother's voice, exasperation laced with concern, cut through Cecilia's confusion. She could not afford to expose herself.

"Nothing. Nothing ails me." Even to her own ears her voice sounded sickly and weak.

Her mother's eyes narrowed speculatively. Cecilia braced herself. She should have known she could not fool her mother.

"Michael, my heart, I must speak to Cecilia privately," her mother said, going to Cecilia's father and laying her hand on his sleeve in a gesture of surprising tenderness. Sometimes, when enduring the brunt of her mother's shrewd wit and sharp temper, Cecilia lost sight of her loving heart.

"Is something wrong?" her father said, looking from one to the other.

"No. No, I must speak privately to her. This is the first time we have mentioned marriage to her. I wish to allay her concerns."

"Can you not do that here and now? I do not see the need for secrecy." Annoyance darkened his face. Cecilia suspected that the conversation was about to cut very close to the truth and she wished her father would leave. She loved him with her whole heart, but there were some things he would never understand or countenance. He was not as fierce as her mother, but he could be hard-hearted. *Listen to her, Papa.*

"Women's knowledge, my heart. I must tell her of a woman's duties and responsibilities."

"She has been raised to know all that."

"There are things that only a wife may know. Do you trust me, Michael?"

His look softened. "I do."

"Then go."

"You have cozened me," he growled, but he took her chin in his hand and kissed her as he always did when he left her, regardless of how short their parting was to be.

This is what I wanted for myself, Cecilia thought, her heart aching as he left the room. To love and be loved as they have. Edmund, Edmund, her heart beat; she felt empty, like a flower stem with the pith blown out.

Her mother walked to the door and barred it. Turning, she leaned her back against the door panel. Cecilia braced herself. From the hard look in her mother's blue eyes, this was not going to be easy or pleasant.

"Tell me the truth, Cecilia. Are you a maid?"

Cecilia swallowed, her stomach tied in a knot and her craven heart crying out for her to nod, just nod.

No.

She knew her life might depend on her answer, but she could not lie. Not because her mother would know the truth anyway, not because her mother trusted her honesty. She could not deny what she and Edmund had shared by pretending it had not happened.

"No."

Her mother nodded as if she had expected Cecilia's answer. "It was Somerset?"

"Yes." She could not imagine how her mother knew, or even how she had learned enough to guess. She did not dare ask.

"Do you love him?"

Cecilia paused, surprised by the compassion in her mother's eyes and voice as much by the question itself. That she loved the man she had lain with meant nothing;

she was not any less ruined for it. She looked at her mother and for a dizzying instant, something shifted and instead of the great lady of her childhood, Cecilia saw her mother simply as a woman with the same fears and joys she herself had. "I do."

"You cannot marry him. The only reason he is not married today is that Anne of Bavaria died. How many times has your father journeyed across the sea to make a treaty that included some provision for Somerset's marriage? You must know from that alone that the king has plans for his brother's future. Even if the king had not contemplated marriage alliances, you know Somerset cannot marry without the king's leave. Nor can you marry because your heart tells you so. That is for laborers." Her mother's voice was firm and very kind, not the tone of a judge making a ruling but of a friend gently breaking unwelcome news.

"I know." She took a deep breath, the dizziness of surprise overtaking her again. She could no longer predict what would happen next. "I never thought to. I thought to take the veil."

Her mother nodded again. "It would be a good life for you. Work and study, both to please you. If you found a good house."

"But you have found me a husband instead."

"Yes, we have." Her mother walked away from the door. Cecilia braced herself for the blow she knew she deserved. Her mother enfolded her in her arms, holding her tightly. "You have been a great fool, my girl," she whispered.

Cecilia burst into tears. Her mother's tenderness had broken her as punishment would not have. What had she done? She had risked shaming her family, all to satisfy her selfish wants. She had been wrong, terribly wrong.

Her mother soothed her, pushing her hood off her head and stroking her hair. Cecilia wept from the strain of confession, the shocks bursting over her one by one, the pain of leaving Edmund. She sobbed harder. She had not been wrong to love Edmund, love him wholly. How could it be wrong when it hurt to know she would never be with him in happy intimacy again? She did not miss the lovemaking—though her body craved his with a persistent ache—as much as she did the quiet evenings and mornings spent in his arms behind the bedcurtains.

Lying behind the bedcurtains as she would soon lie with Sebastian.

She recoiled involuntarily at the thought. She loved Sebastian dearly, but how could she endure his touch?

"I cannot marry Sebastian, Mama," she whispered, easing out of her mother's arms. She could not speak what lay in her mind while her mother held and comforted her. "I cannot do it."

"Ceci, do not be more of a fool than you already have been," her mother said gently, reaching out to wipe away Cecilia's tears with her fingers.

"I am no maid." She blinked away more tears. Her reluctance had nothing to do with that, but it was her best argument. Her mother would have no patience with an argument based on love, and rightly so.

"That can be overcome."

What could she say to convince her mother? "If Sebastian is willing to stab my foot, but I cannot see him conniving like that."

Her mother gasped and then laughed breathlessly. "Wherever did you hear about that old trick?"

"Beatrice. She says that is what Lord Manners did." She walked to the bench underneath the window and sat down. Discussing Beatrice now seemed no stranger than anything else that had happened to her today.

"Did she? Hmm." Her mother moved to her chair and picked up the cushion, patting it to plump it. "That explains a great deal about Beatrice. However, it has no bearing on you or Sebastian. We have two choices here, Cecilia. We can try to fool Sebastian. Or we can be honest with him." She laid the cushion on the chair and sat down.

"Tell him I am not a virgin?"

"Yes. And tell him why. If we wait to be sure you are not with child—"

"I am not. My courses have begun," Cecilia interrupted.

"If we wait to be sure you are not with child," her mother continued sternly, lifting her hand palm out, "Sebastian may be content to have you as you are. You will not be the first girl to go to her marriage bed less pure than she ought to be."

"You do not know that," Cecilia said.

Her mother's eyebrows rose. "Child, how do you think I know of the knife in the foot trick, except that I once helped a friend employ it?"

Cecilia ran the palm of her hand underneath her pomander chain, the metal cool on her skin. Even if her mother spoke the truth, what bearing did it have on her situation? She had always trusted Sebastian, but she had never asked so much of him before. She was afraid his honor would not allow him to stomach an unchaste bride. And she feared what would happen to her if he accepted her now and hated her later.

I need to know Sebastian will not hate me. I cannot marry him unless I know that.

She looked into her mother's eyes. "He must know before he agrees to marry me."

"He may refuse," her mother warned, her brows straightening in a frown.

Cecilia looked away, her gaze fixed on the whitewashed wall opposite while she felt her way forward word by word. She could not say what she needed to and watch her mother's face. "I should prefer him to refuse rather than feel we had deceived him. He will not betray me, whatever he thinks of the marriage."

"You risk your name, child."

She knew she risked her name. She did not fear for her name as much as she feared for her life. Now she looked at her mother. "I risk more if I am dishonest with him."

Her mother answered her look with cool thoughtful eyes. "As you will. Your father shall send for him—"

"You will not tell my father!" Cecilia cried, her hand tightening on the pomander chain in alarm. She could not trust her soft-hearted father to be as understanding as her mother had been. He would fear for her and his fear would make him angry.

"Cecilia!" Her mother paused. "I am not that much a fool."

"I am sorry," Cecilia replied, contrite.

"God save me, love has made you addlepated. I shall have your father send for him without telling him why we must speak to Sebastian. And I shall leave you to tell Sebastian."

Cecilia's heart stopped, frozen. "I cannot." She could not tell him, see his face as he understood what she had done. She did not want to see him before he had had time to master his expression. If he once looked at her with revulsion, their friendship would be shattered. She did not think she could bear that.

"And I will not. If you cannot bring yourself to tell him, he will not be told."

Cecilia recognized that tone from her childhood, the one that meant her mother would hear no arguments. She released the chain, folding her hands together and squeezing, the discomfort focusing her thoughts. Somehow she would find the courage to tell Sebastian.

"Yes, Mama."

"...so if you do not wish to marry me, Sebastian, I shall understand."

Sebastian, standing by the window, released his white-knuckled grip on the casements and turned to face her. The underwater light of the rainy afternoon framed his head with a silver-gilt halo and obscured his expression. He had left her side and gone to stand with his back to her as soon as she mentioned that there might be an impediment to their wedding. It had felt like abandonment, one more blow bruising her battered heart.

"I cannot abandon you. Not like..." He swallowed.

She opened her mouth to tell him Edmund had not abandoned her but then closed it. What good would come of arguing with him? He would not believe her, anyway. Sebastian would not believe her capable of seduction, capable of anything she had done in these past weeks.

"I shall be well and safe, Sebastian. You need not fear for me."

He came to sit beside her on the bench, taking her hand in one of his. "I am glad you have been frank with me, Ceci. I would not want to hear this from anyone else. Now let me be as frank with you. I do not love you, though I am very fond of you and have a great esteem for you."

"Even after I...?" She could not say it again.

"Even after. I know your heart. I know your family. A Coleville keeps her word. If you promise to be true to me, you will be. You must know that if I promise you fidelity, you will have it.'' His tone was muted, as if he were talking in a sickroom. But who was the gentleness for? Her? Or him?

She laid her free hand over his. ''Oh, Sebastian, I do know it.''

''You also know, have always known, of my feelings for your sister.'' He hesitated and then breathed deeply, like a man preparing himself for the barber's knife. ''She does not return them—''

''I do not think Beatrice knows what she feels!'' she cried.

''Stop interrupting, Ceci,'' he said, smiling and laying a finger against her lips, silencing her. She could not remember a time when he had not done that to quiet her and she was reminded that, before anything else, he was her friend. ''You love, unwisely, the Duke of Somerset. I love, unwisely, your sister Beatrice. You and I have been good companions all our lives. I need a wife and I should prefer one for whom I can feel affection if not love. I approached your father without knowing of your circumstance, but it only makes me more sure that marriage between us would be wise.''

She turned her hand and gripped his. ''You are too good. I pray you will not come to hate me for marrying you.''

''I could never hate you.'' He laid the palm of his free hand against her cheek. ''And I shall always try to be worthy of your trust in me.''

He leaned forward and pressed his lips to hers. The kiss was pleasant, comforting almost, raising none of the heat Edmund's touch did. Cecilia fought down the wave of longing for another man that surged through her. If she once gave way to those feelings, she would be undone.

Sebastian's lips parted. She jerked away before she

could stop herself. God help her, she was not ready to kiss any man but Edmund. Sebastian's face reddened.

"I beg your pardon—I moved too fast. But you are very sweet, Ceci."

She stood, driven to her feet by forces she could not understand. She went to the window and watched the rain glimmering as it flowed across the tiny panes. She could not tell Sebastian that compelling herself to accept him physically would take time, but she still owed him some kind of explanation.

"I am sorry, Sebastian. You are right—this has moved too quickly for me. Please, be patient with me." She turned to face him.

"Say no more, dearling. We will leave it at this. You do not object to me, nor I to you. Your father and I will put off negotiating for a fortnight or so, to give you time to grow accustomed to the idea."

She had once been infatuated with him, but time had erased her childish passion. Could it return? Could she, given enough time, come to love him with the ardor he deserved? With the devotion she owed him if she became his wife? Her heart contracted. No, she would never give Sebastian the fierce, passionate love she had given Edmund, but Sebastian already had her steady affection. Surely he and her parents knew that.

Cecilia hesitated for a moment, then asked, "Sebastian, will you not wait for Beatrice? My mother would have the tongue out of my head for saying this, but Lord Manners is a very old man. She will be a widow one day, perhaps soon."

His face shuttered. "I will not take George Conyers's leavings."

A spurt of anger shot up, burning away her pity. "She has done less than I have, Sebastian. She is still a maid!"

"It is not the same." His hand, resting on his knee, closed in a fist.

"No, she has sinned less!" She gripped her skirt so she would not strike him.

His mouth thinned to a white line, his eyes glittering like sapphires. "Cecilia, I will not speak of this." His voice was very soft, as if he rode his temper on a short rein.

She wanted to tell him he was a great fool, but the words refused to come. After all, weren't they both fools for love?

"I beg your pardon," she said after a moment. "I did not mean to intrude where I am not wanted."

He sighed and relaxed as if he had let all his anger out on a breath. When he spoke, his voice was weary and sad. "There are some things I cannot speak of, Ceci. You surely understand."

Edmund's mouth against hers. The way his eyes had shone when he looked at her. His weight and warmth in her arms. She looked away, afraid of what her eyes might reveal. Oh, yes, she had secrets, too.

Chapter Seventeen

While Edmund waited for Arthur's response to his request for an audience, he paced restlessly from one end of his rooms at Windsor Castle to the other. Antechamber, main chamber, bedchamber and back. Piers crouched in the doorway between his bedchamber and main chamber, watchful eyes following Edmund as he moved from room to room.

He could not leave lest he miss Arthur's summons. Unable to think of the future, his mind drifted to the past. He missed her, his longing as raw as a toothache. Traveling without her had been strange, as if he had somehow mislaid a great piece of himself. In the beds along the way, he found himself turning toward a warmth that did not exist, awakening to find himself clutching a coverlet. The worst of it was not knowing when he might see her again.

At last, one of the king's ushers arrived, bidding him to the king's privy closet, the small room where Arthur found the little solitude afforded a king. Edmund signed for Piers to remain where he was and left his rooms. He did not want anyone treading on his heels on this walk.

The king was alone, except for one frightened-looking page standing rigidly in a corner. Edmund took a moment to nod at the boy, who merely blinked in response. Someone must have warned him Arthur could not abide fidgeting; the boy looked as stiff as stone.

"You have returned sooner than expected," Arthur said. "You must have discovered something to have hurried back."

"Nothing I thought to find," Edmund said, and pulled the letter from his sleeve where he had stored it for safekeeping. He thrust it at Arthur, eager to be shed of it.

Arthur accepted it, turning it over to examine the seal first. His lips compressed after a moment. Had he seen as quickly as Ceci? He unfolded the letter and read it quickly. A muscle jumped in his cheek. He folded the letter and laid it before him on the table, staring at it for a long, uncomfortable moment before glancing at the page.

"Find the Duke of York. Tell him the king wishes to see him immediately. And alone."

"Yes, Sire," the page said with more firmness than Edmund would have expected. He slipped out the door, shutting it softly behind him.

"Pour yourself some wine," Arthur said. "Harry is unlikely to hurry."

"I cannot drink it. My belly is griping."

"Afraid?" Arthur asked. His mouth was tight at the corners but the expression in his gray eyes was understanding.

"Should I not be?" He did not want to know what had driven Harry to writing that damning letter and he dreaded the outcome of this interview.

"There is nothing to fear. You need not remain if you do not wish to," Arthur said calmly.

That stung him. How could Arthur think so very little of his courage? Had he not proven his loyalty over and over again? "I will remain. I cannot leave."

"As you wish." Arthur picked up a deck of playing cards laid to one side on the table and began idly shuffling it. "A game of Primero?"

The offer jerked a startled laugh out of Edmund. Playing cards was the last thing he expected to do now. "I do not think I can concentrate on my cards, Sire."

Arthur grinned, laughter sparkling in the depths of his eyes. "There is no better time to play cards with you."

Edmund smiled in response. "It might be speedier if I simply hand you my purse."

"But not as much fun." The cards made a soft *chik-chik* noise as Arthur tossed them from hand to hand.

"Very well, I shall play, but I do not think it will be a good game."

Arthur dealt the cards swiftly, the rings on his fingers flashing in the candlelight. Edmund picked up his cards and began sorting them.

"I am glad for another reason that you have returned before time." Arthur stared at his cards with a faint frown creasing his forehead.

"Sire?" He looked down at his cards, suddenly afraid to meet Arthur's eyes.

"Archduke Maximilian's negotiations with the King of Hungary have come to naught and the Archduchess Margrethe is free to wed. England needs to tilt toward the Holy Roman Empire to offset France and Spain, so I have sent Thomas Boleyn to Vienna."

"Boleyn? He is a good negotiator." He hardly knew what he said, dread burning cold in his belly.

"The best man I have. The plan is to make a marriage between you and the archduchess." His dread growing, Edmund glanced up to see Arthur grin with pleasure. "It is about time you were wed, jackanapes."

Edmund forced himself to smile. "I can wait."

Arthur sobered. "You are too old to keep playing games, Edmund."

Edmund forbore to remind his brother that those games had benefited Arthur for the last five years. He cared nothing for that. He did not want to marry Archduchess Margrethe; he wanted to marry Ceci Coleville.

"I have valued all you have done for me," Arthur said, setting down his cards. "Think of it this way. Your marriage is another way to serve me."

Sweet Mary. Of all the things Arthur might have said, why had he chosen that? Edmund swallowed, biting back hot words that would fling Arthur's service into Arthur's face. He had worked too hard for too long to keep his promise to his father to wreck everything now. There was no choice, there never had been. His thought to marry Ceci had been a fool's dream.

The door opened behind him and the page's voice said, "Your Majesty, His Grace, the Duke of York, waits without."

"Bid him join us in a moment," Arthur said. "Stand over there, Edmund." He pointed to a spot where Edmund would be able to see both Arthur and Harry. "And put on your cap." Only those in very great favor were allowed to wear their caps in the king's presence and even then only at the king's bidding. Edmund so rarely saw Arthur manipulating situations that he forgot his brother was capable of such cunning. Yet he was king, and to be king meant having reins with which to manage your fellow men. Fear was one rein, a crude one; Arthur preferred a lighter, more subtle control.

The door swung open and Harry strode into the room, his cloak swirling around him. In one movement, he swept his cap off, its white plume flashing cleanly, and knelt beside the table, facing the king. His expression was a

blend of deference, curiosity and pride. Edmund repressed
the urge to kneel and wished his wariness had not been
mixed with admiration. Whatever else Harry was, he was
a man with style.

Arthur held out the letter. Harry took it, glanced at it,
then said, ''Sire, if we might be private...''

''We are as private as we need to be, Harry. There
should be no secrets in a family. Which is just one of the
reasons this letter distresses me.'' Arthur's tone was mild,
with just an edge of unpleasantness. ''That is your fist, is
it not?''

''If I may explain...'' Harry was pale and the plume on
his hat trembled. Edmund looked away. He despised and
admired, hated and loved his brother; he did not want to
see Harry shame himself.

''In time, you may. First, answer my question. Is this
your hand?''

''Yes, Sire.'' Harry's voice was low, the voice of a child
confessing a sin. Edmund glanced at him, unable to look
away any longer. Harry had bent his head and the plume
no longer trembled, for Harry had crumpled the hat in a
fist so tight that the skin across his knuckles shone white.

''This is quite a letter. I had not known you trafficked
with heretics.'' Still Arthur's tone was gentle, his mildness
more unnerving than rage.

Harry lifted his head. ''I am a true son of the Church.''

''That is not what that letter says.''

''That letter is deceiving.''

''Certainly. But whom does it deceive, eh?'' Arthur
lifted a hand and rubbed his eyes. Pinching the bridge of
his nose, he added, ''Oh, do sit down, Harry. You, too,
Edmund. We will all sit like brothers at this table and we
will work this matter out.''

Edmund sat at Arthur's right, with Harry on his left.

The table was small; they sat so closely he could see the reddish hairs of Harry's stubble glinting like wheat.

"What possessed you to write this letter?" Arthur asked. "Unless, of course, you lie when you say you are a true son of the Church. Are you a heretic, Harry?"

"No! I despise them."

"That is not very Christian of you," Arthur said. "So. When you advised me to rip the heretics out of England, root and stock, you were sincere."

"Yes, Sire."

"Harry, that makes no sense," Edmund said, his nerves strung tight.

Arthur laid a monitory hand on his arm. "Allow me, Edmund."

"Yes, Sire." Edmund laid his hands flat on the table and counseled himself to remain patient.

"Yet Edmund has a point. Your letter makes no sense if you hate heretics. On the other hand, if the letter is true, then you are lying now." Arthur steepled his forefingers and pressed them to his lips. For a long moment he stared at Harry but his eyes were unfocused, as if he read an unseen text. He turned to Edmund. "Tell me, Edmund, what do you make of this?"

Edmund thought for a moment of Cecilia and the long discussion they had had when she found the letter. Everything made him think of her; every thought of her hurt. He cleared his throat.

"I do not believe Harry is a heretic, Sire. I do not think he is curious enough or foolish enough. I think he is what he says he is, a good son of the Church. Once I recognized that, I looked for another reason for a letter such as this. I think the letter is meant to bring someone down, someone like the Bishop of Lincoln or the Duke of Buckingham."

"Stafford? Hmm, interesting theory." Arthur looked at Harry. "Well, which is it? Lincoln or Buckingham?"

"Neither. Edmund is a lackwit to suggest anything of the kind," Harry said gruffly. "I meant it when I said heretics must be destroyed. I am trying to draw them into the open."

"By pretending to be one of them?" Arthur laughed softly. "What foolishness is this? Life is not one of your court masques, Harry. You cannot pretend to be something you are not in order to catch my enemies."

"Why can I not?" Harry demanded, his face turning dark red as he leaned toward Arthur. "Edmund does."

"It is not the same thing!" Edmund cried. "For one thing, I do nothing without the king's knowledge and approval. I do not take it into my head—"

"Edmund, be still." Arthur raised his hand. Edmund closed his mouth, annoyed that he had let his tongue run away with him. "Hotheaded as he is, he does have a point, Harry. Why could you not come to me with this?"

"How can you ask that? You would pat my head and tell me that life was not a court masque, as if I did not know." Arthur flushed. Edmund looked down at his hands, ashamed of himself. It had never occurred to him that Harry knew how they laughed at his love of playacting. Harry clenched his fists and then laid his hands flat on the tabletop. "I wanted to show you that Edmund is not the only one who can be of value to you."

How could Harry be jealous of him? For as long as Edmund could remember, Harry had been the golden one, admired for his endless talents, his charm and his beauty. Even Arthur, with his aura of royal dignity, was sometimes cast into the shade by Harry's splendor.

"Harry, never think Edmund is the only brother whom I value. He has special gifts but he has them because he was wayward and disobedient as a child. You have gifts, too, gifts befitting a king's son.''

''You trust Edmund more than you trust me,'' Harry said, his voice low as if he thought barely audible was the same thing as barely true.

''I do not, Harry. Though, after this adventure of yours, I ought not trust you at all.'' Arthur sighed. ''Remind me. Why did you write this letter?''

''I wanted to bring you the names of heretics, so you could root them out, all of them. If you sent the Bishop of Lincoln after them, some would slip through the net.'' Harry looked at Arthur as if expecting him to change his first negative reaction to Harry's behavior.

''I see.'' Arthur traced the pattern brocaded into the tablecloth with his forefinger. ''The kind offers of my Spanish in-laws notwithstanding, we have no Inquisition in England and I should prefer to keep it that way. I thank you for your good offices, but never do anything like this again.'' Harry took a deep breath and opened his mouth. Arthur looked up. Harry shut his mouth again, quelled by whatever he saw in Arthur's eyes. ''However, I am not fool enough to throw away something of value simply because I am annoyed by the way it was obtained. I direct you to reveal all you know about these heretics to the Bishop of Lincoln and I also direct you to explain your methods of obtaining this information. Perhaps he can make use of what you have learned.'' He stood and, with a gesture, bade Harry rise, also. ''You fool, if you become Edmund, who will be my brother Harry?'' he asked roughly, stepping around the table and pulling Harry into a back-thumping embrace.

''Edmund?'' Harry joked. Arthur grinned and released him.

''I think not. A Harry who can neither sing nor tilt nor

give me a good fight at the archery butts is no Harry at all.''

Edmund smiled a little, willing to let his inadequacies be used to smooth the moment over. He was still surprised at Harry's jealousy.

Arthur sobered. "I want your word, Harry. No more letters like this.''

"On my honor, Sire, no more.''

"Good," Arthur said. He pulled Harry's head down and kissed his cheek, then struck a playful blow to Harry's strong arm. "Go now, dear brother. Make a song for me. You have not lightened my heart with your music in some time now.''

"As you will, Sire," Harry said, with a bow more flourishing than the one he had offered on entering.

When the door closed after Harry's departure, the king picked up the cards again.

"Play with me, Edmund.''

Edmund smiled ruefully. "You have won all my money, Sire.''

"Then we will play for chestnuts.''

Edmund grinned. When he had been a small boy, short of spending money, Arthur had let him wager common items such as chestnuts, buttons, goose quills, lute strings—all the things Edmund had access to in lieu of money. He had forgotten those stakes until now.

"Chestnuts are as yet unripe, Sire, but if you will accept my promise of payment, I shall make good on my debt.''

"And if Dame Fortune smiles on you, it may be you will win back what you have lost.''

Arthur shuffled the cards, dealing them slowly as if he were weary. Edmund accepted his cards and shot a quick glance at his brother's face. It was expressionless, Arthur gone into hiding behind his royal mask. Edmund looked away. He had hated it as a child when Arthur looked like that; it made him feel adrift and alone. *Is that why you spent your time with men not of your class and station?* The thought came out of nowhere. He rearranged the cards in his hands, unwilling to search for an answer.

"Do you think Harry will obey you?" Edmund asked when he had his cards settled.

"I will watch him to be sure he does," Arthur replied.

Edmund's skin crawled into gooseflesh at Arthur's flat tone. He knew Arthur loved Harry, just as he knew Arthur loved him. Yet Arthur's love had nothing of trust in it. Nor had their father's. Was this what it meant to be a king?

"Thank God and all the saints I need never worry about you." Arthur laid his cards facedown on the table. "Whatever else may fail me in the world, I know I may trust you."

"That need not be said. I shall never betray you," Edmund replied, answering the question in Arthur's tone instead of the certainty in his words. *Ceci.* He clenched his jaw, surprised by the realization he had not quite given up. He still thought to marry Cecilia, despite knowing it was impossible: was that not a betrayal? How could he assure his brother he was worthy of trust and still dream of marrying as he willed?

"No, it needs to be said. I trust two people in this world, Edmund. You and my wife. You cannot imagine what a gift it is to me to know that I can rely on you."

He ought to be flattered by Arthur's trust. Instead, in his mind's eye he saw his prison door swinging shut. "I love you as my king and my brother," he said stiffly, the words sticking in his throat. "I will never do anything to hurt you."

Arthur's smile should have been all the reward he needed but he could only think of what he had lost. He had once again pledged himself to Arthur's service, making an unspoken promise to sacrifice everything to the king's needs. How easy that promise had been to make when he was a child of nine, half in love with the romance of dying for the king. Angry grief rose like a flood tide. He schooled his features into calm when all he wanted to do was smash something, nearly hating his brothers and his birth for what they cost him.

Cecilia slipped away from him as his dreams dissolved, leaving desolation behind. He had kept his word, he had done what honor demanded.

And he felt like a hollow man.

Chapter Eighteen

Sebastian took Cecilia's hand, tucked it into the crook of his elbow and began strolling with her along the pleached alley stretching along the far wall of the garden. Hazy sunshine sparkled on the windows and prodded the herbs and flowers to release their scents into the air. Bees glided past them, humming drowsily. She wished the peace of the scene could find its way into her heart.

Sebastian said, "I did not know you dislike Lord Manners so much."

Cecilia looked up at him, noting the faint shadows under his eyes, the grim set to the corners of his mouth. She sighed. He was no better pleased than she that Beatrice and her husband were staying at Coleville House. "Is it so obvious? If we marry, promise me he will not visit us at Benbury."

His mouth twitched in an expression that was half a smile and half a grimace. "I should prefer it if neither of them came to us."

Raucous laughter rippled across the water. Out on the river, the Duke of Somerset's pleasure barge skimmed by, loaded with merry, drunken gentlemen. Involuntarily, Cecilia searched for Edmund in their midst. Unable to resist

listening to the serving maids' gossip, she had heard that
he had left the Court at Windsor and was living riotously
in London. She could not find him on the barge. The distance was too great, the barge too crowded. She thought
of lying in his arms in Aylesbury, so close she could see
the night-dark flecks in his eyes. *You will never see him
so closely ever again.* For Sebastian's sake she should not
regret the thought as much as she did. The barge followed
the bend in the river and sailed out of sight.

She looked up at Sebastian. "If I marry you, will you
permit me to retire from Court?"

"If it will speed my suit, I shall insist on it." His gaze
returned to her from where it had followed the pleasure
barge's journey upriver. There was pity in his eyes, as if
he, too, had noticed Edmund's merriment and drawn the
same conclusion as she: Edmund did not miss her the way
she missed him. Her mouth twisted. Sebastian knew too
much, saw too much. Marriage to him might be more uncomfortable than she had imagined. They retraced their
steps toward the far side of the garden.

"Lady Cecilia!"

She turned, releasing Sebastian, and lifted her hand to
her brow, shading her eyes against the July glare. A servitor stood just inside the garden gate, waving his arm. At
her nod of permission, he ran forward until he was close
enough to be heard without shouting. "Lady Cecilia, Lady
Manners bids you come. Lord Manners is fallen sick."

Cecilia saw Manners was dead as soon as she and Sebastian entered the hall. Beatrice sat on the hearth with her
husband's head in her lap, ashes smeared across his livid
cheek. Beatrice's hands hung limp at her sides as if she
could not bring herself to touch her husband. Cecilia knelt

beside them and touched her hand to Manners's throat, without expecting a pulse.

"He is dead, Beatrice."

Beatrice looked at her with eyes as blank as a cloudless summer sky. She nodded slowly. Cecilia turned to the servitor who had called her.

"Peter, send Mistress Emma to me. We will need some stout men and a door to bring Lord Manners to his chamber. And we will need Father Francis to shrive him, too. He must be prepared. And a coffin. We will need a coffin built." She felt no sorrow, only a distant relief. He had been old, older than anyone she knew, and she had not liked him. What mattered now was Beatrice and making sure all was done as it should be. With their mother at Court and Beatrice saying and doing nothing, Cecilia must step into the breach.

Her parents. They would have to come back to Coleville House. Cecilia turned to Sebastian. "I need your help."

"I will do anything you ask."

"Go to Court and find my parents. Tell them what has happened. And ask them to come home."

He nodded. "I shall return as soon as I have found them."

"Bless you, Sebastian." She saw him look briefly at Beatrice, his eyes unreadable, his expression closed. He bowed in her direction and then left. She sighed, their enmity chafing her.

Servitors appeared bearing a hurdle, Mistress Emma bustling behind them. They laid the hurdle on the floor beside Beatrice and stretched out their hands to lift Manners onto it. Beatrice's hands came up and clutched his shoulders; she looked wildly at Cecilia.

"No."

"Beatrice—" Cecilia's voice broke off, words deserting her.

Mistress Emma knelt behind Beatrice and gripped her shoulders. "Child, let him go. We must attend to him properly and to do it you must let him go."

"I cannot. I am his wife. I cannot." Tears filled her eyes and her fingers twisted in the fur of his long gown. Her behavior, so like that of a heartbroken widow, baffled Cecilia. What lived in her sister's heart that she could be so unnerved by the death of her unloved husband?

Patiently, Mistress Emma pried Beatrice's fingers loose and enfolded her in her arms. Beatrice slumped against her, crying openly now. Mistress Emma nodded sharply at the servitors. Moving forward, they knelt and shifted Manners onto the hurdle.

"Take him to his bedchamber. I shall be along presently," Mistress Emma said.

"And I shall, too," Cecilia said. Mistress Emma should not be left to shoulder the task alone, but Beatrice was in no state to help lay out the body.

Speaking in a low tone, Mistress Emma said, "I can manage on my own. Someone will need to stay with your sister."

"I have sent for my lady mother."

Mistress Emma shook her head. "She will be of more help to me than to Beatrice. She does not have the patience to console your sister." She tightened her hold on Beatrice, rocking on her haunches. "Hush, my love, hush. My little lamb, hush," she crooned. "Come with Emma, come lie down and weep in peace, there's a good girl." Slowly and awkwardly, she stood, drawing Beatrice to her feet as she did so. "Help me, Cecilia. She will not walk on her own."

They supported Beatrice up the stairs to the solar, depositing her in the earl's big chair. "She needs hot wine.

I will send a boy up.'' Mistress Emma left the room, closing the door behind her. The bar rattled in its socket.

Beatrice's weeping slowed to weary hiccups. Cecilia, almost brought to tears herself by Beatrice's distress, knelt before her sister and took her hands. They were cold, the fingertips icy.

''Why do I weep so when I am glad he is gone?'' Beatrice whispered, her voice roughened and clogged by her weeping.

''I do not know, Bea,'' Cecilia replied, John's old nickname slipping out. She rubbed Beatrice's hands, still chilly, between her own.

Beatrice turned her head where it rested against the back of the chair and looked at Cecilia curiously. ''Are you sad?''

''No. I hated him.'' Beatrice needed the truth now, she needed to hear that she was not the only one relieved by Manners's death.

''I cannot remember why I married him.'' Beatrice looked away, her gaze wandering the solar, pausing to examine its well-known features as if she had never seen them before. ''It seems like such a long time ago.''

''To me, as well.''

They sat in silence for a moment. Beatrice's hands were warmer, resting in Cecilia's.

''Where is he?'' Beatrice asked suddenly, turning her head to look at Cecilia again.

''In the chamber you shared with him.''

Beatrice slipped her hands free and braced them on the chair arms. ''I should go to him.''

Cecilia remained on her knees in front of the chair, blocking Beatrice's exit. ''Do you want to do it?''

''No, but that is of no—''

"Leave it to Mistress Emma. Do not distress yourself more than is needful."

Tears welling up in her eyes, Beatrice leaned forward and rested her forehead on Cecilia's shoulder. "I am glad he is dead, Ceci. And I hate myself for it." She shook with renewed sobs.

Helplessly, Cecilia put her arms around her sister, holding her tightly. She wished she had words of comfort to offer, but there were none. "Hush," she said. "Hush."

Cecilia slipped into the chapel two days after Manners had died and found Beatrice kneeling at the foot of the black-draped bier, candlelight glittering on her jet ornaments, shining on the beads laced through her fingers, gleaming on her pearly skin. The beauty of the scene struck her so forcefully that she checked in midstride. Recovering herself, she walked forward and sank to her knees beside her sister.

They prayed in silence for a while, Cecilia wrestling with her longing for Edmund as she prayed. If she could feel his arms around her for a moment, she could bear her burdens. She did not care what he did while he was away from her, if only he could be with her again.

Stop it. You knew from the beginning how it would be.

Beatrice sighed and lifted her head, rolling it on her shoulders as if to ease tightness in her neck. Cecilia reached out and squeezed her wrist, to offer quiet comfort.

"Sit with me in the back. If I cannot talk to someone, I think I shall run mad," Beatrice whispered.

Cecilia crossed herself and shot a quick look at Manners, as unwanted in death as he had been in life.

Beatrice sat on a bench pushed against the back wall of the chapel and looped her rosary through the gold and pearl chain circling her waist. Folding her hands in her lap, she sighed and said, "I cannot think, Ceci. What is to become of me now?"

"Remarry. When Sir George Conyers returns from Lincoln, you will be free to be with him." Conyers was not an improvement as brother-in-law over Thomas Manners, but if he gave Beatrice some pleasure, Cecilia thought she could bear with him. After everything that had happened, she wanted her sister to know some happiness.

"He is gone to Lincoln? I had not known." Beatrice looked up at the rafters of the ceiling, her mouth pressed thin. "I refused to see him after you found us. I thought if you could discover us so easily, then so could Thomas." Her mouth quirked in a smile full of bitterness. "Thomas did suspect me of betrayal—once I had turned chaste. He accused me of cuckolding him." She laughed without humor. "He said I lay with Sebastian."

"Sebastian!" She could think of nothing else to say.

"A man who would not touch me if I came to him naked."

"No, that is not true. Sebastian—"

Beatrice turned to face Cecilia, her eyes chilly. "Do not tell me Sebastian loves me. He does not. If he loved me, he would have—" She bit her words off short.

"He would have what?" Cecilia demanded.

"It does not matter now. It is too late. He hates me."

"Sebastian can be a great fool sometimes, Beatrice, you know that as well as I. He is angry that—" Cecilia hesitated, searching for a word that was not cruel, and then decided to speak bluntly. Maybe what Beatrice needed was not kindness but the hard slap of truth. "—that you had so little care for your honor or yourself. As I was. I was afraid for you, Beatrice. Do you love Conyers so much that you were willing to die for him?"

"Love him? Oh, Ceci, I never loved him."

"But—"

"Thomas told me he was incapable because I disgusted him. No man had ever said anything like that to me before and I did not know how to defend myself against it except by finding a man I did not disgust. That is why I lay with Conyers, to see if I could rouse a man to passion." Cecilia stared at her, her head whirling. She could not comprehend lying with a man in cold blood, to prove one's desirability. To know a man in such intimacy without the grace of love....

Unwanted, memory cascaded over her: Edmund's skin moving like silk against hers, the tenderness of his mouth and hands as they caressed her. Pain clenched her, the same hungry pain as always. She missed him, she missed him so much she did not know how she was going to survive his loss. *Will this never ease?*

Beatrice eyed her curiously. Her feelings must be showing on her face, feelings too intense to be in response to Beatrice's revelation though Beatrice had no way to know that. "Ceci, what I have done is bad, but not so bad as that."

Cecilia rose and walked away from her sister. She stopped by the chapel door and pressed her forehead against the wall, relishing the scrape of the rough stone against her skin. She heard the bench creak and then the rustle of cloth. She braced herself without knowing why. Beatrice's arms went around her. "Ceci, what is it? Tell me. This is not about me and George Conyers. Something else ails you."

Cecilia's throat was sore; it hurt to push words out. "Did you know that our father is negotiating my marriage contract?" She pulled free of Beatrice's embrace; she could not discuss this with her sister's arms around her. She went to the prie-dieu standing against the far wall.

"No. Ceci! To whom?"

Cecilia rubbed her thumb on the lamb carved into the side of the prie-dieu. "Sebastian."

"Sebastian Benbury? You are to marry Sebastian Benbury?"

Cecilia lifted her head to look at her sister. "Is that such a surprise?"

"Yes."

"Why? Am I not fit to take what you discard?" Cecilia said fiercely.

Pink filled Beatrice's pale cheeks. "That is not what I meant. I know you and Sebastian are great friends, better friends than he and I ever were, so I expect you will suit very well. I had never thought of it."

"You thought that if he married one of us, it would be you." She did not want Sebastian, she wanted Edmund. What did it matter what she wanted? She had allowed herself to be trapped. She wrapped her arms around her waist and leaned against the wall.

"Who among us did not?" Beatrice's mouth twisted. "But when I told Sebastian that Thomas intended to approach our father, he wished me happy. If he had spoken one word of protest, I should have gone to our father and asked him to refuse Thomas. But he did not. So I accepted Thomas." Beatrice sighed. "And now he thinks I am a whore."

"How did he find out about Conyers? I heard no whisper of it, so it is not common knowledge. And I kept my ears pricked for it." Let them talk of this, hard as it was; anything was easier than thinking of Edmund.

"To taunt me?" Beatrice's expression was wary.

"No! To warn you, that you might save yourself."

Beatrice blushed again, the same faint wash of pink as before. Then it deepened, so that her face and neck were red. "I told Sebastian."

Chapter Nineteen

"**Y**ou? Why? What madness possessed you?"

Beatrice turned so that Cecilia could only see her profile. The corner of her mouth lifted in disbelieving smile. "I lost my temper. He found me in a corner of the garden alone with George and took it upon himself to lecture me on what I might do to my reputation. He was—his manner was unendurable to me. I would barely tolerate such treatment from Thomas, who had the right to do much worse. So we quarreled and in the course of our fight I said something that gave Sebastian the idea that George was my lover. I cannot even remember what it was. I was so angry that I remember nothing. When Sebastian asked me if I was George's leman, I said yes."

"Oh, Beatrice, what if he had told Thomas?"

"I was too angry at his presumption to care."

Emotions jostled for expression in Cecilia's heart, so many she could hardly tell what she felt. Beatrice had always had the capacity for fierce, consuming anger, but the conflagration was only touched off by matters close to her heart. Why had Sebastian's behavior hurt her so? There was more to this than Beatrice had told. It is none of your affair, she thought.

But it is your affair, another voice said, *if Sebastian is to be your husband.*

"Beatrice, why did you think Sebastian would protest your betrothal to Thomas?"

"We always said when we were children that we would marry," Beatrice replied, walking to the bench. She looked over her shoulder. "Plainly he never meant it."

"But it might be binding."

Beatrice sat back down on the bench. "We were children, too young to make contracts on our own."

Cecilia went to sit beside her. "Did you ever tell anyone?"

"About a child's game? No. If Sebastian wanted no part of me, then why should I mention my folly?"

"He wanted you." Cecilia took Beatrice's hand. If only she could help her sister see past the barrier of her hurt, she might bring them together. *Sebastian will never abandon you.* But he might, if he were offered Beatrice.

Beatrice slipped her hand free. "He may like to think so, but if he had felt as much for me as he said, he would have claimed me."

"Why should he have when you argued *for* your betrothal to Thomas?"

"I did not speak in favor of my betrothal until it was clear Sebastian would not claim me. I wanted Sebastian, Ceci. I always thought I would marry him, but he had done nothing to win me. So I told him about Thomas in the hope it would spur him into speaking. And when it did not, I had no choice but to marry Thomas. I could not let Sebastian think I pined for him."

"Why not?" Cecilia said, irritated by the vanity and pride that had driven Beatrice into making such a mess of her life. "You have let him pine for you for all the world to see for years. Could you not set aside your pride for one hour to show him your heart?''

''Not then, I could not.''

''Then claim him now, Beatrice. Go to him and tell him all that you have told me!''

''He will spurn me,'' Beatrice said quietly. ''I tell you, he hates me. He will not want George Conyers's leavings.''

''You are not Conyers's leavings, Beatrice. Go to Sebastian. Tell him you are still a maid. Tell him everything you have told me. He loves you, Beatrice.''

''No, Ceci, he does not.'' She smiled brightly. ''Besides, you will make him happier than I ever could.''

How can I when I hate the very thought of marrying him? Cecilia shot to her feet and went to kneel by the bier again. There was a storm brewing in her breast, one that would tear her open when it burst free. She lifted shaking hands to her mouth. ''I cannot do it,'' she whispered. ''I cannot.'' She crouched in a ball, the wooden busk in her stays stabbing her with a welcome pain.

Vaguely, she heard the scuffle of footsteps on the flagstones and then Beatrice knelt beside her, her arms embracing Cecilia's shoulders. ''Ceci, what is it? Tell me! Are you ill? What is it?''

Cecilia fought the storm back down into her heart. She would not break down, she would not let her emotions rule her. She had made the decision to marry Sebastian because he was a good choice. Only a fool would fail to recognize that. Swallowing and blinking her itchy eyes, she straightened.

''It is nothing,'' she said and tried to smile. ''I am well.''

''You are as green as glass,'' Beatrice said, frowning.

Cecilia gripped her sister's hand. ''Let us pray for poor

Thomas Manners. Neither of us loved him, but we can pray for him. Please.''

Beatrice stared at her for a long moment, hesitation plain in every line of her face. Cecilia returned look for look, willing Beatrice to let it go. Finally her sister nodded and freed her gleaming beads from her belt.

A week later, she and Beatrice sat together in the solar, pretending to be busy. Cecilia, sitting on a bench against the whitewashed wall, had quit stringing her lute when she began to grow drowsy; she still held the instrument in her lap but she could not compel herself to finish. She felt as if she waited for something, but for what? Lord Manners's eldest son had claimed his father four days ago, taking him home to be buried; it could not be that. Did she expect some signal to return to Court? She did not think she would ever go back, Sebastian or no. Beatrice sat at the accounting table with a breviary open before her, lazily turning the pages. Since she did not like to read, Cecilia suspected she only examined the pictures.

One day, she thought. That is all it takes to change a life. Once his son had taken Thomas's body away, it was as if Thomas had never been a part of their lives. She slid a glance at Beatrice, intently examining something on a page brilliant with illumination. Did her sister feel the same way? Did she, too, feel as if Thomas might never have been?

No, that was not possible, not after what Thomas had done to her.

The solar door opened and a manservant slid into the room. He bowed and said, ''My ladies, there is a gentleman below claiming to be Lord John—''

''John?'' Beatrice asked, sitting up. ''What does he look like, Peter?''

Sunshine flooded Cecilia's heart, casting out the darkness. She dropped the lute on the bench and stood. "Never mind that, Beatrice. It is John, I know it is."

Without waiting for Beatrice, Cecilia rushed from the room. John was home far earlier than she had hoped but that did not mean she could wait another moment to see him. She flew down the stairs.

In the hall, a man and a woman stood beside the elaborate screen that masked the outside door from the hall. One swift glance absorbed details, as if time had stopped and she could look to her heart's content. Both man and woman were dressed with a slope-shouldered elegance unlike anything Cecilia had ever seen. The man was dark, like John, but for a moment, he was a stranger to her. She had a quick impression of an impatient temper kept on an uncertain tether, as if he might erupt into scornful irritation at any moment. This was not a man who suffered fools gladly and while that was very like her memory of John, the arrogant tilt of the stranger's head was not. Cecilia took a step toward them, wondering if perhaps she had been mistaken.

He turned his head from examining at the hammer-beam ceiling and looked at her. His face lit in a smile, arrogance and irritability dropping away and her own John coming home. At last, at long last. Her heart broke open into aching emotion. Pain or joy, she could not tell which.

He opened his arms and she ran into them. "John! Oh, John!"

She clung to him, solid and warm under his foreign finery. His arms crushed the breath from her body and his voice in her ear, deeper than she remembered, murmured her name. If he had not held her until her ribs hurt, she would not have believed he was real. For a long moment, not nearly long enough, they clung together. Then he set her down and touched her cheek, holding up a finger she was surprised to see was damp. She had not felt the tears. "You were weeping the last time I saw you. Have you never stopped?"

It was so like John to tease at this kind of moment that a watery laugh was shaken out of her. "I am happy."

"I generally laugh for happiness, poppet. Tears I save for grief." The old endearment, so long unheard, started her tears afresh. The laughter in his face dissolved, replaced by something like pain. "I have missed you." He looked past her and the laughter returned. "Beatrice, my love, still as beautiful as ever, I see." Cecilia turned so he could move forward, but she clutched the back of his gown, half afraid that if she let go, he would disappear again. Beatrice stepped into John's arms and began sobbing. Tears dropped on Cecilia's breast and trickled down her breastbone. The laughter left John's face, driven away by tenderness. His arms went around his sister, one hand rubbing her back. "Hush, Bea, hush. You will spoil your face with tears."

"I do not care!" Beatrice lifted her face and seized the collar of his short gown. "You have come home and that is more to me than my face shall ever be." Cecilia released his doublet and wiped her tear-wet face on her linen cuff, her full heart overflowing. It only wanted Sebastian to make John's homecoming complete.

John's eyes narrowed thoughtfully. "You are not the Beatrice I left behind."

Beatrice flushed. Cecilia glanced at her sister, noting the circles under her eyes and the faint marks of unhappiness bracketing her mouth. How was it that suffering had made her more beautiful?

"No, I am not." She let him go and folded her hands on her waist, lifting her chin. "Nor you the John who left.

Your manners, for one thing, have gotten worse. Who have you brought with you?''

''You sound exactly like our mother.'' John turned to his companion and held out his hand to her, his face softening in an expression Cecilia had never seen before. ''Lucia.'' The woman came forward.

She was tall, her cloud of silver-gilt hair held back by a fillet, her green eyes wary. She looked at Beatrice, then Cecilia and finally, John. He drew her close, his fingertips caressing her shoulders in a gesture both loving and possessive.

''This is Lucia Coleville. My wife.'' A wife? John was married? The sunshine in her heart dimmed, darkened by something akin to fear. She bit her lip to stop her cry of protest. How could she bear having John restored to her and then snatched away in nearly the same moment?

He murmured something to Lucia in a language Cecilia could not understand. She heard her name and Beatrice's; plainly John was performing the same office for his wife that he had for his sisters. Lucia glanced up at him and replied. When she turned back to face Beatrice and Cecilia, there was such a look of longing and fear in her eyes that Cecilia felt her jealousy begin to dissolve. Lucia frowned and her lips moved briefly before she said, in a halting voice, ''I am glad to meet you both.'' The way she spoke English was full of a strange music, sweet to the ear.

Before she had the chance to begin questioning John—why had he come home? why now?—the butler entered the hall, bearing a tray with a ewer and cups on it. He set the tray on the table against the wall and bowed himself out. John, moving with as much assurance as if he had never left, went to the table and poured himself a cup of wine. Lifting the cup to his nose, he took an appreciative sniff. ''Good English canary. I have missed this.'' He drank, his eyes glittering over the rim of the pewter cup. After setting his cup down, he replenished it and then poured wine into three more cups. "Why are you in black, Bea?"

"My husband died a fortnight ago. God rest his soul." She crossed herself.

John's hand shook and wine splattered on the floor. He set the ewer down and wiped his damp fingers on his travel-stained gown. "Then Sebastian Benbury is dead."

"I am alive as anyone in this room," Sebastian said, entering the hall from behind the entry screen. His gaze flicked over all of them, lingering on Beatrice instead of John and Lucia. "Who says I am dead?"

"John does," Cecilia said. She ought to bring him a cup of wine, see to his needs like a good wife, but not now. Once she was used to John being home, once the contracts were signed, then she would act as Sebastian's wife. Not before.

You are unfair, the voice of her conscience said.

I do not care. I want Edmund and I do not care for anything but that.

"John!" Sebastian rushed forward and embraced John, laughing and pounding John's back. "Thank God! Thank God for it!"

John's expression, anything but joyous, caught Cecilia's eye. His mouth was set in a grim line and the laughter had faded from his eyes. She frowned, a worm of disquiet wriggling through the rest of her emotions.

"You do not seem happy to see me, my friend. What ails you?" Sebastian said, holding John from him at arm's length. Half his mouth still smiled, while his eyebrows had lifted in a look of inquiry. Every fleeting thought marked its passage on his mobile face.

"I am glad, more glad than you can know, to see you,"

John said. He reached up and gripped Sebastian's wrists as if to brace both of them.

Cecilia's uneasiness deepened, driving every other emotion before it.

"You look it," Sebastian mocked, pulling free. "It cannot be grief for poor Thomas Manners that makes you look so black. You never knew the man. Come, tell me, tell us all. Why the long face?" Across the hall, she could see his worry. He had hardly noticed Lucia, standing quietly near the fireplace and watching them with narrowed, wary eyes.

"Because Bea says she is the widow of a man she cannot have married." John rubbed his forehead as if it pained him. Cecilia's heart began to pound against her ribs. That her heart knew something she did not frightened her still more. What ailed John? Why had this joyous occasion turned grim? She did not want to know, but she did not dare leave.

"I witnessed their marriage and Ceci attended her," Sebastian said, an edge to his voice. "Do you tell us we were not there, that it was all a dream?"

John met his eyes. "No. I am sure there was a wedding. I am telling you that the marriage was invalid."

Cecilia remembered what Beatrice had said about childhood promises she and Sebastian had made. Had John witnessed them? A monstrous notion rose up in the back of her mind; she refused to face it.

"Invalid? On what grounds?"

"That she was promised to another man," John said. "Promised in a binding betrothal."

"Another man?" Sebastian asked coldly. "Are you saying she has known yet *another* man?"

Cecilia's hands came together in a tight grip. *No, no, no.*

"Another man? What are you babbling about?" John said. He shook his head. "She is betrothed to you, Sebastian."

Chapter Twenty

Cecilia's head reeled.

"Are you mad?" Beatrice cried. "We are no more betrothed than…than— We are not betrothed. Do you think I could make such a mistake?"

Sweet Mary…

"Or I?" Sebastian demanded. "This is not funny, John."

…can this be true?

"It is not jest, Sebastian, and I do not think it funny. Do you not remember that Twelfth Night when you and your family joined us at Wednesfield? I filched a ewer of mead and the three of us drank it in the old tower. You and Beatrice promised to marry when you were grown and then we all laughed and drank some more."

I should not pray for this.

"Oh, blessed Virgin," Beatrice said, closing her eyes.

But, Jesú, I wish it were true.

"I do not re—" Sebastian's brows drew together briefly then relaxed as his mouth tightened. "Aye, now I do! What foolishness is this? We made no promises that bound."

"That is not what I remember, Sebastian. Think. Think

what you said, the words you used. The promises you made bind you.''

"You are no churchman. How can you know for certain?'' Beatrice demanded, her face white.

Was she free? Cecilia did not dare believe it; she could not bring herself to the sticking point again.

"Do you not remember?'' John asked. "You promised to have Sebastian as your husband and he promised to have you as his wife. Both of you promised without conditions.'' He sighed. "I have lived among churchmen for the last three years, Bea. Canon law fills the air in Rome. A man who has ears cannot help learning a little.''

His voice harsh as a rook's, Sebastian said, "We did not lie together. It cannot be binding.''

"It does not matter in this case. If you never lie with her, she will still be your wife before God.'' In some distant part of her mind, Cecilia noticed his gentleness. When had he learned to set vehemence aside?

"I cannot believe this,'' Beatrice said, her face blank and white, and went to sit on one of the benches pushed against the wall.

"I am betrothed to Cecilia,'' Sebastian said. He stared at John, refusing to look at anyone else.

"You cannot be,'' John said.

At the same moment Cecilia said, "Do not lie, Sebastian. It will only confuse matters.''

"We can pretend it never happened,'' Sebastian said. "If no one knows—''

I will not lie for you, Sebastian. I cannot.

"You will know, Sebastian. And God will know. Can you take another woman to wife, knowing you make a concubine of her? And if you do not marry, who will your heirs be?''

Beatrice spoke from where she sat near the fireplace.

"How do I get out of this?" Her voice was flat, as flat as it had been when Cecilia discovered her with Conyers. The only thing that would save her from marriage to Sebastian was if Beatrice married him.... And Beatrice had been right: Sebastian hated her.

Sebastian walked to the opposite side of the room, his hands balled into fists. He pressed his forehead against the wall. A voice in Cecilia's head said, *You should go to him.* She did not move.

"Ceci, why do they fight this? What has happened in while I have been away?" John asked.

With a start, Cecilia realized that when John had left all those years ago, there had been no hurt rift between Sebastian and Beatrice. How turbulent his homecoming was turning out to be; had so much time gone by he could never truly come home?

"I do not know, John." Here was not the place and now was not the time to tell the tale of their quarrel. And in truth, she did not know in her heart why they fought as they did. She could only accept that they did. She finished with the truth. "I do not now nor have I ever understood why they are at odds."

"It avails you nothing to do this!" Beatrice cried. "You will do most good by telling me how I may escape this!"

"There is no way. You are married to Sebastian." John's voice was low, as if he was weary of their squabbling.

"If I deny it? What then, O brother?" Beatrice snapped.

John stared at her, the old, hard, black-eyed look. "Sebastian can sue you to live with him."

"And how many witnesses will he need? Is one enough? And will you oppose me in this, my brother?" Her voice was as sharp with anger as Cecilia had ever heard it, but underneath the anger was a dragging note, as if hopelessness lapped at the edges of her temper.

"It takes two witnesses to make a case," John replied. "But if you marry another man, you will be committing bigamy and your children will be bastards."

"I do not intend to marry again. Once was enough to last me a lifetime."

"Bea, you know you are married," Cecilia said.

"There are no witnesses!"

"I will be a witness to your admission of the promise," Cecilia said steadily. "With John, that is two witnesses."

Even if she saves you from marriage to Sebastian, you will still not have Edmund, a vile voice whispered.

I cannot fight to save my betrothal. I will not. She must not think of what would become of her after this; that was the road to madness.

Beatrice gasped. "A pox on you!"

Sebastian turned and crossed the hall again, joining them by the hearth once more. He faced Beatrice and spoke in a flat voice. "I cannot marry another woman, knowing the marriage is a lie. I cannot let her risk her life to bear me a son, knowing that son is a bastard. You are my wife, as much as I wish it otherwise, Beatrice, and if you have a particle of honor left, you will come live with me as my wife."

"I will not," Beatrice said, glaring at him. "I will not marry a man who scorns me as you do."

"I do not desire to marry a woman so stupid with pride she will ruin herself rather than yield, but unfortunately, I am betrothed to one and have no choice. In law, Beatrice, you are already my wife and as such you owe me obedience," Sebastian said, staring her down.

"How dare you!"

"Beatrice, be sensible. You cannot win, not if Ceci and

I both bear witness against you. Nor can you wish to spend the rest of your life in limbo, neither wife nor widow nor maid,'' John said. He went to sit beside her on the bench, taking her hand in his. ''I do not know what has happened to estrange you from Sebastian nor do I understand why the pair of you are behaving as if we were all back in the nursery, but surely neither of you is foolish enough to ruin your lives.''

Beatrice stared at John for a long moment, her free hand clutching the front of the bench. ''This means I am trapped.''

''We both are,'' Sebastian said, still in that hard voice.

Cecilia shivered, afraid for both of them, beginning a marriage under the weight of Beatrice's pride and Sebastian's anger. *If I took back my word to witness against them...* A woman who had thrown away her maidenhead ought not to balk at a few lies. She could save Beatrice and Sebastian a great deal of heartache. *I will speak, I will tell them what I shall do.*

But she had not thrown away her maidenhead. She had given it to the only man she would ever love, the only man who would ever touch her. And it had been a good gift. Nothing and no one would ever make her see it otherwise.

''Aye, you are,'' John said, ''but only so long as you both see it so.''

Beatrice stood and pressed her hand to her temple. ''My head aches. I cannot listen to another moment of this. You will please excuse me.'' She left the hall without a backward glance, her back stiff.

Sebastian watched her go, his hands still knotted. Then he turned on John, glaring at him with flame-blue eyes. ''Why did you come back now? Why could you not stay in Rome?''

''I wanted to come home.'' John's voice was soft, the

reproach in his words all the more harsh for his gentleness. He inclined his head toward Lucia. "I wanted to bring my wife home."

Sebastian turned red, the flame dying in his eyes.

John went on, his voice hardening, "I will not apologize for this, Sebastian. I had no way to know you and Beatrice were not married and raising a handful of yellow-headed babies."

"I know, I know. Forgive me, I beg of you." He sighed and put his cap on. "What an accursed garboil this is. I must find your father and explain what has befallen." His mouth curving downward in a dispirited arc, he crossed the hall to where Cecilia stood. He stroked her cheek with the backs of his fingers. "Ceci, I am sorry. What will become of you now?"

I am not sorry, I am glad, so glad. She took his hand and squeezed it, affection thrusting through the turmoil in her heart, balancing her terrible relief at being free of him. "Dear Sebastian, do not worry about me. All will be well."

"I cannot help worrying," he said quietly. "I have loved you for a long time."

She looked into his eyes, seeing the love and pain in their depths. The relief she felt at the end of their betrothal shamed her, as much as she had chafed at the betrothal before. She leaned forward and kissed him, wishing just a little that she could have loved him as she loved Edmund. Sebastian deserved a woman who would love him with heart, body and soul.

He stepped beyond her and embraced John. "I am glad you are home, John. I could wish you had not had such news to bring with you, but I am glad you came before Ceci was utterly ruined. Your parents have kindly given me leave to stay here while I am in London, so I shall see you again later." He bowed to Lucia, put his cap on his head and walked behind the screen without a backward glance.

"I should attend Beatrice." Cecilia glanced at the door to the stairs.

"Beatrice will be well enough alone. I should prefer it if you could arrange for a chamber for Lucia to rest. The journey has been long and she is with child."

Envy stabbed, sharp and bitter as a poisoned blade. It was worse even than the jealousy she had felt when she realized that another woman now came first in her brother's heart. *I want that! I want to bear my beloved's child.* Lucia had everything: John, love, marriage, a child. And all she had were her memories.

The self-pity of that thought jolted her. She gave herself a hard shake, forcing her resentment aside.

You cannot wish to bear a bastard.

She smiled at John, praying her real happiness shone more clearly than the ache of her empty arms. *No, not a bastard. Edmund's son. But I shall be barren all the days of my life.*

"Oh, John!" She kissed him and felt his arms tighten for just a moment, as if to offer comfort. He had always seen too much; did he still speak his mind about what he saw?

Releasing her brother without meeting his eyes, she went to Lucia and embraced her. "I am so happy! I shall put you and my brother in my chamber. I can sleep with my sister. There is no need for us to have separate rooms now that her husband is gone," she said. Leaving her arm around Lucia's waist as if acts of affection could create it, Cecilia turned to John. "Shall I send Mistress Emma to her? Although I think Mistress Emma will prefer to see you."

"Let me go with you and see Lucia settled. It is not easy to rest in a strange place, especially when you don't speak the language well and you cannot see a familiar face." As he spoke, his gaze turned inward, as if he reviewed old memories. From the way his lips set, they were not pleasant.

Cecilia stretched out her hand and grasped his wrist. "It seems to me that Lucia is not the only one wearied by her long journey," she said. "Come, lie down and rest. You have come home and there is all the time in the world for everything else."

That night the family dined in the solar, everyone but Cecilia talking and laughing long past the lighting of the candles. She was too busy watching them to speak, her heart too full of dark emotion to pretend happiness. Her parents stared at John as if they could not look enough. After the meal, her mother made Lucia sit beside her on a low stool, as if Lucia were one of her children; from time to time, her hand reached out and stroked Lucia's cloud of silvery curls. Lucia caught Cecilia watching them. She cocked her head and lifted her eyebrows as if to say, Am I taking your place? Do you want it back? The kindness in Lucia's eyes eased Cecilia's heart. Lucia had not taken her place, nor did she wish to sit at her mother's feet. She smiled at her sister-in-law and shook her head, feeling the first tentative thread of true affection working its way into her heart.

Sebastian and Beatrice sat at opposite ends of the room from one another and did not speak directly to one another all evening. Cecilia wanted to slap them both. Beatrice retired for the night first, followed shortly afterward by Sebastian. Even when her parents departed, Cecilia lingered, her irritation still smoldering. She suspected Beatrice would want to talk to her when she went to bed; she did not have the patience to listen to a kitten purr. But when Lucia rose and went into John's arms as if they were alone, Cecilia realized she had outlasted her welcome.

She rose to leave, but John said, "Stay a moment and talk to me."

Lucia smiled at her, understanding warm in the cool depths of her eyes. "Do stay. I am weary and go now." She kissed Cecilia on the cheek and slipped out of the room.

"Sit with me, here," John said, indicating the seat beside him.

Her tiredness giving way to a low thrum of pleasure, she obeyed him and sat in their mother's chair. She had not had him to herself since his return. Above all, she had missed time alone with him.

"What did Sebastian mean when he said he was glad I came before you were utterly ruined? And why did he ask what will become of you now?" John asked. His voice was pitched low, so low that it took a moment for her to understand exactly what he asked.

She had forgotten how clever he was, and how he held on to anything that engaged his interest. He had always done this, referring to remarks made hours before as if they had just been spoken. She had also forgotten how determined he could be to have his way. Anger sparked as well as amusement, old quarrels echoing in her memory. They had fought like puppies all through her childhood, occasionally biting hard enough to hurt. But she was not a child anymore and her secrets were not free for the asking.

"I am not sure I want you to know." She looked down at her hands. She dared not look at him, remembering the stare that had bent her to his will.

"Ceci, please look at me."

She turned her head, unable to resist the pleading note in his voice. "You cannot go away for five years and then come back expecting that nothing will have changed."

He winced. "I know."

"I am not your little Ceci anymore. I have been to Court, I have—" She stopped before she confessed more than she wanted to.

"You have become a great lady, but you have done things that make Sebastian fear for you." He took her hand, his dark eyes kinder than she remembered. Something had gentled him, bringing his wildness to earth. She ought to be saddened, for she had treasured that part of him, but she was not.

She searched his eyes, weighing old trust and time apart. In the dark depths, she found her beloved brother, not the Italianate stranger who had waited in the hall. Taking a deep breath, she said, "I fell in love and I am no longer a maid."

Nothing flickered in his eyes: not shock, not condemnation. He waited for her to go on, his relaxed stillness comforting. Something tight eased in her chest, words and pain welling up where there had been none before. She had always been able to tell him what was in her heart, as he had always told her; that was the source of their bond.

Telling him about Edmund took some time. He asked questions when she did not explain herself clearly, nothing in his face or voice leading her to believe he thought less of her for what she had done. As she spoke, her heart eased, the pain lanced by words.

"What will you do?" he asked when she finished.

"I do not know." The whitewashed walls of the solar wobbled, the candlelight blurring. She shut her eyes. "I do not wish to return to Court, but I expect I must. Mama and Papa are disappointed, though neither of them will say so.''

''What do you want to do?''

That opened her eyes again. ''I want to be with him.'' She blinked hard to clear her gathering tears. Words would not speak her heart, nor could music tell of the ache that never went away. She wished she had never met Edmund. She wished she had never left him.

''Then be with him,'' John said.

She stared at him. ''Are you mad? I cannot.'' She could not, in honor, be less than Edmund's wife, not without irretrievably harming the family. She had chosen to break every rule she knew about men and maids, and this heartache was her punishment.

''Why not?''

She opened and shut her mouth. How could he ask? The answer must be plain. He raised one brow in a mocking question. She said the first thing that came into her head. ''Because—because it will be a great scandal.''

''And?''

''What do you mean, 'and'?'' She stood up, her torpor burned away in shock. ''You cannot throw everything away to follow your passions.''

''I did.''

She opened her mouth to argue, but how could she dispute the truth? He had turned away from everything they had been taught was right and proper, and had prospered. Yet what he had done could not apply to her. She was a woman, the rules were different for her. Were they not? She walked away from John, toward her lute. If she could, if there were no consequences, would she go to Edmund? Only the impact of her behavior on her parents gave her pause. She might dare anything if she believed it would not hurt the family.

Very well, the voice in her head said. *Imagine you could go to him without a soul knowing. Would you do it?*

If he wanted me to.

The words came out of nowhere, sounding in her head. She ran her fingers lightly over the half-strung lute. It was out of tune from the restringing; what should have been music was only a discordant jangle. The corner of her mouth lifted. The lute sounded like her heart. She turned to face John. "I will not go to him because I do not know if he still wants me."

"And if he does?"

She laughed unwillingly, her voice catching when her heart skipped a beat. If only she knew Edmund did want her. "Are you trying to corrupt me?" she asked. "Are you really my brother John, or are you the devil?"

His mouth quirked up in the old mischievous smile. "Perhaps I am both." She crossed herself. "It was a jape, Ceci."

"Perhaps. But you tempt me as if you were the devil." She feared the power of her longing for Edmund, the way her flesh urged her to run to him. It was madness, all of it, and she could not get free of it.

He looked thoughtful. "Do you wish to avoid Court because you do not dare find out the truth of what he wants?"

"No!" The question sank into her mind and heart, stronger than her denial. "Perhaps." She sighed. *So that is the truth.* She was a coward, hiding behind words like honor and duty, pretending to herself that she wanted Edmund with her whole heart.

"You cannot hide from pain, Ceci. It finds you."

"I am afraid." The words escaped her on a gasp.

He rose from his chair and pulled her into his arms, his embrace full of strength and comfort. "I know, poppet. I know." His voice rumbled in her ear. "But you always had courage. It will not fail you now."

"Promise me you will stay until I come back," she whispered.

"I promise. I promised I'd come home and I did. Now I promise not to leave."

She leaned back in his arms. "What of Lucia? Will she want to stay in England?" *Will she want me running to you when my heart is broken?*

"She cannot return to Rome, nor can I." He drew her close and kissed her forehead. "For good or ill, I am home to stay."

If John were in England, if she knew she could find refuge with him should she need it, she thought she could dare anything. She was afraid and would be until she saw Edmund again and knew what was in his heart. But John had given her strength by reminding her of her courage. She buried her face in his doublet.

"Bless you," she whispered fiercely.

His hands were firm as they rubbed her back. "Trust your heart, Ceci. It was always wiser than your head."

Chapter Twenty-One

Edmund adjusted his cap on his head, watching himself in the mirror held up by one of his gentleman ushers. Abruptly, he remembered preparing to meet Black Margery. He had been sick of too much wine earlier that day, wine taken to scrub away the knowledge of what he and Ceci had nearly done. And that had not been as painful to recall as the memories of Ceci that rose up now: her merry, mischievous smile; the intelligence shining in her dark eyes; her warmth as he held her in his arms. Closing his eyes and clamping his mouth shut, he thrust the recollections away.

Do not think of her.

He shoved his short gown back on his shoulders so it sat more comfortably while one gentleman usher tied cloth-of-gold bases around his waist and another handed him the chain he had chosen to wear across his shoulders. Dressing with only Piers to attend him was far more pleasant than being swarmed over by half a dozen ushers. For a moment he dreamed of ordering everyone from the room. He blinked and recollected himself. He was Duke of Somerset and he had a position to maintain. The whole fabric of the world would unravel if he did not do his duty and behave as a royal duke ought.

He sighed and rubbed his eyes. Feeling sorry for himself would not help, though God knew he was unhappy enough, his misery following him as he traveled with the Court from Windsor to Richmond. He spent his days and nights in a pretense of merriness, forcing his lips to smile, his voice to laugh, lying without words, all to disguise the simmering anger that was his constant companion. He was angry with Ceci for leaving, angry with Arthur for arranging his marriage, angry with his life for turning gray and sour when Ceci left it.

But mostly, he was bitterly angry with himself for his cowardice. He had not been man enough to stand fast. *I should have told Arthur I wanted to marry Ceci.* A voice in his head responded, *And by doing so, you would betray both your brother and your promise to your father.*

It was the voice of duty and common sense. He opened his eyes. He would not listen to that voice, he would not hear it. It only made him angrier, a tide of rage surging toward his memory of his father, threatening to swamp it in hurt and bitterness. If he hated his father now, all he had sacrificed to his father's memory would have been for nothing.

"I have not seen Benbury in an age. Has he left York's service?" one of his men asked.

"I should hope not. No one has a readier wit," another said.

"Or loses so often at dice and cards."

There was a burst of laughter. Edmund curved his mouth in a smile. He would smile at that, would he not? He could not smile from the heart, so he must smile from habit.

"I do not know if he will be back. I have heard he is betrothed."

"Betrothed? This is sudden. Who is the woman?"

"Coleville's daughter, the one who attended the queen until her disgrace—" The voice fell abruptly silent, as if the speaker had suddenly remembered that Ceci had been "disgraced" for "dallying" with Edmund.

The conversation went on, the words in his ears simple noise. His mind was blank, white as a snowstorm; his heart was empty. Ceci was marrying Sebastian Benbury—

I will kill him. All the anger that had simmered far below the surface of his life boiled into consciousness, directed at one man.

"Your Grace?" the usher asked doubtfully.

Edmund became aware of his lips, pulled back in a snarl, and smoothed his expression. He nodded at the usher. He had eaten too much anger in the last fortnight to stop swallowing it now.

"Let us go," he said. He strode out of his chambers. Let them follow as they might; he could wait for no man.

The lackeys lounging in the antechamber leaped up and hurried before him, bellowing in their brassy voices, "Way! Way! Make way for the Duke of Somerset!" His ushers laughed and jostled in a pack behind him, everything a man might wish for in attendants. At any other time he would be grateful for their insensitivity; tonight their noise, even in a noisy Court, scraped his raw nerves. He clenched his teeth against his desire to shout them silent.

He had no right to be angry with Ceci. She had not promised him fidelity nor had he offered her marriage. In agreeing to marry Benbury, she had done all that was right and proper, following all the women who had gone to Court before her to obtain royal favor and meet marriageable men. He ought to be happy that she had found a man who would take proper care of her. What ailed him that he begrudged her a little happiness?

Thank God, I will not see her again. Yet he wanted to see her more than anything else on earth. If he were a woman, he would weep for the contradiction in his heart, the anger and pain and longing that churned together in such a mess that he wanted to howl.

He and his attendants passed into the king's Great Chamber, his lackeys shoving a path to the royal dais through the glittering throng. Edmund knelt before the king and queen until Arthur bade him rise. Kati smiled at him and gestured for him to come forward, holding out her hand to be kissed. He brushed his mouth against her knuckles while a treacherous voice murmured, *If you tell her what happened to you, perhaps you will be eased.* Oh, to be shed of his burden, to have the release of confession... He had always been able to trust her. Perhaps tomorrow, after her morning devotions—he rose, his gaze sweeping across the visible rounding of Kati's latest pregnancy. The walls closed around him once more. He could not tell her what worked in him.

Her pleased smile faded. "What ails you, *mi hermano?*"

"Nothing ails me, Kati. I am well." Smile, he thought. His lips would not move.

Frowning at him with worry in the hazel depths of her eyes, she said, "I do not believe you."

"My head aches from the noise, that is all. I will be well." Concentrating, he made himself smile, though it felt like a grimace.

"Edmund..."

He looked away, gritting his teeth against the temptation to start talking. He let his gaze wander over the queen's ladies and maids of honor. Perhaps one or two of them would distract him. One might even be pretty enough to catch his eye, and if he were truly lucky, she would also be clever enough to divert him for a day or two.

Ceci.

He stiffened, the shock of seeing her slamming him from head to foot.

She stood at the edge of the crowd of maids, her head turned so only her profile was visible. He had thought she was still away from Court. Aching as if it had been crushed, his heart turned over while his hands tightened into fists. *How could you? How could you agree to marry him?* The white blindness of his rage shocked him and he turned his head, unable to master the pain of seeing her.

Kati dismissed him and he turned toward the crowd. In a far corner, Harry's wife Madeleine stood with one or two attendants. She swayed a little, moving in time with the music and the dancers in the middle of the floor. Releasing his ushers from attending him, he threaded his way through the crowd. Dancing with Madeleine would give him time to think. And to calm his temper.

Madeleine smiled when she saw him, the smile widening when he invited her to dance. Taking her outstretched hand, he led her onto the floor. Ceci had also joined the dance, turning in the measures of the lively courante with one of the king's gentlemen. Her smile was fixed and a little cool; she did not look happy. If she had rejoined the Court, Benbury must have returned, as well. Edmund scanned the crowd for him but could not see him. Thank God. If the sight of Ceci made him this angry, what would seeing Benbury be like? And what might he do if he saw them together? He forced his mind away from the thought and concentrated on partnering Madeleine.

He stumbled and then turned the wrong way. Madeleine

lifted her brows and said, "You are not yourself, Edmund."

"I am well enough," he said. She nodded and smiled, the smile as false as most of his. He sighed, knowing he had offended her. "Forgive me, *ma mie*. My head aches." He was beginning to sound like a sickly babe. How many more times would he claim a headache?

"You are not sickening for anything…" She followed the turn of the dance and returned to face him with a look of concern.

"No. I am well."

"You do not seem so," she said.

"Ma mie…"

"I am sorry, I have been prying."

She did not speak again. The courante ended, the dancers bowing to one another. Edmund led Madeleine back to her corner and then, moved by a compulsion he could neither name nor resist, he took up a position where he could watch the dancers. Or rather, two dancers: Ceci and Benbury. Despite his dread of the pain it would cause him, he had to see them together. He wanted to know she was as unhappy as he.

Ceci moved past him in an intricate measure, her face white and set. He followed her with his eyes while she returned to her partner and braced himself.

Her partner was Conyers, not Benbury. Edmund's brows lifted; he had not known Conyers was back. The expression on Conyers's face, avid and malicious, raised the hackles on his neck, made his stomach clench with nameless dread. He could not take his eyes off them.

The dancers moved in the final lifting leap. Conyers did not set Ceci down correctly, but dropped her so that she fell against him and slid down the length of his body. When her feet touched the ground, Conyers smiled at her and bent to whisper in her ear. Color washed Ceci's face and she pushed futilely on his shoulders. Conyers's smile broadened.

Edmund was beside them before he knew he had moved. "Unhand her," he said in a low, furious voice.

Conyers jerked in surprise, his arms falling away from Ceci. All the anger that Edmund had held confined for the last month struggled for release. He wanted to flatten Conyers, to beat him until he whimpered for mercy. Instead he narrowed his eyes and let his rage harden his face.

"I believe I once told you that if you forced your attentions on this lady again, you would have to answer to me. Do I misremember?"

Conyers swallowed, his arrogance draining away. "No, Your Grace."

"Then you ignored my warning. Did you not believe me?"

Conyers swallowed again and something ugly in Edmund enjoyed the sight of his fear.

"Yes, Your Grace, I believed you."

"Then you are truly a fool for disobeying me. Begone."

Conyers started. "But, Your Grace, I am in the king's household. I may not depart without his leave. He—he will be angry."

Edmund smiled. Conyers paled. Of course Arthur would be angry. That was the point, to injure him in the king's eyes and make him vulnerable to disgrace. It was the most he could do now, but this was not the end of it. Not by any reckoning.

"You will depart now at my bidding. Or you and I will go to His Majesty to explain why your presence is a stench in my nose. I do not care which it is." Arthur would surely dismiss him if Edmund asked it; perhaps they ought to go to Arthur in any case. But before Edmund could change his mind, Conyers bowed and scurried away, leaving him with Ceci. He looked at her, seeing her clearly for the first time this night.

She was pale and thin, unhappiness in the set of her mouth and the way she seemed braced against a blow. His anger at her faltered. Perhaps she had had no choice in her betrothal. God knew, she did not seem pleased by it. She looked up at him, her eyes full of love and pain, and his furious resentment weakened still more.

He held out his hand. "Walk with me."

"I should be glad to." She did not seem to hear the harshness of his tone.

They moved to the outer part of the room as they had on that night when he had first seen her at Court. How long ago that seemed, longer than the whole of his life. How much longer would a life without her seem? He shook the thought off, knowing it would return as it always did.

"When did you return to Court?" he asked, breaking the silence between them.

"This morning," she replied.

Silence again, awkward with thoughts unspoken. She was tense, as was he, but he could not tell if she was angry with him for his neglect of her. Did she think he had abandoned her? *You did, you lackwit,* a sharp voice in the back of his head gibed. He thought, And she left me, promising herself to Benbury. His anger began to rise again.

"Where is Benbury? He should have saved you from that," he snapped.

"Sebastian has gone home."

"Abandoning you to that cur." *If you were mine, I would never leave you.* He flinched at the thought.

"Sebastian has other things to worry about," she said, and sighed.

"Other things? What can be more important than his betrothed wife?" With an effort, he kept his voice low. There were too many ears pricked to hear what they had to say to one another. He did not want this all over Court.

She stopped short, staring at him with wide eyes. "I am not betrothed to Sebastian."

"Not— But I heard—" His head rang with silence as if it had been struck with the flat side of a sword.

"He is marrying my sister Beatrice."

"She is married." Nothing made sense, his thoughts as slippery and elusive as river weed.

"He died."

Joy stabbed him, as fierce as pain. She was free, free to— Free to what? Marry him? *Do not be a fool. If it is not Benbury, then it will be someone else.* He caught Mary Butler watching them with a worried look in her eye. If he and Cecilia were seen to dally again, what would come of it?

A wicked voice murmured, *She would not become betrothed to anyone else.*

She belongs to me. But I cannot claim her. He would not think of that.

"But I heard— You and Benbury—"

"Sebastian thought to offer for me, that is true, but when Lord Manners died, he chose my sister instead. I am free."

"Free." He tried to think of what that might mean, but her voice saying, "I am not betrothed to Sebastian," echoed through his head and drove coherent thought away. Carefully, he schooled his face to indifference, afraid of that his unseemly joy might show if he did not. With a great effort, he made himself say, "I should find Benbury to congratulate him."

"He has gone home."

"You said that." He shook his head as if he could jostle his thoughts into order.

"Yes." She looked up at him, amber light sparking in the depths of her eyes and color rising into her face. He wanted to kiss her even as he was intensely aware of the eyes all around them. He thought, I should leave her.

"Meet me." It was not at all what he had intended to say. He did not care.

"Yes." Her lips were parted and the pinched look had vanished, leaving her glowing and fresh.

"Noonday, in the pleached alley."

"I will be there."

"Kati will not stop you?"

"Nothing shall."

Chapter Twenty-Two

Cecilia set the lute aside, yawning. Unsettled by the tumult of meeting Edmund again last night, she had been unable to sleep, tossing and turning until the other maid in the bed jabbed her and hissed at her to be still.

"Oh, do not stop, please," Mary Butler said, looking up from her needle.

They sat together in a windowed alcove. They were both supposed to be stitching an altar cloth but Mary preferred to stitch alone while Cecilia played to speed the time.

Cecilia sighed and reclaimed the lute. Mary had not yet said anything about the unwisdom of dancing with Edmund last night, and perhaps if she continued to play, Mary never would. She had played and practiced the lute enough that she ought to be able to think while her fingers moved. She wanted to remember the sound of Edmund's voice, to remember the way his eyes had seemed to see nothing and no one but her. They were memories that soothed her fears.

"I am so happy you have returned," Mary said, spreading the altar cloth across her lap, smoothing it with a careful hand.

"I am glad to be back." Cecilia's fingers danced over

the lute strings, spinning a merry tune into the air. She only lied a little bit. She was not glad to be back at Court, but she was happy to see Mary again. It was the only pleasure she had expected to find in returning.

"It has not been the same without you." Mary lifted the cloth close to her eyes, examining her stitches with a critical air.

"No one to play the lute while you stitch?"

"Not so well as you, nor anyone to talk to."

"All the queen's women do all day long is talk." A note rang sour and she sighed; the lute had gone out of tune again. She began adjusting the pegs.

"It is not the same thing," Mary said. She held the cloth out at arm's length, cocking her head from one side to the other. "Does that green match?"

Cecilia laid the lute down. "Where?"

Mary pointed out a pair of leaves. "Here."

Cecilia took the cloth and held it up. "It looks well enough to me."

"Turn it this way," Mary said fretfully, and adjusted Cecilia's hands so that the light fell across the stitches rather than full on them. Now the greens neither matched nor flattered one another.

"I see what you mean." She handed the cloth back. "Do you have any other green?"

"No, just this skein—" She stopped and turned pale, the skin around her mouth and eyes nearly greenish. "Oh, no." She dropped the altar cloth and pressed her fist to her mouth. Shooting Cecilia a look of apology, she fled the alcove.

Cecilia retrieved the altar cloth from the floor where it had drifted. After spreading it on her lap, she looked up to find Sir George Conyers leaning against the wall at the entrance to the alcove, watching her intently.

"Sir," she said, setting the cloth aside and folding her hands against her waist.

"I had not thought to find you," he said lightly. "But it seems my luck is turning." He entered the alcove and sat next to her. She fought the urge to shift away from him.

"As is mine," she said. "But not for the better."

His lip lifted in the semblance of a smile. "Such a pretty wit you have."

She looked away. "I thank you, kind sir." Get up, she thought, but she would not run from him. The chamber beyond was empty and in some dim part of her mind, she marveled at his ability to find her when she was alone.

Except for last night. He had shamed her, first by dropping her so that she rubbed along the length of him in full view of the Court and then by whispering, "I had not known you were such a toothsome armful, my lady." Her cheeks grew hot at the memory.

"I enjoy it, although it might please me more if you used its sharp edge on other men," Conyers murmured.

"I am not concerned with what pleases you, sirrah," she said while she tried to remember what they had been discussing. Ah, her wit. *If I had any wit, I would not have to endure you.*

"But you should be, my dear."

She turned to face him, her brows raised and her chin lifted so she looked down her nose at him. "I do not believe I heard you aright, sir."

"So proud," he murmured, and took her chin in his hand, pulling it down. She jerked it free. "Will you be so proud when we are wed?"

She stiffened, cold cat's feet walking up her spine. "Wed? We? I think not."

"Think again, alder-liefest. As I said last night, you are

sweeter to hold than I had imagined. Not only that, I expect you have as rich a dowry as Beatrice. I need that money.''

She laughed, half angered and half entertained by his effrontery. Something whispered that she ought to be afraid. ''I have no doubt that my dowry tempts you, sir,'' she said, looking down at her brocade sleeve and picking bits of dust from the wide cuffs. ''But nothing about you tempts me. Choose another for your bride.''

He leaned close, so close she could feel the warmth of his breath on her breast, her nose filling with the scent of cloves. Her stomach rolled, the hair on the back of her neck standing on end. She gathered all her strength and did not lean away from him.

''I have chosen my wife, madam.''

She stood. ''I refuse you, sir.''

Before she could escape, he shot to his feet and seized her about the waist, his mouth curved in a half-moon smile. ''But, my dear, you have no choice.''

She stiffened, refusing to struggle. Her futile effort last night had pleased him; she would not gratify him again. ''I am not without friends, my family is not without power. Without my consent, you cannot force me.'' *Thank you, God, for keeping my voice steady.*

His smile changed to one of genuine amusement. ''But you shall consent, alder-liefest.''

She lifted her eyebrows and curled her mouth in what she hoped was a sneer. *Blessed Jesú, do not let him feel me tremble.* ''Why shall I consent to throw myself away on you?''

The half moon of his smile widened into a grin. ''Because, my pretty little whore, I saw you in Aylesbury.''

She could control her face but she could not stop her jerk of shock. She saw in his eyes that he had felt it, too, but she would not yield to him. "I do not know what you are talking about."

He pulled her more tightly against him and rubbed his cheek against hers. "I admire your spirit," he murmured. "It inflames me." He shifted her so that she was pressed against him, his arousal unmistakable even through her brocade skirts and layers of petticoats. Her gorge rose, bile burning the base of her tongue. "I saw you in Aylesbury with a man. You stayed the night in an inn. You bloodied the sheets in that inn." His voice purred in her ear. Fury and shame and disgust howled through her and her stomach rolled. She did not know how much longer she could keep her composure. "Surprising, how much information a sovereign will buy."

He loosened his grip so that he could look into her face. "I do not mind that you are not a virgin. I dislike virgins." She fought the urge to claw and bite him, refusing to grant him the amusement of an empty struggle. "What? You will not fight me? A pity." Gripping the back of her head so she could not evade him, he bent his head and pressed his mouth to hers, his tongue forcing her lips apart. She closed her teeth against him and clenched her jaw. He lifted his head. "You will yield to me, because if you do not, I shall ruin you. I will tell everyone that you are a whore." He released her waist, smiling gently. "I should far prefer to tell the world you are my betrothed wife."

"I should far prefer to be known as a whore." She prayed he would go before she was sick; he must not see her weak, must not know how badly he frightened her.

"I am sure a moment's reflection will show you how foolish you are being, alder-liefest." He put on a look of sorrow. "Think of the pain your dishonor will bring your mother. Think how this will shame your father. I have no doubt you would happily cast your own reputation to the wind—but what of the harm to your family?''

"I am not the first maid of honor to be led astray," she said. "Nor, I warrant, will I be the last."

He laughed. "Had you been deflowered by a nobleman, I am sure your family should have survived the scandal. But a poor gentleman from Wales? I think not."

She lowered her eyelids to conceal her sudden hope. He did not know whom she had lain with.... Somehow she could use his ignorance to her benefit, if only she had a moment to think.

"I should like to swive you here," he murmured, lifting his hand to trail his fingers along the edge of her deep neckline. She stepped back before she could stop herself. He laughed softly. "But I shall not. Anyone might discover us. Better by far to keep your name clean until it is no longer your name. I want more than a single tumble, alder-liefest."

"Go," she whispered.

"It is not easy to part from you now that I have found you, Cecilia. Yet perhaps you need some time to consider your position."

She could not answer him, not when all she wanted to do was spit in his face. He waited for a moment, then bowed and left the alcove.

Her stomach heaved and she was abruptly sick. She staggered away from the mess in the rushes, collapsing as blackness overcame her and her knees gave way. Voices hissed and roared in her ear as her vision whirled darkly. She lay still, stunned and afraid to think, for a long time.

Footsteps. She opened her eyes and pushed herself to a sitting position, afraid he had come back to find her in this state. Blessedly, it was Mary, returning from her abrupt departure.

"Cecilia? What happened? Why are you sitting on the floor?" Mary rushed forward and knelt beside her. Cecilia struggled to her feet. What was she going to do? She could not marry George Conyers. She could not put her life in his hands. Yet if she did not she would be ruined and her family shamed. She was trapped, trapped as surely as the mouse impaled on the cat's claws.

"What happened?" Mary asked again.

Tears filled Cecilia's eyes before she could prevent them. Mary abandoned her look of skepticism and took her in her arms.

"No, sweeting, do not cry. Tell me. Tell me what happened."

Cecilia shook her head. She could not tell anyone. She opened her mouth to tell Mary she was well enough. A sob escaped before she could speak and then a storm of weeping overcame her. Mary held her while it raged, her arms strong, her shoulder plump and comfortable.

When it had passed and she was calm, she pushed out of Mary's embrace and dried her eyes on her shirt cuffs. Somehow, her burst of tears had restored her and while she still feared and hated Conyers, she did not doubt she would find a way to thwart him. Somehow. Glancing at the sunlight flooding the window, she calculated the time. She could not linger if she wanted to meet Edmund at the promised hour. God willing, he would not notice her reddened eyes.

"I beg your pardon for weeping all over you," she said, summoning a smile for Mary.

"It is of no matter." She looked thoughtfully at Cecilia. "Let us walk outdoors. The rain has stopped and I do not think the queen will grudge me a chance to walk off my greensickness with your attendance."

How could she accompany Mary and still meet Edmund? Her mouth opened and shut while she wondered why she could not think quickly enough to avoid this.

"I do not know…" She had no excuse, not even a feeble one.

"You need the summer air, child," Mary said, folding her hands at her waist. "As do I."

Cecilia laughed a little unwillingly at Mary's tone. "I am no child."

"You still need the air. Come, what reason can you offer to refuse me?"

She looked into Mary's eyes and took a deep breath, balancing on the edge of a decision as she used to balance on the riverbank before plunging in. "I have promised to meet Ed—the Duke of Somerset at noon."

Mary nodded briskly, neither surprised nor disapproving. "Where?"

"The garden. The pleached alley."

"We have no time to waste. Come, let us go." Mary pulled her out of the alcove and then tucked her hand into the crook of Cecilia's elbow as if she relied on her friend for support.

"He does not expect I shall be escorted," Cecilia said faintly as they walked.

"It is better this way," Mary said serenely. "If anyone sees us meet, it will more surely seem happenstance. And if anyone questions you, you can say I led you there. You need to manage these things better."

Chapter Twenty-Three

Edmund paced the length of the pleached alley, his gaze fixed on the lattice of shadows cast on the path underfoot. Would she come? Or would she think better of it and leave him to wait? Was it noon yet? Or was it later? He turned and turned again. *She will come.* His good sense asserted itself and reminded him that she was a member of the queen's household, unable to come and go as she pleased. She would come as soon as she could. He looked up at the tangled branches overhead, rolling his shoulders to relax them. It was warm here, the sunny air full of the smell of green leaves and brown earth.

He hungered for her touch, even if it was no more than the clasp of her hand. Being parted from her had been a foretaste of hell, nothing he ever wanted to experience again. *What of your vow?* He pushed the voice away, as he had so many times since Ceci had come to Court, and then drew the thought back. Indeed, what of his vow?

He had been too young to know what he pledged. He stepped over the border into unknown territory, a life without his promise. His heart pounded against his ribs.

"Edmund?"

Cecilia stood at the end of the alley, limned in gold. Her

arm was linked with Mary Butler's, her sharply shadowed face impossible to read. He glanced at Mary, wondering why she had joined them. She slipped her arm free of Cecilia's and dipped gracefully into a curtsy. Rising, she turned her back on them, affording them some privacy as well as the protection of a lookout.

He opened his arms. Cecilia walked into them, sweet and warm in his embrace. For a moment he savored the bliss of holding her before raising his hands to tilt her face up. She had been weeping, her eyes reddened and the tip of her nose shiny and pink.

His heart clenched. "Tell me."

"I cannot." Tears rimmed her eyelids. She blinked hard, holding them in.

"You can. Anything. You can tell me anything."

"It is of no matter." Her voice shook on the last word and she would not meet his eyes.

As if he could see into her heart, he suddenly knew. Rage ignited. "Is it Conyers?"

She nodded and caught her breath on a sob. He pulled her into his arms, lifting her bulky gable hood from her head so he could cradle her more closely. "Hush, Ceci. Hush." He rubbed her back, swallowing the sudden burn in his throat.

"He saw us—me in Aylesbury. He knows we... He thinks I lay with a Welshman..." Her voice was soft, hardly louder than the breeze tossing leaves and spangling sun and shadows all around them. He would have heard her in a gale. She stopped, took a deep breath and said, "He will ruin me if I will not marry him. He knows enough to do it." All at once, she broke and wept, clutching the edge of his doublet. He had never seen her so overset; murder crept into his bones.

"When did this come about?" he asked, careful to speak softly, careful not to frighten her.

"Th-this morning. He cornered me when I was alone and told me we were to wed." She stopped, her hands tightening. He soothed her, kissing her hairline, murmuring soft words against the skin of her forehead while his blood, hot with violence, surged through his body. Cecilia gulped and shuddered. Her tears had stopped. "He said he liked my spirit and he was glad I am not a virgin."

"A pox on him." He had not known Conyers was so vile.

"I am sorry!" She pushed at his shoulders. "I did not mean to tell you. I will find a way out of this, you need not worry yourself."

Her words cut him, but he would not let her go. "Not worry myself! Ceci, you are my very heart. Whatever harms you harms me, do you not know that?"

She pushed herself out of his arms. "How? We are neither married nor kin. How is my harm your affair?"

Her words slashed him. Oh, she was right, but she was also utterly wrong. He could not help saving her from harm; it did not matter if he was neither brother nor husband. He loved her too much to let any ill come to her. "I cannot stand by and watch while you are hurt."

"But you have no right." Tears trickled across her cheeks, escaping her before she could blink them away. Each one scored his heart with acid.

"I love you. That gives me right enough." He pulled her against him, wishing that she could melt into him, that they might be as one forever. "Do not you fight me, too. Let me do this, Ceci. Let me defend you."

"What can you do?" she cried, and let him enfold her in his arms.

He laughed softly. "Oh, my heart. I am the Duke of Somerset and the king's beloved brother. What can I not do?"

Edmund nocked his arrow and drew on the bowstring, the heavy bow fighting his pull. The sun's heat released the clean, pungent smell of Dame Joan's herbs; he stood in his Southwark garden surrounded by a cloud of fragrance. Sighting along the arrow shaft, he took a deep breath to steady himself and released the string. With a satisfying *thunk* the arrow went home in the center of the target Piers had set up on the far side of the garden.

Breathing deeply, he took another arrow from the case over his shoulder. Taking aim, he pictured Conyers standing in place of the target. He smiled and let the arrow fly. It, too, struck the target's center. Killing Conyers might satisfy the cold anger hissing in his heart, but it would cause no end of difficulties afterward. His smile spread into a grin. *I will not kill him, but I will make him wish I had.*

The garden gate creaked. "He is coming, Your Grace," Piers said.

Edmund sighted along a third arrow shaft. "Send him to see me as soon as he arrives."

"And if he brings a guard?"

Edmund loosed the bowstring, releasing the arrow to flight. "Admit only Conyers." The arrow struck within an inch of the other two.

He had sent a message to Conyers, promising him that he would learn something to his profit if he came to Southwark. Edmund counted on Conyers's greed, but he had additional plans if Conyers's caution proved greater than his courage. He smiled softly to himself. If Piers spoke truly, greed drove Conyers more strongly than prudence.

The garden gate groaned again. Edmund glanced at it

as he drew his bow a fourth time. "Sir George Conyers,"
Piers announced, and stepped aside.

Conyers strode through the gate and stopped short.
"Your Grace!"

Edmund swung around, the bow still drawn and the arrow pointed at his guest. Conyers blanched. "It would be
so easy to shoot you," Edmund said. "Piers would throw
your corpse in the river and I would have done with your
endless impertinence." He slowly lowered the bow so the
arrow pointed at the ground and then relaxed his pull on
the bowstring. "But I shall not."

"Your Grace is pleased to jest," Conyers said, and
choked out a laugh.

"No, you miserable lickspittle, I am not pleased, nor am
I jesting," Edmund said, unstringing his bow and turning
to lay it and the arrow case on the bench behind him.
Violence simmered in his bones, aching for release. Not
yet. Not quite yet. Moving might ease him. He faced Conyers.

"I had a message to meet someone here, I did not mean
to disturb you, I shall leave you in peace, I beg your pardon, if Your Grace will forgive me." Conyers bowed low,
as if they were at Court, and took a step toward the gate.

Edmund frowned. "Halt!"

Conyers froze, one foot behind as the other bore his
weight.

"Did I give you leave to go?" Edmund spoke quietly,
too angry to shout.

"No, Your Grace, you did not," Conyers said, still bent
in his bow.

"Then where do you go?" His hands were clenched in
fists. He loosened them, reaching again for calm.

Conyers gripped his knees. "Nowhere, Your Grace."
He did not lift his head to look at Edmund.

"Stand up."

Conyers straightened. His gaze darted here and there, avoiding Edmund's. Edmund closed the distance between them and seized the front of Conyers's shirt, shaking him just a little to make sure he had his full attention. "Do you know why I sent for you?" he asked. He spoke softly; if he relaxed his grip on his restive temper, it would escape his control. More than anything on earth, he longed to damage Conyers.

"N-no, Your Grace." His voice was hoarse, as if Edmund choked him.

"I have spoken to Lady Cecilia Coleville since your visit to her this morning. She is not given overmuch to chatter, but she did tell me a thing or two." Edmund tightened his grip and watched the livid color darken Conyers's face. "You did not listen to me."

Conyers clawed at Edmund's hand. "Your Grace, I can explain." Edmund looked into his frightened eyes and then flung him away. Conyers fell to his knees and reached up to rub his throat, his breath coming in gasps.

"Explain, then. I am listening," Edmund said, folding his arms across his chest. There was nothing Conyers could say that would excuse what he had done, but Edmund was curious to hear what tale he would spin.

"I had hoped the jade would take warning, but I see she has not," Conyers said, clambering to his feet. The fear had left his eyes, replaced by a look of calculation. He licked his lips. "I do not know what lies she has told you, but—"

Edmund's hands curled again into fists as a great hot weight settled on his chest. Calm, he thought, be calm.

"—I have never laid a hand on Lady Cecilia Coleville."

"So you did not threaten to ruin her if she would not consent to marry you?" The effort of containing his fury leached the emotion from his voice, but Conyers did not seem to hear anything odd in his tone.

He spread his arms wide, his eyes wide and innocent. "Your Grace! It was the other way about! Lady Cecilia threatened to claim I had ruined her if I would not consent to marry her." His tone was perfect, embarrassment and outrage mingled. At any other time, in any other circumstance, Edmund would have been amused by his smooth performance.

The weight in his chest shattered, and he swung at Conyers before he had time to think. Conyers made no attempt to dodge his fist, falling to the ground in a heap. Cowering, he stared up at Edmund with terrified eyes while blood ran in a gleaming thread from the corner of his mouth.

"Get up and fight like a man," Edmund said.

Conyers dug his fingers into the turf as if he feared Edmund would force him to his feet. "You are the king's brother, Your Grace. I may not strike you as easily as you strike me."

Edmund laughed. Conyers must have heard the contempt in it; dull red shot into his face, masking the mark of Edmund's fist. "A reasonable excuse. Except here I am not the king's brother. Fight me like a man. I promise you I will not use my rank against you."

"No, Your Grace."

Edmund kicked him in the ribs, taking ugly pleasure in the sound of Conyers's grunt of pain. "Get up or I will kick you to death like a dog."

"Your Grace…"

Edmund kicked him again, angered and disgusted by the man's craven mewling. "Get up and fight me."

Conyers got up, groaning a little as he rose. Swaying and holding his ribs, he narrowed his eyes in an expression of surprising unpleasantness. The thought of what Ceci had

had to endure at this man's hands sent anger surging anew through Edmund. He tamped it down, saving it.

Conyers drew a wheezing breath. "Before we begin, I should like to know why you are so concerned."

"I do not give a damn for what you want," Edmund said, feinting with his right and striking a quick, hard blow to Conyers's head with his left. Conyers staggered to the right. Edmund shifted so that he faced him, his back to the house. Conyers swung a blow at Edmund's ribs, moving so slowly that Edmund easily avoided his fist. "So. I am not as easily affrighted as Lady Cecilia."

Conyers swung and missed again. Behind him, Edmund heard a creak and thump as a shutter was flung open.

"Surely you can do better than that, my little caitiff." Conyers's blow grazed his chin. "Much better."

He hit Conyers in the ribs, drawing a muffled groan. He heard cloth flapping, Daisy or Dame Joan shaking out a cloth of some kind. He refused to be distracted, certain Conyers was a more dangerous opponent than he had so far appeared.

Conyers looked up at the house. His eyes widened and he stumbled back, out of Edmund's reach. "I see it now. Your Grace, you could have been frank with me."

What game was this? Afraid that Conyers meant to rush him if his attention wandered, Edmund moved so he could see both Conyers and the back of his house. Daisy leaned out of an upstairs window, vigorously shaking out a coverlet. She had gained a little weight and a little color; Edmund realized that at a distance she could pass for Cecilia. Coldness settled in the depths of his stomach. Had his attempt to protect Cecilia only made it worse for her?

He turned back to Conyers, lifting his brows, becoming a prince once more. But Conyers, greed and glee kindling in his eyes, did not seem to notice.

"I beg your pardon, I did not know, Your Grace. Lady Cecilia did not lie. I do wish her for my wife but you are welcome to her bed. Indeed I am willing to share to please—"

Something snapped inside Edmund. Roaring in fury, he hurled himself across the lawn, giving Conyers no time to avoid him. Edmund knocked him down and straddled him, pinning his arms against the turf with his knees. Reaching down past the ineffectual flapping of Conyers's hands, he gripped his throat and squeezed with all his strength. "I will kill you!" Conyers bucked underneath him; grimly Edmund held on. Strangling was not enough; he began beating Conyers's head against the ground. Conyers's face turned red, then purple, his eyes and tongue starting from his head.

Hands reached out to pull on his arms and Piers cried in a shrill voice, "My lord, my lord, you must not kill him." Edmund tightened his grip. Conyers must pay for his insults with his life.

A blow that made his head clang slammed his jaw and jarred him loose. Piers filled the gap between him and Conyers, shaking his right hand as if it hurt him while he seized the front of Edmund's shirt with his left.

Edmund jerked his fist back. "You dare? Get out of my way." Wheezing breaths whooped behind Piers.

"No, sir, I shall not," Piers said, his face whey pale.

"I will kill him."

"Not while I live to stop you." Piers clamped his mouth shut and stared at Edmund.

Edmund met his eyes. Piers did not flinch, his unwavering gaze penetrating the red haze in Edmund's head. The moment when he might have killed Conyers passed.

He pushed off Conyers's body and staggered to the bench, shoving the bow and the arrow case aside. Propping his elbows on his knees, he buried his face in his hands and fought a rush of nausea. *Sweet Mary, I came so close...*

Conyers began coughing, great racking coughs that ended in choking sickness. Edmund lifted his head and looked at him, lying on his side and spitting matter onto the grass. He felt nothing, no shame, no regret, nothing but a vast weariness. "I could have killed you today and no one would have ever known what befell you. Remember that."

"I shall go to the king," Conyers said, and began coughing again.

"Go and be damned to you." Edmund's fatigue deepened. "You will be lucky if all he does is lock you in the Tower and forget the key." He put his hands over his eyes and rubbed them. "Piers, get him out of here before I do kill him."

He heard Piers murmuring and Conyers replying. When the garden gate creaked, he removed his hands from his eyes and stared at Conyers being helped out of the garden with his arm across Piers's shoulders.

"Conyers," Edmund said. Both men turned. "If you so much as look at Lady Cecilia, nothing will prevent me from killing you. Do you understand?"

"Yes, Your Grace," Conyers said.

"Good. Now begone."

They disappeared through the gate. Sensation awakened throughout Edmund's body and the bruises on his knees and hands began to ache. He sighed and rubbed his knuckles. He had wanted Conyers to die and only Piers's intervention had saved them both: Conyers from death and himself from the sin of murder. Thank God for Piers.

The gate whined again as it swung open. Piers stepped

through it, his mouth compressed into a thin line. Edmund sat up and frowned at him.

"I have no desire to hear what you have to say, Piers, so you must not speak it."

Piers crossed to the bench and sat down. "I shall have my say."

"Piers—"

"And you will listen to me."

Edmund opened his mouth to reprimand Piers for his impertinence but the disapproving look in Piers's eyes checked him. Piers would neither listen nor obey, that much was clear. Edmund shut his mouth and sat back. The sooner Piers began, the sooner he would be finished. And afterward, Edmund would blister his ears.

"What ails you?" Piers demanded.

Edmund sat up. "Ails—"

Piers did not listen. "Have you run mad? What has Sir George Conyers done to make you assault him?"

"He insulted Lady Cecilia Coleville," Edmund said. He had never seen Piers angry, had not even known Piers had a temper. Refusing to meet Piers's gaze, he plucked his hose where they had loosened at the knee.

"What affair is that of yours? Let her father or her brothers avenge her honor. Better yet, let her make a complaint to the queen."

Abandon Cecilia when she was in need? "I cannot do that."

"Why not?"

The garden walls leaned over him, crowding him, and the breeze died, leaving the air flat and close. "Leave me be, Piers."

"I will not."

Edmund turned to glare at him. "You forget who you are."

"Do I? Or is it you who forgets?"

"How dare you!" He did not want to be angry at Piers, but Piers seemed determined to provoke him. He tightened his grip on his temper. "Do not pursue this, Piers, I warn you."

"Cecilia Coleville is none of yours," Piers said.

"She is everything of mine!" Edmund shouted, leaping to his feet.

"Then claim her and have done!" Piers shouted back.

Edmund dropped onto the bench. "I cannot." He was a coward and a fool, but he spoke the truth.

"You can, if you will," Piers said. His voice had resumed its ordinary mildness. Edmund closed his eyes and let his head fall back on his shoulders. Tears burned his eyes. "What keeps you from it?"

"I am not free to marry as I list," Edmund said. The words resisted him; he had to fight to speak. "Even now, the king makes a marriage for me with Margrethe of Austria."

"If you betroth yourself to Lady Cecilia, no one will be able to part you."

"I promised my father before he died that I would do whatever I must to protect the king."

"You keep that promise every day you ride to gather information for him," Piers said.

Piers had not said anything he had not known, yet everything changed. He saw his promise and the dilemma it had created in an entirely new light, as if the sun had left its customary path to travel a new way across the sky.

"If I marry Margrethe, I will not be able to ride for him," Edmund said slowly.

"No, you will not."

He had been a fool, a blind fool. He wanted to rush to Cecilia and lay his heart at her feet, to tell her how stupid he had been. But he could not, not yet. He needed to think this through. He had done enough harm as it was because he had not thought anything through.

"I can marry Cecilia and keep my promise."

"I cannot see who else you can marry," Piers replied.

Eight simple words. Yet they turned things yet again and he saw his way clear.

"Piers, fetch me a waterman. I must go back to Court."

Chapter Twenty-Four

"The king will see you now, my lord," the page said. "He awaits you in his chamber."

Edmund shot to his feet. He had requested an audience with the king as soon as he arrived at Court, expecting the usual delay. Instead, the page he had sent returned within half an hour. He had no time to reconsider his plan, no time to reshape the words of his plea. And no time to become fearful. Sending his lackeys before him, he went to wait on his brother.

As he walked, his confidence mounted and he began to think this might be possible, that he might win Ceci without displeasing his brother too much. Then he arrived at the door to the king's private chamber and his hope fled, replaced by doubt. What if he failed? What if the king laughed in his face? What if Arthur had him arrested?

Do not think of it. Whatever he felt in his deepest heart, he could not show fear when a confident mien might make all the difference to his cause. He must enter the king's presence without hesitation or timidity. Removing his cap, he nodded to the lackey at the door, who swung it open and announced him.

Yet despite his determination to march boldly into the

room and declare himself, he checked in midstride almost as soon as he entered the small room. Arthur was not alone. Kati sat beside him, stitching a tiny cap. Arthur rested one hand on the growing bulge of Kati's pregnancy and, as Edmund approached to kneel before them, he leaned toward his wife and murmured something that made her laugh and blush. Edmund knelt, his throat closing in a surprising spurt of jealousy. *That is what I want.*

Arthur looked up and smiled, removing his hand from his wife. "Ah, Edmund. You came swiftly. Rise, rise. And put on your cap—there is no ceremony between us here."

Wordlessly, Edmund obeyed. This was going to be harder than he imagined, Arthur's warmth all the more precious now that Edmund was about to fling it away.

"There is wine on that table, a good canary," Kati said.

"I thank you, but I am not thirsty." Where to begin? This might be the last time he joined his brother in perfect amity; he was loath to begin the conversation that would shatter their relationship.

"So." Arthur clasped his hands and rested them on the knot tying the skirt of his bases. "What has befallen that you must see me so soon? It must be a matter of some urgency if you come to disturb my hour of peace."

The humor in his tone and the smile that lingered on his lips blunted the reproach hidden in his words. Guilt threaded its way through the mess in Edmund's heart. How could he be so sure of what he was about to do and still be so uneasy? "I wish to talk to you about my marriage to Margrethe of Austria."

Arthur's mouth remained curved yet somehow his smile was gone. "What is there to discuss?"

Edmund swallowed, his throat thick and mouth dry. "I do not wish to marry Margrethe." He gripped his courage. "I wish to marry Cecilia Coleville."

The king's eyes grew as cold and gray as snow clouds. "I see."

Arthur's frigid calm reminded Edmund of that afternoon with Harry. *I am afraid of him.* Strangely, the admission eased him. What was a king if he could not inspire fear?

"This alliance with Austria is important," Arthur remarked.

Beside him, Kati set the cap aside and folded her hands on the mound of her belly, her hazel eyes watchful in her smooth, unreadable face. It was as if the woman he knew as his friend had left the room. Gooseflesh prickled along Edmund's forearms, and going forward with this began to resemble walking up a river in full spate. Yet he forged on. "I know that," he said. "I do not speak idly or without forethought."

"I did not think you did," Arthur replied. His voice was colorless, as Edmund's had been when he'd faced Conyers, so angry that he had been unable to moderate his feelings. To hear the same flat tone from Arthur made his soul shift uneasily in his body, made him see the abyss opening at his feet as he chose Ceci over his king. "Yet you speak as a child."

He could not answer this. He itched to adjust his knife belt, to shift his gown on his shoulders, anything rather than standing still, but he would not betray himself by fidgeting. For a moment, quicker than a flash of lightning, he hesitated. It would be so simple... *Withdraw your words and you can end this. No woman is worth it.*

And then, as suddenly as it had tilted, the world righted. The treacherous voice was wrong. One woman was worth whatever it cost him: Ceci.

"I had hoped you might find the same happiness in your marriage as I have with the queen." Arthur took Kati's hand and smiled at her. She smiled in return. Edmund, who had seen them dazzle those new to Court with this display of affection, was unmoved. Arthur looked at him again. "I still hope it, but if you do not, it cannot be helped. You will marry Margrethe of Austria. Or anyone else I deem fit."

Edmund took a deep breath, gathering his strength. "No."

Arthur laughed, a startled sound bereft of amusement. "What did you say?"

"No."

Light caught in Arthur's eyes, glittering like diamonds. "You are mad."

"Perhaps. But I shall not marry anyone but Cecilia Coleville."

"You will do as I command."

Regret leaked warmth through his muscles. "I cannot."

Arthur leaped to his feet and snatched the cap off Edmund's head, crushing the plumes and velvet in a shaking fist. The fist remained high, as if Arthur fought the urge to strike him. Edmund released his breath in a silent sigh, his hands hanging loosely at his sides, his shoulders relaxed. If Arthur wanted to strike him, so be it. He would bear it, not because Arthur was his king and must be obeyed, but because Arthur was his brother whom he loved.

"I could have your head for this," Arthur said through his teeth.

Edmund compelled himself to meet his brother's eyes, to face the fury in them without flinching. "I know. If that is the price I must pay, I shall pay it." He did not want to die, he wanted to live and love Ceci until God saw fit to take him, but he could not deny Arthur's right to do what he chose. "I shall obey you in all things but this."

Arthur threw the cap in Edmund's face; Edmund let it

fall to the ground. "Conditional obedience is not obedience at all."

He was right. It was all or nothing. "Then I am a disobedient subject, dependent on your mercy."

"I have none for you. None." Arthur flung himself in his chair and, resting his elbows on his knees, buried his face in his hands.

Kati spoke. "You risk your life for her and for your selfish wants. Why?"

"Because I love her."

She made an impatient noise and waved her hand as if brushing away an importunate insect. "Love is a luxury you cannot afford."

It was hard to argue with them when so much of what they said was right. He was a king's son. He should not marry for anything as ephemeral as love; a vow for life should be founded on something sturdy and lasting, like property. Yet Arthur proposed to marry him for the sake of a treaty that would likely be broken before the ink dried. The arguments could go on forever and still mean nothing. He loved Ceci; he would marry her or die trying.

"Kati—" Her face tightened while her hand reached out and caressed Arthur's shoulder in a gesture of absent-minded tenderness. The words he had planned to speak fled as a new idea sparked to life. He hesitated, thinking swiftly, assessing the risk. If he offended Kati completely... He had no choice. "—Your Grace, may I ask you a question?"

Her eyes narrowed. "You may."

He took a deep breath and plunged. "If God plucked my brother from his throne tomorrow and cast him down among the poorest of the poor, would you search him out? Would you find him and share his portion?"

"What foolishness is this?" she cried. "Do you speculate on the king's death? That is treason!"

He lifted his hands, palm out, in a placating gesture. "No, no, never that." This was like walking across the moors of Devon, where a misplaced foot could mean death in a sinking bog. He took another deep breath, trying to ease the pounding of his heart. "No, it is simply that I believe my brother means enough to you that you would follow him wherever he went."

There. It was said. What she did now was in the hands of God.

Arthur lifted his head and stared at his wife, his mouth set in a hard line. Kati's gaze lost its shrewd focus and turned inward. Edmund held his breath, knowing that her lightest word had more influence with Arthur than all the arguments he could muster. *Please, God, let me be right.* His heart thumped against his ribs, beat in his ears; for a brief moment it seemed to say, Ceci, Ceci.

Kati looked at Edmund, the corner of her mouth curling upward. "How did you know?" she asked softly. "You are right—I would follow him to the ends of the earth."

"Whither thou goest," he said in Latin.

"Yes." Her hand skimmed Arthur's sleeve, down to his hand, where her fingers twined through his. "Cecilita?"

"Yes. I cannot help it. I have tried." He took a breath to say more, but there were no words.

"I do not care," Arthur said flatly.

Kati stood and lumbered to her knees at his feet, her hands on his thighs. "*Mi querido, mi corazón.* Listen."

Arthur sat back in his chair and folded his arms across his chest. "Get up, Kati. There is nothing you can say to me that will change my mind."

"My heart—"

"Madam, I have bidden you sit. Do you disobey me?"

He glared at her, his mouth pulled tight. Edmund took a step forward with some half-formed notion of protecting her, but Arthur checked him with a cold glance. For good or for ill, Kati would fight alone.

"Yes, my lord, I do," she said.

"This does nothing to endear you to me," Arthur said. His voice was flat, unlike his own.

The hair on the back of Edmund's neck rose, the flesh prickling. *Papa.* He had forgotten the sound of his father's voice; why did it return to him now?

"I will not sit until you hear me out," Kati said.

"You waste your time, madam." Arthur shifted in the chair, looking over Kati's head.

"I think it a fine use of my time. I besieged Moors with my mother, my lord. I know a thing or two about patience."

What would his father say about this situation? "Women!" Edmund's mother, a fainter memory, had often knelt as Kati did, cozening his father into some act he did not want to perform, charming him out of doing something he would regret. Would Ceci kneel before him in the same way someday? *Please God, let it be so.*

What, moreover, would his father say about his adventures as a common man? Little good, no doubt. Something loosened in his heart. His father had not known everything, had not been able to anticipate everything. Edmund abruptly remembered Piers asking him who else he could marry but Ceci.

"As do I, madam, as do I. This is not your battle to fight. Edmund must do his duty."

"Which duty?" Edmund said, and started at the sound of his own voice. He had not meant to speak his thought out loud.

Kati twisted on her knees to stare at him while Arthur's

brows lifted in a look of chilly annoyance. "You interrupt us," he said.

"Which duty must I do, Your Grace?" Edmund asked despite the warning in Arthur's eyes. "If I marry Margrethe of Austria, how shall I be your ears and eyes in England? Have you no more use for those services?"

"You will do as I bid you," Arthur said, but he spoke slowly, as if he thought as he spoke.

"Assuredly," Edmund said. "But will what I do have any value? If I tell my wife I must leave her but I cannot tell her where I go, will she keep her tongue still? Or will she clack all over the Court that I have disappeared? How shall I keep my secret then?"

Arthur's mouth curled. "I doubt it is entirely a secret."

Edmund nodded. He had long suspected rumor chased him. "As do I. But it is not entirely known, either. Will that still be true when I am wed to the archduke's daughter?"

He stopped, to give Arthur time to think through his argument. Kati heaved herself to her feet and stood beside Arthur's chair, her hand resting on her husband's shoulder. Her eyes met Edmund's for moment, a twinkle in their depths, before she lowered her lids.

Arthur stared at the floor, his brows drawn together and his teeth massaging his lip. The itch to adjust his knife belt or shift his gown on his shoulders returned to Edmund, crawling more insistently than before. He forced himself to be patient. Arthur could be persuaded but he could not be compelled; anything that smacked of coercion would plunge him into obstinacy.

Arthur looked up at Edmund, something like humor lurking in the depths of his eyes. He shook his head. "Not even More could be that clever," he said. "I daresay you could argue the stars out of the sky."

"Only if they belonged on earth," Edmund said. The bunched muscles in his neck and shoulders began to loosen their knots. He wanted to say it was not so ill a match, the Duke of Somerset and the Earl of Wednesfield's daughter, but he feared that the decision still lay in the balance.

"Tell the boy outside to fetch Lady Cecilia." Edmund's heart beat so strongly he thought it might crash through his ribs. "Tell her the king wishes to speak to her."

When he had done as Arthur commanded, Edmund returned and knelt before his brother. "Does this mean…?"

"Get up!" Arthur said irritably. "No, it does not. It means I have not yet decided to send you to the Tower. Get behind that tapestry—" he pointed to the hanging in the corner "—and do not reveal yourself until I give you leave."

The page found Cecilia pacing in the pleached alley while Mary Butler sat on a bench in the sunny garden. The queen's ladies and maids were free to do as they listed while the queen dallied with the king and they had taken the opportunity to scatter to the Court's four corners.

"My lady…the king…wishes…to see you…in his chamber…. Now," the page said. He bent over, ostensibly in a respectful bow, but by the way he rested his hands on his knees, Cecilia suspected he was simply trying to catch his breath.

"Bring me to him," Cecilia said.

The page bent his neck to look up at her and nodded. "Yes, my lady."

He kept a swift pace, breaking into a trot now and then. She hurried as best she could, but tight stays and voluminous skirts were not as easy to move in as doublet and hose. Her heart throbbed against her ribs but she did not know if it was fear or exertion. Why did the king wish to see her? And why the hurry? She could ask, but the pages were notorious tale-bearers; she did not want her anxiety sped from lip to lip. Had this to do with Conyers? Her stomach rolled and she gripped the chain around her waist. Damn Conyers! Whatever it cost her, she meant to see him destroyed.

She and the page arrived at the door to the king's private rooms out of breath but the boy did not wait to compose himself. He slipped into the room with sweat gleaming on his smooth apple-red face, his breath wheezing in his throat. A brief instant later he was back in the antechamber. "The king bids you enter."

She was trembling, sick; her heart choked her. She took two steps into the room and sank into a deep curtsy, staring modestly at the floor.

"You may rise, Lady Cecilia."

That was the queen's voice. Cecilia stood, lifting her head. All her half-formed speculations jumbled in her head. What could the king want that required the queen's presence? What did he want that the queen could not ask? She breathed deeply to still the pattering of her heart, to calm her stormy stomach. Perhaps it was another marriage... Let it be. She would not accept it, not again. Anything was better than that.

The king examined her with a gray gaze that returned nothing, not even curiosity. She had never seen him so coldly disposed. Her courage trickled out of her, her ideas of defiance fading. "I expect you wonder why I have sent for you."

"I should be a fool if I did not, Your Grace," she said, and then bit her lip. Had that come out of her mouth? Sweet Mary, save her.

"I have heard you love my brother. Is that true?" His eyes were as hard as granite. What would he do to her if she told the truth? Oh, it did not matter, her blush answered clearly enough. She lifted her chin. *Claim the truth with pride.*

"I do."

The king sat back in his chair and the queen stared at her hands.

"Does he love you?"

She remembered his arms around her as she wept, the way her trembling had awakened tremors in him. He had been angrier than she had dreamed possible, all because someone had threatened harm to her. She did not know how deep or true his feelings were, but she knew he loved her.

"He does."

"Do you expect to wed him?" The king did not sound as scornful as she might have expected.

Oh, to spend the rest of her life with Edmund, to lie with him openly, to bear his sons... *The truth will set you free.* "No. I do not."

The king leaned forward. "Then why did you allow yourself to love him? Why did you let him come to love you?"

What was the expedient answer? She did not care; it was hard to worry about the repercussions of this conversation just now. Besides, had she not cast the king's favor to the wind when she admitted his brother loved her? For the king would not blame Edmund for that; he would blame her. Such were the capricious ways of kings.

She spread her hands. "Sire, I did not allow anything. It was beyond my ability to prevent. Love cannot be commanded to go or stay."

"Nonsense." The king sat back again.

She remembered the way he had looked at the queen that day in April. The love, the passion, the longing. Was it nonsense, the idea that love struck where it willed? *What of you, Sire?* If only she dared speak her question out loud. ... Why not? She was surely disgraced; a little impertinence could not make things worse.

"Sire, may I be frank?"

His eyebrows lifted. "You may."

"Is it nonsense? I believe the queen would be your love if she was a goosegirl. And I do not think you could change the way you feel about her if you wanted to."

The king scowled. "You are impertinent."

She swallowed the stickiness in her mouth. "Yes, Sire. But I stand by what I say. As you love the queen, I love your brother. I would love him if he was the lowest yeoman in the land."

"You risk a great deal by this, mistress," the king said, his frown deepening. "Not only your own future but that of your family depends on my pleasure. And I could be made most displeased by malapert behavior."

Cecilia clenched her hands, concealed in the folds of her dress. If she had any kind of wit or shrewdness, she would speak soothingly. "I am sorry to anger you, Sire, more sorry than you can know. But I cannot lie to you. I wish the Duke of Somerset had been born a yeoman and I a yeoman's daughter, so we might wed freely."

From behind the tapestry in the corner, she heard a faint, "Ha!" Who was behind there, listening to her bare her soul? Would this tale be all over Court by midday? Well, of course it would. Disgrace was not a quiet matter and she had surely disgraced herself.

The king glanced at the queen. "I knew I should have sent him out, but I was afraid she would see him." He sighed. Raising his voice, he said, "Come out, jackanapes, now that you have revealed yourself."

The tapestry lifted and Edmund stepped into the room,

his face illuminated by a grin. She blinked, unable to believe her eyes. Edmund? Somewhere, far away, she trembled, her heart jumping in shock. He crossed to her and took her hand, lifting it to his lips. His fingers were warm and strong, his touch making him real.

"You argue our case beautifully, my heart," he said. It was the first time he had shown his feelings so clearly before anyone but Piers. *You will betray us.* Then she realized she was a fool. *We betrayed ourselves long ago.*

"You are right, Edmund. She is most eloquent on your behalf and almost inclines me to grant your petition. If we can settle the matter of punishment for defying my will…" the king said in a voice that made the hair on the back of her neck stand up.

Edmund did not seem to hear the menace in his brother's voice. There was a smile playing in the corners of his mouth as he gazed at her. "Fine me, Sire. Take every groat I have. If you let me marry this woman, I can never be poor."

Feeling broke through to her, her heart swelling, suffocating her with joy. He had risked himself for her, risked his brother's love for hers. She could hardly trust that what she saw and heard was truly happening. *I am dreaming.*

"You were right, lady, when you said that I would choose the queen for my love if she were a goosegirl. But I would also have done my duty." The king's voice barely impinged on her awareness. The world was confined to Edmund's blue-gray eyes, staring into her own.

"I tried, Sire," Edmund said. "God knows, I tried. But my love for her was too great."

"You are lucky that I love you well, Edmund. I might have been very angry."

Edmund turned to his brother, still holding her hand, his thumb caressing the sensitive inside of her wrist. Desire flared. She had missed his touch. "I know it, Sire, and I thank God you were not."

"Do not thank Him too soon. I intend to fine you," the king said. "And it shall not be a small one. Oh, I shall not take everything, but you will feel the pinch of it."

"I do not care, Sire. She is all the wealth I desire." His hand tightened.

"You are a fool!"

"Perhaps, Sire. But if you give us leave to wed, we shall be happy fools."

The king looked at his wife. "Kati, what am I to do with such a lackwit?"

"Let him have his way. He has risked too much not to let him marry as he desires."

The king looked at them. "The queen's lightest wish commands me. You have my leave to wed."

"Bless you, Sire." Edmund turned to her, taking her other hand. The laughter had left his gaze, leaving love. Blood rushed through her ears, almost deafening her, and her heart trembled against her ribs. *This cannot be happening.* "Ceci, I cannot bear to live without you. I want you for my duchess, I want you to bear my sons. Marry me."

Tears stung her eyes as a wave of emotion crashed over her, joy and pain in one aching flood. "Yes." She wanted to say so much more but there were no words, they had all deserted her. She looked away from his eyes, unable to bear the tenderness in them.

How could this be happening to her? A moment ago she had been certain she was ruined. Now she was to marry the man she loved and ascend to a position higher than she had dreamed possible. She remembered Mistress Emma's vision, that she would go further than anyone imagined. It was true in more ways than one.

Edmund's hands cupped her jaw and tilted her face up. "I will love you until I die," he said, and kissed her.

Heat curled through her, heat and longing. She clutched his sleeves, giving herself up to the caress of his mouth and the love in her heart. She forgot the king and queen, forgot everything. A voice said, *You should not do this* and another voice cried joyously, *Oh, but I can.*

She could do this. No more longing, no more denial. She would have him in her bed and at her board all the days of her life; his sons would emerge from her body. Desire rolled a long hot wave from her heart to the depths of her belly.

"Ahem."

Edmund lifted his head, breaking their kiss. Cecilia remembered where they were and blushed.

The king stared at them with laughter sparkling in eyes that were no longer granite-hard. "This can wait, jackanapes. You will have time enough for loving."

Edmund did not take his arms from around her. "Why, yes, Sire, you are right." He began laughing. "I have the rest of my life."

* * * * *

**Praise for 1998 Golden Heart Finalist
Katy Cooper and her terrific new book,
PRINCE OF HEARTS**

"With a rare magic and grace, Katy Cooper creates a
vivid world of history and passion that readers are
bound to adore. An unforgettable debut!"

—Miranda Jarrett

PRINCE OF HEARTS
Harlequin Historical #525—August 2000

HARLEQUIN

Duets™

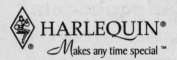

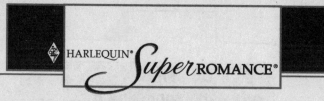

KATY COOPER

Ever since she picked up one of her father's history books because the cover was so beautiful, Katy Cooper has been fascinated with people who lived in the past. Writing historical romance is her way of exploring the glories of history while also honoring the glories of true love. A military brat who has traveled the world, Katy now lives in Massachusetts with her own true love, her husband, Jim.

HH525IBC